MW01199432

VIA ÁPIA

"Geovani Martins has written a funny, tender, kinetic, often brutal debut novel. *Via Ápia* cracks open a favela—built on a hill whose slope suggests both aspiration and danger—revealing a teeming, vivid motion that can only be found by observing real life without pity or fear. Martins's eye is sharp, his ear true. Julia Sanches's translation is hip and contemporary. This book is the beginning of something big."
> —Vinson Cunningham, author of *Great Expectations*

"Vivid, electric, and so immersive you'll catch a contact high, *Via Ápia* pulls you into the wild world of Rocinha, the largest favela in Latin America, and never lets go. A celebration of life and all the beauty and pain that come with it, Geovani Martins's novel is transformed into a portal to new sights, sounds, smells, and tastes—all of which initially seem foreign but are more familiar than we know. From alleyway confrontations to bumping bailes, Martins masterfully highlights the heart-wrenching conflict of a changing home full of people who are forced to change with it. An inner-city epic that will echo through the ages."
> —Mateo Askaripour, author of *This Great Hemisphere*

"This is a war novel like no other, an unflinching portrayal of the militarized police occupation and 'cleanup' of Rio de Janeiro's Rocinha. And Julia Sanches handles Afro-Brasilidade, class, and favela slang with so much care and brilliance. I don't know how she did it. Her translation is sheer sorcery."
> —Bruna Dantas Lobato, winner of the National Book Award for Translated Literature and author of *Blue Light Hours*

"Geovani Martins documents the marvelous beauty and tragedy of lives on the periphery of Rio de Janeiro with the humor, perspicacity, and expansive detail of Machado de Assis. But check it: the thumping, boiling heart of this book is the sick-ass, incisive, *malandra* narrative voice brought to crackling life by Julia Sanches's wonderful translation. *Via Ápia* is about carving out a space for joy, love, and friendship in a death-haunted, dangerous place. Martins imbues every corner of this book with grace and light; it's this dazzling quality that cements *Via Ápia* as a contemporary Brazilian classic."   —Harold Rogers, author of *Tropicália*

"*Via Ápia* is absolutely alive with the rhythm of Rio, of youth, of community. With an incredible dexterity, Geovani Martins flows between characters who together make a wondrous novel of great heart and ambition."
—Nana Kwame Adjei-Brenyah, author of *Chain-Gang All-Stars*

Ana Alexandrino

GEOVANI MARTINS

VIA ÁPIA

Translated from the Portuguese by
Julia Sanches

Geovani Martins was born in 1991 in Rio de Janeiro, Brazil. He is the author of *The Sun on My Head*. He grew up living with his mother in the Rio neighborhood of Vidigal. He supported his writing by working as a sandwich-board man and selling drinks on the beach, and was discovered during creative writing workshops at FLUP, the literary festival of the Rio favelas. *Via Ápia* is his first novel.

Julia Sanches has translated more than twenty books from the Spanish, Portuguese, and Catalan into English, including Geovani Martins's debut short-story collection, *The Sun on My Head*. Born in São Paulo, Brazil, she currently lives in Providence, Rhode Island.

ALSO BY GEOVANI MARTINS

The Sun on My Head

VIA ÁPIA

VIA ÁPIA

A Novel

GEOVANI MARTINS

*Translated from the Portuguese
by Julia Sanches*

FSG Originals
Farrar, Straus and Giroux
New York

FSG Originals
Farrar, Straus and Giroux
120 Broadway, New York 10271

Copyright © 2022 by Geovani Martins
Translation copyright © 2025 by Julia Sanches
All rights reserved
Printed in the United States of America
Originally published in Portuguese in 2022 by Companhia das Letras, Brazil,
as *Via Ápia*
English translation published in the United States by
Farrar, Straus and Giroux
First American edition, 2025

Art facing the title page and the table of contents by Miloje / Shutterstock.com.

Library of Congress Cataloging-in-Publication Data
Names: Martins, Geovani, 1991– author. | Sanches, Julia, translator.
Title: Via Ápia : a novel / Geovani Martins ; translated from the Portuguese
by Julia Sanches.
Other titles: Via Ápia. English
Description: First American edition. | New York : FSG Originals / Farrar,
Straus and Giroux, 2025. |
Identifiers: LCCN 2024056840 | ISBN 9780374612986 (paperback)
Subjects: LCGFT: Novels.
Classification: LCC PQ9698.423.A7556 V5313 2025 | DDC 869.3/5—dc23/
eng/20241129
LC record available at https://lccn.loc.gov/2024056840

Designed by Patrice Sheridan

Our books may be purchased in bulk for promotional, educational, or
business use. Please contact your local bookseller or the Macmillan Corporate
and Premium Sales Department at 1-800-221-7945, extension 5442, or by email
at MacmillanSpecialMarkets@macmillan.com.

www.fsgoriginals.com • www.fsgbooks.com
Follow us on social media at @fsgoriginals and @fsgbooks

1   3   5   7   9   10   8   6   4   2

This is a work of fiction. Names, characters, places, organizations, and
incidents either are products of the author's imagination or are used
fictitiously. Any resemblance to actual events, places, organizations,
or persons, living or dead, is entirely coincidental.

*In memory of Ecio Salles—
a Vasco da Gama fan who sparked a revolution
in the lives of so many people, including mine*

CONTENTS

PART II

PART III

PART I

RIO—July 27, 2011

They aren't singing "Happy Birthday" for another hour. Washington paces up and down the room, eyes the clock. It's the same old story: when you're kicking back on your time off, the pointer shows no mercy, a month vanishes in five minutes. But when you're at a shit job, everything drags. More so when the munchies are ramping up. He serves whole wheat pastries at the tables, with zero enthusiasm. Those ricotta pastels never looked more appetizing.

The guests were on a different wavelength. After eating like pigs the first hour, they started turning everything down with a frown, before they'd even heard what it was. To make matters worse, the birthday boy got it in his head to start bawling and refused to let up. His cries were shrill, annoying, and echoed all over the room while guests, parents, and staff pretended not to hear them. The nanny pulled out all the stops. She danced with the animal decorations, goofed around, made his favorite faces, and didn't let out a single God-given shut-your-mouth. His wailing mixed with the soundtrack to Lottie Dottie Chicken, and the din of the party, the toys, the chatter. Famished and surrounded by chaos, Washington stopped to take a deep breath and visualize the end of his day.

Munchies are the craziest thing. On the one hand, they make anything you eat taste out of this world; on the other, they have the power to strain your body, cloud your vision, sap all your energy, and lower your blood pressure. What sucks is that it's always the same: when Washington was stoned, the first couple of hours zipped by and, depending on the party, he sometimes even had fun with the kids. But then there was the comedown, the crushing hunger.

Given the choice, Washington would have gone straight to bartending. Everybody knew the trays were heavier, but it was still worth it. Things were a lot mellower behind the bar, the managers barely ever checked in on you, and time slipped away. Besides, then he wouldn't have to deal with the smell of food wafting up from the tray all four hours of the party.

Washington still wasn't used to those people. He only put up with them because he knew that, without money in his pocket, he was a nobody. It was supposed to be short-term, something to tide him over until he aged out of military service. That was three years ago. What was keeping him from finally looking for a real job? A signed work card, RioCard, Sodexo.

After another lap around the room, Washington headed over to the kitchen. He was glancing around for the wall clock when he walked straight into the events manager. With a full tray.

"Are you offering everyone food?" she asked before shoving a ricotta pastel into her mouth.

"I am. But people are stuffed, Ângela. You saw the way they were eating at the start. You gotta give them some breathing room now," Washington said, dumping the pastries into a container with the other leftovers.

Ângela frowned like she didn't like what she was hearing but only spoke after gulping down the pastel.

"Believe me, Washington, I do. I give them a whole lot of it. But then they complain to the bosses upstairs, and who do you think those guys take it out on . . ."

"All I'm saying is—"

"You don't need to be saying shit, Washington. What you need is to be serving people right. Think I didn't catch you walking around the hall with that look on your face? Nobody should have to put up with a pissy waiter. Feeling stressed? Stay home. I'm tired of reminding people. But if you come into work, I'd better see you smiling, happy, and energized. We're in the party business. How would you feel if some wet blanket was working *your* kid's birthday?"

"You know what everybody's ordering? Burgers. Loads of guests have asked. It'd be cool if we could send some around."

"Then let's give the people what they want. I was wondering why we never make burgers in this place . . ."

"I'll wait here, then send them out soon as they're ready."

"Nuh-uh," Francisca, the cook, interrupted. "Take this before it gets cold. The other kid left and never came back."

Unlike his brother, Wesley was digging the party. After lazing around a while, he went back to the play area with Talia, a dime on her first shift at the venue. Wesley was feeling cocky. The party was for a one-year-old, so there were more grown-ups than kids and plenty of time to kick back and talk. He didn't want to scare away Talia by coming on too strong but also knew he'd have to act fast if he wanted a chance with her. The party hall was crawling with Romeos ready to pounce on new hires the second they walked through the door, each one more fired up than the last.

"You ever worked a party for somebody famous?" Talia asked once they'd finished discussing their favorite bailes and pagodes.

"Oh, yeah, loads. Tons of actors and soccer players throw parties here . . . One time I worked this gig for Luciano Huck and Angélica's kids. It was wild. There were so many celebrities, the place looked like the season finale of a telenovela or something. The managers were all twitchy cause everything had to be perfect and shit, but it was pretty low-key in the end."

"Did anybody ask for a picture?"

"Nah, it's not allowed. If one of the managers catches you doing that, you're fucked. We're supposed to pretend we never seen them in our lives, that it's totally normal for people like them to be, like, in the real world, outside our TVs."

Talia laughed. Convinced she was enjoying the subject, Wesley confessed:

"I did ask for a picture this one time. It was at a birthday

bash for the daughter of this guy who plays for Flamengo—
Luiz Antônio or Júnior César, I can't remember. All I know
is Léo Moura was here. I couldn't help myself, brother's my
idol. I just had to get a pic. But I did it outside, after the party."
Talia clearly didn't care and pretended not to hear him.
Maybe she wasn't into soccer, or worse yet, maybe she pulled
for Vasco. Wesley was trying to control the ball by changing
the subject when she asked:

"Any idea how much it costs to throw a party here?"

"Word is they won't let you through the door for less than
eight stacks."

"Are you for real? Eight thousand reais for, like, a four-
hour party?"

"That's if the family doesn't hire a magician or a clown or
something. One time this couple got a troupe to perform *The
Little Mermaid*. Shit lasted less than an hour, I swear. Between
the performance and the rental hall, I hear it cost, like, thirty
grand. Can you fucking believe it?"

Washington left the kitchen with the tray of hamburger sliders. His hunger had soured to hatred. He walked past the play
area and told his brother about his plan to boost the whole
tray. Magal was hiding in the restroom. Washington just had
to slip past the guests, walk down the hall like he was headed
to the kitchen, and drop the food off with his buddy. Wesley's
job was to keep an eye on the manager and, if necessary, distract her with some small talk about the party.

The plan was a success. Magal ate his share of the loot
right away. Washington informed his brother he was up next.

Knowing Ângela had her eye on him, he decided to do another loop around the main room.

As soon as Washington left, Talia approached Wesley, curious to know what was going on. He asked if she was hungry. Talia said she hadn't eaten since lunch, that she hated mortadella so she didn't touch the snacks given to the staff. Wesley told her about the hamburger operation. Talia was very interested. Before leaving, Wesley said he'd figure out a way of getting her in on the food.

Washington could hardly believe his nose when he walked into the restroom. It smelled like victory. He started with the cheeseburgers, his favorite, though only while they were still warm. Truth told, all the food at the venue sucked once it went cold. That's another reason Washington never waited around for leftovers like the other servers. Besides, as far as he was concerned, fighting over scraps was even more pathetic than sneaking food in the restroom.

He put away four cheeseburgers in record time. There were another four burgers with lettuce left. He'd eat two and leave the rest for his brother's new girlfriend. But the second the burger touched his mouth, somebody knocked on the door.

"Busy," he said with a full mouth.

"What're you doing in there?" It was Ângela.

Washington spat out bits of burger into the toilet.

"I'm taking a leak. Or is that not allowed anymore?" He grabbed the three remaining burgers, wrapped them in an apron and dropped them in a corner of the restroom, then flushed and walked out. The manager was waiting for him right outside the door.

"I know, I know. It's time to sing 'Happy Birthday.' I'm on it, Ângela. Let me go deal with dessert first."

Washington was still shaking when he got to the kitchen. He stood next to Magal and began arranging the desserts on the trays. Steadily, he felt calmer. He'd always found that part of the job relaxing; getting the desserts ready was as good as getting ready to leave. It was magical, really, how the same forty-five minutes that felt like an eternity in the thick of the party just flew by after "Happy Birthday."

"What's all this about?" Ângela walked into the kitchen with the burgers.

She didn't wait for Washington to answer before reaming him out in front of everyone. The thing that really pissed him off in those moments was knowing that it would all come to nothing, just like every other time he'd been caught stealing food. Washington had worked there for years, and though he was no employee-of-the-month, he knew the job inside out, was always available, and had the managers' backs when they needed it. It didn't make sense to fire someone like him over a dozen measly hamburger sliders. All the managers knew this, which is why they went to town when it was time to call him out.

"Are you gonna fire me already or just talk a big game?"

Ângela couldn't hide her shock at his response.

"Up until yesterday, you were bussing tables just like the rest of us. You've stolen tons of food. Now you want to get all high-and-mighty about it? Please! There's nothing but snakes in this joint. I'm sick and tired of it. I am so fucking sick and tired of this bullshit."

Washington had no trouble speaking his mind. The same

words he'd held in for so long seemed to be leaping out of him now, one after the other. The kitchen staff watched in shock. Everyone had apparently forgotten there was a family outside waiting to sing their kid "Happy Birthday."

"Washington, all I was trying to say—"

"We're done here, Ângela. Don't sweat it. I'll just take my paycheck and bounce." The second he finished that sentence, he snapped back into his body, which simmered with rage.

Washington gazed at the objects in the kitchen where he'd spent nearly every weekend over the past few years. All of it looked strange. Soon enough, he began to feel relieved; it was over. He'd never have to see that play area again in his life, or listen to that dumb music, or serve people who couldn't even sing their own kids "Happy Birthday" without professional help.

"You'll have to wait until the party's over to get paid. I'm busy," Ângela finally said, slamming the door on her way out of the kitchen.

Wesley didn't notice his brother wasn't there for "Happy Birthday." He was too preoccupied with other things. Guys pulling all kinds of stunts. Singing, busting moves and shit, all to get Talia's attention. The problem was she seemed to like it and kept smiling at them clowning around. Backstabbing assholes.

He only remembered Washington when they brought out the cake. He was used to his brother stopping by to say something, pocket desserts, kick around as the party wound down.

"Did you get to eat, Talia?"

"Damn. With all this birthday stuff, I totally forgot."

One of the servers came over to fill them in on what had happened. That's party venues for you: gossip spreads like a common cold. Ângela and Washington's argument would go down in the books as a classic party-hall dustup. The birthday ended. As always, the staff piled up at the kitchen door. Washington sat on a gas canister off to the side, smoking a cigarette. Wesley went over to him; his brother seemed calmer than he'd expected. Several people had filled Wesley in on the altercation, and with every new version, the story grew more and more intense.

"Sup, menó. Let's bounce."

"I'm still waiting for my paycheck, man. Ângela's being a little bitch. Thinks I'll give up if she keeps jerking me around. No way in hell I'm leaving without my money."

"Whatever, menó, get that shit later. It's nine. The Flamengo match is starting soon."

"Fuck. I totally forgot about the game. Gimme a sec to track her down."

Wesley considered ditching his brother and running out of there to catch the kickoff. He couldn't wait to watch Ronaldinho Gaúcho and Neymar battle it out. They were two of the best players he'd ever seen. Flamengo haters loved to claim Ronaldinho Gaúcho was old news, that he was only in Rio to hit bailes in favelas and orgies at VIPS, that he'd left the game in Europe. But Wesley thought he had potential. He'd followed Ronaldinho's career in Barcelona and watched a couple of his matches for Milan. Age slows people down, no doubt, but no one who does what Ronaldinho could do straight-up forgets how to play ball from one day to the next. It was just a matter of adapting. In a way, Wesley believed this was the match where Ronaldinho would finally shine. Besides, even without a stellar performance from their new hotshot player, the team remained undefeated, in the running for the semi-finals. If Ronaldinho did what he'd come there to do, they may as well hand Flamengo the cup.

Ângela was still working through her checklist in the empty room, casting a calm eye over everything, as though managing a party hall were the greatest responsibility in the world. Washington followed her around, insisting he had to leave. This went on for a while. Finally, she asked Washington to follow her upstairs. She filled in a receipt for him to sign but only handed it over after apologizing for the scene in the kitchen. It wasn't a big deal, if he was stressed, he should just say so, they could call in somebody else. Washington half-listened. All he cared about was that stuffed envelope. As he counted the money, the ball hit the grass in Vila Belmiro stadium.

"Holy shit, menó. You put two hundred down on Flamengo? You're even crazier than me."

"Whatever, man. How was I supposed to know I was gonna be out of a job? I had a ton of parties lined up this month. I was meant to be raking it in, pô. So I put a little faith in my team."

"See, that's why I don't gamble, menó. It's serious shit, you just never know . . . How much she give you?"

"Sixty. Only worked two parties this week."

After waiting fifteen minutes at the stop, the 557 rolled up. As they sat on the bus, Washington finally filled his brother in on what happened. It was better to let him bring it up. As much as Wesley had been dying to know, he didn't want to put pressure on his brother. If Washington decided to talk about something else instead, he would play along.

"And that's when I flipped out. To be honest, I'm not even sure what happened. It was all so fast. Everybody was staring at me, and I was just talking, letting it all out. You know the rest. Fuck it. I was sick of working there. Time to move on to the next thing."

"That's right, menó. Gotta keep on keeping on. Real talk, I'm not sure how you lasted as long as you did. I'm sticking around, but only till the end of the year. Take on a shit-ton of parties, save up for a motorbike, a junker or whatever. Then I'll work as a mototaxi driver. Be on my feet in no time. I'll get my license. Buy a Twister, a Fazer, something. I don't wanna work for anybody ever again."

The bus was racing through Joá. Sometimes Washington stressed himself out thinking about this accident he'd only ever heard about, where a van flew off the road and landed right in the ocean. Now and then he'd yell at the driver: We're not cattle back here, asshole! But only if the bus was full and he could count on the other passengers to have his back. One time, this kid cussed a driver out on an empty bus, and shit got ugly. The driver pulled into São Conrado, parked the bus, and started whaling on him. A city cop had to break them up. This time, Washington said nothing, not only because the bus was empty, but because he couldn't wait to get back to Rocinha.

"I just can't work out how she knew I was in the can. Since getting promoted, Ângela only uses the office bathroom. So what the fuck was she doing down there?"

"She was tipped off for sure."

"Fuck, man. Of course. Your little girlfriend must've turned me in, the fucking rat. That barbie-doll face doesn't fool me, not for a second. Trust me, that girl is playing you."

"Come on, man. Talia doesn't even know you. Why the hell would she rat you out? You're tripping."

"All right, dude. I won't say another word. You do you, find out for yourself. Just don't come crying to me later."

Wesley didn't want to believe his brother. Talia seemed like good people. She'd even given him an opening in the end. But, if he was honest, his brother's suspicions weren't unfounded. Magal had been tight with the two of them forever, plus he'd eaten some of the loot as well—no way he'd snitch on Washington like that. The manager showing up outside the bathroom was definitely sus, but it wasn't solid proof. Wesley would have to stay on his toes. If Talia was a narc, it wouldn't be long before she showed her true colors.

As they were leaving Joá, one of the older passengers got up. He'd been sitting in a yellow seat, even though the bus was pretty much empty, as if wanting to assert his priority status. When he turned to face the door, they noticed a battery-powered radio held up to his ear. He was probably listening to the game. Another thing they noticed is that he was scowling. Either he supported Flamengo, and their team was losing to Santos, or he was a hater and upset that their team was in the lead. With a face like that, they knew a tie was out of the picture.

When the old man reached the door, Wesley asked him for an update on the game. His eyes were lowered. He glared at the two brothers, like it was all their fault.

"Neymar just scored another two for Santos," he seethed. Then, seeing their reaction, he added, "Santos is leading three–nil."

Ryan Giggs intercepted another ball off the back of a rival winger and then sent an additional crosskick to Chicharito Hernández's head with his left foot.

"Fuck you, man. Same scoring move *every time!*" Douglas was playing for Barcelona, and he was pissed.

"Cool it, cuz. Drink up so we can get back to the game."

The match was almost over. That last goal, the third by the Mexican striker, brought the score to five for Manchester United, Murilo's team, and four for Barça. Biel was sitting there beside them, rolling a joint. His friends were already heavy on the sauce. Not that it was unusual for them to be drunk-gaming with vodka. In fact, it was a regular pastime of theirs. But the floodgates were wide open that night. To give you an idea, Murilo had beat Biel eight to six in the last match, meaning he was already loaded by the time he had to play Douglas, his biggest Bomba Patch rival. And that wasn't even counting the first game, which went to penalties after a measly one–one draw. Penalties are always worse because the players have to take several shots, one after the other, alternating with their opponent.

When Murilo scored his fifth goal, Douglas thought they should call it a day. Things could get weird if they went to penalties in that state. The problem was that Murilo couldn't just win and leave it be. He had to demolish his opponent. Worst of all, the thing that really riled Douglas up: the guy always scored with the same move.

While Murilo messed around in added time, Douglas, blood boiling, sent a right pass to Messi. The Argentinian star ran diagonally into the box, cleared two opponents, and took a cross shot at the goal. The Manchester United keeper didn't even make the snapshot. A five–five draw, and the second half ended.

The fifth shot of vodka knocked out Murilo who, for all his swagger, was the biggest lightweight of them all. Douglas figured he could use this to his advantage. He wanted to score another two in OT, just to put Murilo in his place. But with both teams worn down and some players injured, the score stayed the same.

The moment before a penalty kick is always tense. Douglas glanced at the bottle of Kovak, now half-empty, and regretted scoring that last goal. All of a sudden, he started tripping. It was Wednesday night, he was on shift the next day, and there they were, getting plastered again. Nothing they could do now, though. Biel lit up. As Murilo geared up to take his next shot, Douglas shouted:

"Shit, fuck! The game!"

Murilo didn't think twice before dropping the controller and switching on Globo. Fucking dead-ass brain cells. They'd turned on the PlayStation just to kill ten minutes before the Flamengo–Santos match.

"Guess it's back to the PS," Murilo declared in a somber tone when he saw that Santos was winning three–nil.

"C'mon, dude! Didn't you say you wanted to watch the game? Then let's watch it, pô!" said Biel, the resident Vasco supporter.

The three had met at the start of that year. Murilo's mother had just relocated to Campo Grande with her husband, leaving the apartment to Murilo and his sister Monique. Things were quiet until Douglas moved into a room on the floor below them at the end of the previous year. At first, they didn't have a lot to say to each other besides the usual neighborly stuff, *sup, sup, thanks, thanks.* Things went on like that until Murilo came home from the barracks one day simmering with rage and desperate to clear his head. He went straight to the boca in Via Ápia, but all they had was hash. So he dropped by the one in Valão—same deal. He wasn't into mixing weed and to-bacco, but it was looking like he wouldn't have a choice. Word on the block was the only weed in the area was up the hill. He was crossing Travessa Kátia toward his building when he bumped into his neighbor lighting up on the street. Douglas caught the over-the-shoulder look and called out to Murilo, offering him a toke. Even though they'd never talked much, they were already on the same level. From that day on, they always burned one together—sharing joints, pitching in. It wasn't long before Douglas brought up his PS2. The rest was history. Every day was turned up.

Monique couldn't deal. She was prepping for the ENEM and had to constantly shut them up on the few occasions she found time to study. After she left the apartment to live with a friend, Douglas inevitably moved in. It made practical sense. Sharing chores and expenses made life easier on both of them. A big place in Rocinha was a rare find; two bedrooms, living room, kitchen, bathroom. Pricey but totally worth it. Some landlords in the area charged the same for a studio.

It was around then that Douglas decided to take up tattooing. He'd been into drawing since he was a kid, even done a few courses, and he never lost the knack. With all the tattoo parlors opening on the hill, he saw it as an opportunity to make money doing something he'd always loved. That was another reason the move upstairs had been such a big deal. There was more room for him to practice. Plus, it'd be perfect for when he eventually started inking his guinea pigs.

Biel came later. They'd met him slinging acid at Carnaval. You had to be there—dude laid on his playboy pitch so thick that Murilo and Douglas didn't even know what hit them. In all the years they'd gone to Carnaval, no playboy had ever tried pushing drugs on them. Buying, sure, now and then some fool would rock up and ask if they had any, but selling? Only among themselves. Straight away, Murilo said he wasn't interested. He'd been scared of the stuff ever since another soldier at the barracks told him about a guy tripping so hard he was never the same again.

Douglas had never done it either, but he was game. Ev-

erybody knew playboys on the blacktop were the only ones
with good candy, that in the favelas it was straight-up meth-
amphetamine. Same for E. Look hard, and you could probably dig up some decent candy in the favelas, but the general
consensus was that blacktop candy was on a different level.
Truth told, when it comes to drugs, money makes everything
easier. Murilo couldn't help telling the story about the dude
in the barracks. Biel joined the conversation:

"Nah, brother. Listen, I'm reading this book about the guy
that invented LSD, right? Name's Albert Hofmann. The book's
a trip. He talks about all kinds of things, like the first time he
dropped acid. So, like, he and his assistant take a dose, and
they're so fried they can't even get the car out. Dude climbs
in, next thing he knows, he's got no idea how to start it. That's
how spun he is. So the two of them bike home instead. That's
the best part, for real, when he goes into all the shit he saw,
these forest-like colors, creepy-ass sounds from trees, animals, that kind of stuff. All this on his bike, tripping balls.
That's why this acid here is called Bike 100, in honor of that
day."

He finished his story and pulled out half a tab sheet.
The picture was easy to make out, even though there were
squares missing: a man on a bike with his eyes closed and
face angled up, one of his legs sticking out behind him. In
the background, a mountain separated night and day while
the cyclist cruised along lost in time. At least one guy in
every Carnaval bloco was wearing a T-shirt with that design. The second he saw that, Douglas started counting out
money. If Murilo didn't want to drop paper with him, then
fuck it, he'd do it alone. The issue was he only had fifteen

reais, and the playboy was charging twenty-five a tab. Murilo fished a twenty out of his pocket. Seeing him waver, Biel went in for the kill.

"The wildest thing about acid, according to the author, is that it blocks off part of your brain, so then your neurons have to, like, find another way of communicating, right? You gotta relearn everything. So, when this dude rides his bike, it's like he's doing it for the first time. So what I'm saying is: you ever thought of experiencing this bloco all over again, but like it's the first time?"

Murilo gazed at the crowd around him, everyone in their own world, and felt he could stand to go a bit crazier.

"I only got twenty. If I give you ten, that leaves me with just enough to get home."

"Where y'all live?"

Douglas and Murilo glanced at each other, then told Biel they lived in Rocinha.

"Cool. What you're gonna do is use the change to buy water and walk home instead."

They handed the money to Biel, who pulled scissors out of his drug kit and helped them cut the paper. They placed the tabs on their tongues. Biel instructed them to let the squares dissolve until the bitterness faded, then have a sip of water to wash down the rest. Biel lit up a joint. Skunk, by the smell of it. He gave each of them a hit. Good weed helps the acid kick in faster, he explained. Murilo and Douglas turned to face one another, trying to wrap their heads around what was going on. Who *was* this guy? A rich white boy who sold drugs *and* rolled his own joints? They hadn't started tripping yet, and the whole situation already felt surreal.

They'd been watching the match for about a minute when Flamengo scored its first goal. Luiz Antônio crossed right, Rafael, the goalkeeper, missed, and Ronaldinho Gaúcho pushed the ball into the back of the net from the goalbox. Murilo started cheering, but it was too soon. Ronaldo picked up the ball and carried it himself centerfield without celebrating. He wanted a real match.

The ball hit the grass, and Flamengo kept up the pressure. The three friends watched wide-eyed. The team didn't seem to care that they weren't playing on their home turf and Santos had already scored three goals against them. Less than five minutes later, thanks to a header from Thiago Neves, the gap narrowed. To Murilo, Douglas, and Biel, it almost felt like a trick of the eye. The players were fired up, rushing this way and that, it looked more like a kick-around than a championship game. Another five minutes, and Deivid controlled a high ball, then scored Flamengo its third goal. The goal snapped them out of the shock, and both Douglas and Murilo leaped up from the sofa to celebrate the draw. Murilo screamed out the window:

"Flamengo, motherfuckers! Y'all can take your hate and shove it!"

Douglas joined in. Biel watched them and cracked up: on TV, the sports commentator had just announced the goal was disallowed.

They'd barely made sense of the offside when they saw Neymar fall in the penalty box. Penalty kick for Santos. Their joy curdled into agony in a matter of seconds; the most crushing defeats always come after the pinnacle of hope. They dragged their feet back to the sofa. Borges, the player behind two of Santos's goals, grabbed the ball in the hopes of pulling off a hat trick. But Elano, who'd flubbed a penalty kick just days ago for the national team, asked Borges for the ball. It was a gesture of redemption, the commentator said with emotion.

Not one of the friends blinked as they watched Elano prepare to take the penalty kick. Murilo grabbed the bottle of vodka and took another swig. Elano tried his hand at a Panenka and shat the bed. Felipe, the Flamengo goalkeeper, anticipated the play and held the ball, then paid Elano back for his cheek by doing a series of kick-ups before sending the ball into the game again. After a stunt like that one, even Biel, who not only pulled for Vasco but didn't really care about soccer, couldn't peel his eyes away from the screen.

It wasn't long before Flamengo tied with Santos. It felt like the hill would explode from all the shouting, gunshots, and fireworks. As they clumsily celebrated, they realized there was no way they could watch the second half in the apartment without breaking something. They grabbed the vodka and some money, then headed for the streets.

The second the two brothers set foot on Via Ápia, they knew something was up. In the largest favela in Latin America, high foot traffic was normal, and there was noise around the clock. But something was different that day. When they walked into the crowded bar and looked up at the screen, it all started to make sense. The first half had ended on a three–three draw; Flamengo fans were seized with hope while the rest stuck around out of curiosity. The hill was gearing up for a celebration.

"Go get us some weed, bro. In a game like this, if we don't have something to mellow us out, we're gonna have a heart attack," Washington said as if he'd watched the whole match. In the time it took his brother to go to the boca, Washington polished off a can of beer. The enthusiasm in the bar helped dispel his worries about his job situation and the bet he'd placed.

"You haven't even smoked yet, and you're already zonked." Wesley walked in, rolling the joint. "Folks are putting a lot down on this game. We're talking hundreds."

"Santos doesn't stand a chance. When a team gets tied like that in the first half, they can't see straight for the rest of the game. Trust, if Flamengo keeps it up, this match is in the bag. Maranhão must be wigging out right now. Dude's gonna lose two hundred to big daddy."

The ball hit the grass again. Wesley lit up, eyes fixed on the screen. He took a couple of hits, then passed the joint in what seemed like a well-rehearsed move, right as Neymar tore up the left side of the field and scored Santos a fourth goal. Washington took it, annoyed. As he pulled on the joint, all his worries flooded back into his head.

With the match cranked up to eleven, the fans couldn't catch a break. Thanks to the two inspired offenses, and Ronaldinho and Neymar putting on their own show, opportunities multiplied onscreen. The most diehard supporters looked on the verge of cardiac arrest, Wesley included. Unlike his brother, Washington could barely look at the screen after Santos scored another goal.

He started thinking about life, the incident at work, the bet—it was all such a mess, not even the most exciting game of the season could hold his attention. He thought about what he'd accomplished in his twenty-two years of life. Nothing. If he died that day, there wasn't a thing he'd leave behind. For anyone. His mom would still have to pay rent on her apartment. He was starting to regret dropping out of high school two years shy of graduation and leaving the technical course his uncle had signed him up for in the city, all on account of the long commute. Now, there he was, no job to speak of, minutes from losing a bet on the blacktop. He was spiraling so hard he didn't see Ronaldinho take a foul in the penalty box and only realized what had happened when the fans reacted to Flamengo's chance to even the score.

No one breathed as Ronaldinho took the shot. In a stroke of genius, the star player did the opposite of what everyone expected—even Santos, even his teammates. Instead of aiming over the barrier, he kicked a through-ball low to the ground, sinking it in the left corner of the goal. Four–four and all of Rocinha came crashing down.

Less than ten minutes later, Ronaldinho scored a comeback goal, cementing his team's victory and clinching their place in that year's championship. The final whistle sparked more shouting, gunshots, and fireworks—not to mention the urge to hug everyone in sight, at least on the part of Flamengo fans. Total strangers greeted each other and bought rounds of drinks. Smokers took hits of whatever was passed to them. The line for coke was around the corner. Loló was thick on the ground. If an oblivious gringo wandered into the favela, he'd tell everyone at home that he'd seen the world's largest fan base celebrating an important victory. The only thing missing was Mestre setting up speakers and calling an impromptu baile, which hadn't even happened in the 2009 Brazilian championship.

Washington hugged his brother. He almost couldn't believe it. A day he thought for sure would end in shit had started looking up, toward hope and victory. Not only had he witnessed his team win the most important match of the season, but he'd also won some money to keep him afloat while he hunted around for a new job. It almost felt pre-written, like a script or something, Washington thought as he walked up Cachopa. When they got home, he dropped his clothes on his bedroom floor and collapsed on his mattress, confident he was one lucky motherfucker.

RIO—July 28, 2011

A loud, inconsiderate knock. It took Douglas a while to realize it was coming from their front door. When he finally opened his eyes, he felt it rattling in his head. The previous night's activities, which in the depths of sleep seemed as distant as a dream, were beginning to take their toll. It was shaping up to be one of those days when he swore off drinking for good.

Before answering the door, he went to the kitchen and chugged an entire bottle of water. He wanted to wet his throat and also wait a beat. If it was a neighbor come to say something or complain, they'd eventually give up and try again later. But the knocking persisted. It could only be Biel; he'd probably lost his keys again.

"Fuck's sake. Coming!" he shouted, placing the empty bottle in the fridge.

He opened the door and jumped. He'd been so sure it was his friend that he hadn't even put on shorts. Instead, standing at the door was Coroa, the owner of their building and a few others around Valão: a fat, tight-lipped man who walked around with a mean mug, ignoring any hellos, good-mornings, how-are-yous, and keeping quiet about what he did with his money. When he saw Coroa, Douglas wasn't sure what to do, whether to go back inside and throw on some clothes or pretend he was cool with talking in his briefs. Coroa didn't look too comfortable either. He gave his tenant a once-over, lingering on his hips, like he'd never seen a guy sporting morning wood.

"Murilo home, is he?"

"Hey, Mr. Coroa. Murilo's on duty today. Left for the barracks early this morning."

Douglas emphasized the words "duty" and "barracks," as if they could instill some respect.

"Do me a favor and send him up to see me when he gets home, okay?"

"Is it just him you wanna talk to? If it's about the apartment, you can talk to me too."

"All right then. I'm letting you know, and you should tell your friends, that I'll be needing the apartment. You've got until the end of the month to find another place."

"What do you mean, Coroa, sir? If something's the matter, then give it to me straight. We're not kids here, we can talk things through, pô. Don't we pay you rent every month, sir?"

"Listen, you two are lucky I've got a lot of respect for Murilo's mother. It's only on her account—I know she left a lot of furniture here—that you're getting another month. But things have gone too far. If I wasn't a professional, I'd turn you out on the street right now."

Douglas was stunned. When he'd opened the door and

seen Coroa there, he'd been ready for an earful, if only because Coroa was always complaining, but he'd never imagined the guy would want the apartment back, like that, from
one minute to the next.

"I'm renting the place to a couple—no kids, no pets, nothing. And the woman works. Folks who don't muck around
and make a mess like you and your friends, understand? All
day the stink of your old weed, the racket. Nobody can stand
it. The wife's got lung issues. There's days she can barely
breathe. To think I was telling her about wanting to kick you
out, and she goes and stands up for you! That's what she's
like—she stood up for you, the woman. Said there's no getting
away from the devil's grass on this hill, that either the smoke
comes from your neighbor's or from the street or from the
bar, folks like it too much, she said to me. But I'm done with
all your clowning, my building's no circus. This is a place
for families, understand? Working people who need rest. I've
given you a chance. There's no more talking. No talking and
no understanding. It's over."

Coroa spoke fast, jittery. His yellow face reddened. Douglas tried to find the right time to cut in and stand up for himself, but Coroa didn't stop talking, not for a second.

"This morning, I hadn't even had coffee yet or breakfast,
and I thought I saw my wife keel over, dead, right in front of
me. You know what that does to a man's head, big guy?"

The more Coroa talked, the less Douglas understood.

"By your dumb look, I'm guessing your pal, the blond
one, didn't tell you what he did." At his mention of Biel, Coroa
had to stop for a second to breathe out his hatred. "My wife
was standing there making coffee, and I was feeding my little

birds, when your friend shows up out of nowhere, for God only knows what reason. Face like a goat's from all the drugs. She was bringing over my cup, my wife, when she looked up and there he was in the hallway, like a ghost. She got so scared she fainted from all the screaming and sent everything crashing onto the floor. And I almost let one of the canaries out in the rush to get to her. To top it off, your little pal didn't move a finger to help, the peeping Tom. He just stood there watching me with his junkie, wild-eyed face. I sat my wife down in a chair, and by the time I turned around to give him a piece of my mind, he was gone, just as sudden as he came, the scum."

Coroa had no reason to lie or make any of that up. Considering the kind of shit Biel was always pulling, his story seemed plausible. Douglas got nervous. It wouldn't be easy to get the old man to back down, he realized.

"I'm gonna be straight with you, Mr. Coroa, in a situation like this, there's not much anybody can say, you know? We're in the wrong, for real, no use denying it." Douglas was trying to find the right words, to win back Coroa's trust. "All I can say is that I'm sorry about your missus, I mean it, from the heart. We all like her here, you know. But yesterday, there was no helping it, we went off the rails. Everybody did, didn't they? You catch the game?" Coroa was looking at him sternly, his head still. "But, for real, Coroa, just yesterday I was telling the guys that we gotta start taking it easy, lay off the booze, the weed, be chill, just work and stuff. So you can relax now, sir, I'm giving you my word, nothing like that will ever happen again."

"I said what I came here to say. You can tell Murilo you

got a month to leave." Coroa turned on his heel and walked upstairs.

Douglas still tried to talk his way out, but Coroa kept walking. He slammed the door, still feeling a bit woozy. When he closed his eyes, he saw flashes from the night before: the second half of the match at the bar, the empty bottle of vodka, the beer chaser, another bottle of vodka (even cheaper than the first), a cougar getting handsy with Murilo at Mamédio's liquor store, Biel snorting blow with a stranger.

Douglas started really freaking out about his life. He'd been on that rock for twenty years, lived alone since he was seventeen. He couldn't keep acting like that forever, letting loose on a workday. Just to show up at the pharmacy hungover, face crumpled. The manager had been giving him a hard time for a while now. Cracking nasty jokes, making quips about how late and red-eyed he was. Douglas knew it was his time, but not even that could get him to clean up his act.

Besides, that was one of the best gigs he'd ever had. He'd always enjoyed biking, zipping through traffic, feeling the wind on his face. He often cycled down to São Conrado just to kick back and cruise from one end of the coastline to the other. At this job, he got to smoke up between deliveries, didn't have to carry heavy shit, and even had time to sketch between orders.

If he thought about it, the worst part of the job, barring the minimum wage, was going into the buildings. He could just as easily give the package to the doorman, but these people don't leave their apartments for anything in the world. When Douglas walked into those places, he felt like smashing everything to pieces. Vases, paintings, mirrors, all of it. Not that he wanted to leave the hill, live the way they do. But when he saw those patterned tiles, spotless hallways, high-quality wood doors, and lavender-scented trash bags, he was filled with downright hate.

Worried as Douglas was about work, the thing that stuck in his head now was the talk with Coroa. Why had they gone and let Biel crash with them? It was becoming clearer by the day that he was one of those guys who drags his friends down. Sure, the dude was funny, easy to talk to, generous in his own way, but it's hard to do things right when your whole life is a lie. How could a kid born and raised in the favela, a kid who went to public school and everything, live among playboys, dress and talk like them, just because he happened to be born white? Biel lied through his teeth 24/7. And it wasn't a couple white lies a day like everybody else, it was all the time. About where he'd come up, his mom, school, everything. How did he do it? For a while, after moving in with them in Rocinha, he'd kept his playboy act going. It was like Biel couldn't see his true self when he looked in the mirror, which is why he was always going off the rails. All those thoughts had Douglas feeling sorry for his friend, but there was no turning back now. He'd have to talk it through with Murilo, fill him in on the conversation he'd had with Coroa, and explain that the only way to keep the apartment was to ditch Biel. Nothing personal, it wasn't their fault he was constantly high, being his own worst enemy. Murilo would understand, it was the only way.

The thought of losing the apartment was straight-up terrifying. The place was spacious, well-located, awesome all-round. Travessa Kátia was one of the best streets in Via Ápia.

There was a bus stop less than two minutes away, a 24-hour bakery, and a bunch of other eateries, including classic PF joints that served up set meals, Japanese restaurants, pizzerias, and more. Not to mention they were a short, twenty-minute walk from São Conrado beach. The only thing that made it less than perfect was the building being located between a whore-house and an Evangelical church; when it wasn't whoring on the one side, it was praise-the-lord on the other. Things got particularly unhinged on Good Fry-day, when the two sides went at it at the same time. Besides that small detail, it was a great time. They didn't have to worry about spending money on mototaxis, and they never ran out of water, two issues most other residents couldn't escape.

Douglas got more and more anxious. Not only would it be hard to find an apartment as cool as their current one, but they'd also have to *move*. Haul a fridge through an alley, take apart a wardrobe only to put it together again, carry a mattress, the usual crap. Douglas's mind was set: he would do whatever it took to stay put.

With Biel out of the picture, they'd be shouldering a larger portion of the bills, but it'd also be a lot easier to lay off the booze, hold on to their money. With that, Douglas could afford to buy tattoo equipment, set his plan in motion. Before he knew it, he'd be working at a parlor and making money from ink; then he'd only ride his bike for pleasure. He'd get to make his own schedule, wear dope threads, meet girls. His phone alarm started going off in his room. It was time to wake up and get to work.

RIO—August 3, 2011

Dude didn't show face for a week. When Washington stopped by his place, it was crickets. Lights off around the clock. He started thinking Maranhão had skipped town for his namesake, that there was no hope, he was going to come away empty-handed. Worst yet, he understood the guy, for real. If things had gone the other way, and Flamengo lost the match, he had no idea where he would've found the cash. He'd probably have lain low as well, either while scaring up the dough or waiting for everybody to forget.

Lesson learned: gambling's a headache. No matter who won, the stress was shared fifty-fifty. Half for the person coughing it up and half for the person chasing it up. If he was in a better place, he'd have left it alone.

It was mountain-mellow in Cachopa. In Larguinho, where folks usually hung out at any hour of the night or day, there wasn't a soul he could ask for a toke. Everybody laying low.

His best bet was to head home; it was looking like drizzle again.

Washington got there shivering head to toe. All he wanted was to crawl into bed under a blanket. Instead, the second he set foot in his room, he turned everything upside down again in the hopes of unearthing a roach. Nothing. He'd have to wait for Wesley to get back. Being out of work sucked, with nothing to do in that freezing cold and nothing to help him unwind.

He sat in bed and lit up the loosie he'd gotten on the street, then started mulling over his talk with Dona Marli. As he'd imagined, she wasn't so much annoyed about him quitting as she was about how he'd done it. Dona Marli had always made a point of teaching her sons the importance of keeping your name clean and not burning bridges, not with anyone or in any job, because you might need them someday, and then what? It's good to keep doors open, she was always saying before rattling off a list of the places she'd worked and been allowed back to when she wanted or needed. The problem was that Washington had slammed a door shut. The door to a shit job, no doubt, but a door no less.

He started regretting telling his mom, but what was he supposed to do? It wasn't like he could claim he'd just woken up one day, and the air had felt different, so he'd gone and quit. He couldn't run away or make something up; he had to give it to her straight. Besides, when Washington talked about the argument in the kitchen, about letting out everything he'd held inside for so long, in front of everybody, he felt proud, there was no denying it. Naturally, Dona Marli sided with the manager and even came out with the classic line about how the girl was just doing her job.

Washington and Wesley didn't like how subservient their mother was toward her bosses, all conscientious and grateful. But what could they actually say to her? The woman had never been out of work or asked anybody for a handout, all while raising two kids on her own. The thing to do was listen.

Tired of thinking, Washington switched on his computer so he could activate his contacts. He scanned Facebook chat for friends with online statuses, wrote "HOOK US UP" to a handful, and prayed for a miracle. In the meantime, he checked out the profile of this girl who'd sent him a friend request. Considering the people they knew in common, she must be from the Paula Brito area.

Gleyce Kelly. He scrolled through her photos but couldn't remember if they'd ever met on the hill. Seemed unlikely. From what Washington was seeing, she wasn't someone you forgot. He'd just liked a bunch of her profile pics, so it wouldn't take him long to figure out if she was looking to start something with him or if she was just one of those people who collects friends on social media. Once he was done, he scrolled back to a favorite: Gleyce on the beach in a bikini flashing her tongue ring.

Washington always got horny as hell when he was bored. He put his hand down his briefs. Seconds later, he was pitching a tent. Outside, the rain fell in sheets. He closed his eyes and pictured them fucking on one of the beaches of São Conrado or visualized them going at it in the apartment bathroom, on the sofa, in bed. He was about to come when he heard a knock on the door. He shoved his dick back in his pants, praying the blood would rush out as fast as it'd rushed in.

"Took you long enough, menó! Break out that joint already. I'm fucking dying over here."

After getting no response, he walked out of his room to check that the noise had really come from inside the house. It was Dona Marli. She was home much earlier than usual, soaking wet under her rain poncho, carrying groceries.

"You're hopeless, aren't you, Washington. Not one goddamn cent in your pocket and all you can think about is smoking that shit."

"God bless, Ma."

"God bless and keep you, son."

Washington took the groceries to the kitchen while his mother changed into dry clothes. The second he stepped in there, he became acutely aware of the dishes he'd let pile up throughout the day. Dona Marli had the power to make any mess in the house shriek in despair. She walked into the kitchen and gazed around at everything, scrutinizing the disorder. Then, without saying a word, they began putting away the groceries.

He wanted to tell her he'd gone out looking for Maranhão a bunch of times, but his mom didn't know about the bet, and things stood to get way worse if he brought it up. Still, Washington felt the need to say he'd done something that day, that he'd scoped out a job or chased up an interesting-looking course, anything, even if it was bogus. But nothing came to mind. He was familiar with that silence: his mother was making every effort to hold back, but he knew she'd explode eventually, out of nowhere.

"You stay home all day, and you still got the nerve to leave dishes in the sink for me to do. I must've fucking sinned in some past life!" Dona Marli stood at the sink.

"I was about to get to them. You came back early."

"And the floor? Were you about to sweep as well? Who do you think you're kidding, Washington? If you were gonna make yourself useful round the house, you'd have done it already instead of waiting for me to get home. When your brother's here, he leaves everything spotless. You don't see any of Wesley's clothes or sheets or nothing lying around. And he's younger, a pothead just like you. So what's your excuse?"

His mother had a habit of comparing the two brothers, and it drove Washington crazy. In her head, it was like they were always competing over who the best son was, who helped out more around the house, who brought in more money.

"C'mon, Dona Marli, gimme a break. I swear I was about to do it."

"What about before? Did you take your CV to that place I told you about?"

All that talk was making Washington regret quitting. He knew his mom would be on his case until he got another job. What he should've done, he was only realizing now, was look for work while he was still on the payroll. Then he could've had something else lined up when he quit.

"I don't even have bus fare. What do you want me to do? Been checking if anything needs delivering or moving, but it's tough in this weather. One of my buddies said he'd call tomorrow with a lead," he managed to lie.

"Don't have bus fare? Then walk, ué. Or are you made of

sugar? Go down to São Conrado, drop off some CVs at the mall, the pet shop, in the South Zone . . . then swing by Gávea. Doesn't hurt to try."

"Don't worry, Dona Marli. I'm gonna hustle, promise."

"I already told you not to call me Dona. I'm not even fifty."

"And if you keep turning forty-five every year, you never will be."

They finally smiled at each other. Now that the tension had eased, Washington wanted to jump on his computer, see if anyone had come through for him. But he couldn't help himself.

"Now, be honest, Dona Marli. Would you hire somebody who showed up at your place of business soaking wet, covered in mud, with a sloppy mess of papers? Tell me, would you? I know what you're like. You'd be the first to say that if a guy shows up at an interview looking like that, just think how he's gonna look when he shows up for work."

Washington always had an answer for everything. This both fascinated and irritated the hell out of Dona Marli, who usually just ignored him.

"I went to the bank today. The place is a nightmare, Washington. There's so many people there on the first of the month. It's a madhouse."

"See? You're always changing the subject."

"I even left work earlier than usual." Dona Marli bent over to put away the pots. She continued, eyes averted: "I wanted to talk to the manager about a loan."

"You owe the kingpin money or something?"

Dona Marli ignored him. She finished putting away the dishes, went into the living room, and sat on the sofa. Washington knew she didn't appreciate him joking around like that. As a kid, he'd gotten beaten for a lot less, to teach him not to talk like a thug. But for some reason he thought it'd be funny this time. At least he could go back to his room now, check if someone had offered to hook him up.

Dona Marli seemed restless, legit outraged. Washington acted like he didn't see her and walked straight to his bedroom. One of his friends had DM'ed to say they were all meeting at Moderninho's for a fatty. As he threw on a jacket, he saw his mom still sitting there on the sofa, staring glassy-eyed at a blank TV screen.

"What's all this stuff about a loan, Ma? Is something the matter?" He sat down next to her.

"I don't wanna pay rent all my life, son. Before you know it, I'll be too old to work, and then what? I've got to get settled."

The fact that his mom had started working before she was ten, and still didn't have a house to call her own, always made Washington rage against the world.

"So did the money stuff get worked out?"

"The application's being evaluated. Now we just wait," Dona Marli replied, raising her hands to the sky.

"Cool. But isn't the interest on that kind of thing steep and all?"

"Apparently, it's not too bad if you stay on schedule. At least I'd be putting money toward something that's gonna be mine. That way if anything happens to me tomorrow, or whenever, I can leave you two a house. You never get rent money back, and I'm tired of that bullshit."

As Dona Marli unburdened herself, she seemed like a completely different person. A lot more fragile than her son was used to. Washington wanted to tell his mom not to worry, that soon enough he'd find a good job, and they'd start moving up in the world. It would make his mom happy to hear those words, even proud, but he couldn't get them out because he didn't believe them. They sat in silence for a while.

"I'm gonna talk to Valdir, see if he'll sell us the apartment. We're at home here, wouldn't have to move . . ."

"I don't think Valdir's interested in selling, Mom. The guy owns the whole building. Why sell one unit?"

"Money. I think he'd be open to it for cash. And if he isn't, we find something else. I'm not a plant or anything to be putting down roots."

"It's not easy finding a two-bedroom on the hill. Maybe in Rua 4, but I don't think folks down there can sell yet." Washington wanted to be supportive, but all he could think of were the obstacles.

"Any old thing. I saw a couple new buildings over in Freguesia, near Itanhangá. A bit farther from work, but quiet. There are some nice apartments."

"C'mon, Ma. You wanna live on militia turf now?"

"You're twenty-two years old now, Washington. Time to stop joking around. Talking like a thug. You think you've got what it takes to be a player? No? Then why keep pretending? What's the point? Tell me. By the time I was your age, I already had you, and your brother was on his way. You have any idea what that's like? I didn't think so. So wake the hell up."

"All I mean is that living on militia turf is no joke." Washington didn't want to make his mother more upset. "Me and Wesley, we're potheads, Ma, there's no helping it. We like smoking weed, and we're not gonna stop. So, like, how are we supposed to move over there, with those guys? They're bad people."

"You don't wanna move there, that's on you. Rent a place of your own here in Rocinha, have it your way. I've done my part. You've been raised, thank God. But from now on, as long as you live under my roof, you'd better pitch in. You're too old and too big to be dragging me down. You're grown-ass men. I've worked like a dog all my life to support you and your brother. Either help me steer this ship or get off."

Conversation over. Washington had wanted to ask her for some money to buy a loosie, but he lost the will to do it. Dona Marli got off the sofa and went to her room. Judging by the time, the joint at Moderninho's was long gone. Washington switched on the TV, face burning up. He was more angry about not being able to give his mom a boost than he was about not smoking with his friends. He thought of apologizing several times, but it was like he was nailed to that sofa. Twenty minutes into his mindless channel hopping, Dona Marli walked out of her room with a five-real note.

"Here."

It wasn't raining anymore. Washington took the money, kissed his mother, and left.

RIO—August 8, 2011

Murilo leaped out of the armored car with the other soldiers in his battalion. They headed into the alley, 7.62 rifles held across their chests. Adrenaline was a shield against the night cold, so much that he was sweating through his uniform. Tense, he went with the flow; the only sound he could hear was the duty boots keeping rhythm on the concrete. None of them had asked, none of them wanted to know, but the truth is Murilo was well-acquainted with that alley. He'd been born and raised in that place. It's where he'd learned to run, lie, smoke. But now, as he trailed a line of soldiers through the night, it dawned on him that he might not have anywhere to go home to.

How had he come to be in that situation? Up until then, being in the Army had mostly involved running, surveillance, doing sweeps. And he liked it that way. If he'd wanted to shoot guns, he'd have worked at the boca; it made more sense. While he tried to understand how he'd wound up there, he watched his fellow soldiers advance on high alert, even though the alleys were deserted. The houses were dead quiet too, and all the bars closed. Murilo wondered if there was anyone left on that hill. Then he got his answer: his battalion received orders to drive out the neighborhood's last remaining residents. That's when he noticed the bullet holes in the walls of the houses around him, the blood trickling down the steps as if from a fountain at the very top of the hill.

How long had they been at war? Murilo's body was tired, sore, like he hadn't slept in days. All of a sudden, he heard a burst of gunfire. The fear didn't stop him from immediately getting into combat position and firing his weapon up the hill, despite there being no enemy in sight. A shadow appeared around the corner and was instantly shot. It didn't matter that everyone was firing their rifles at the same time; Murilo felt like *his* bullets were the ones that pierced that body. The man crumpled to the ground. Murilo recognized him: Sparks, an old buddy who'd been working at the boca for a while. Another body appeared and was quickly shot down: Douglas, who dropped his umbrella before falling to his knees. The volley of gunfire didn't stop for a second. Murilo kept firing his rifle through the shock, one bullet after another; it was what he was trained to do. Another person down. At peak adrenaline, Murilo didn't have time to be shocked, his mission was to keep pulling that trigger.

The second Murilo lowered his head to change the magazine, he was immersed in the pin-drop silence that follows a shootout. He quickly reloaded, then looked up and saw a woman standing a little over one meter away. He didn't recognize her and yet, at the same time—it was the strangest thing—he *knew* her.

"It's over. Let's go home," she said.

Murilo thought for a minute, pointed his gun at the woman, and jolted awake.

His sudden movement startled the woman next to him on the bus. She grumbled. Outside, it was pitch dark. Murilo peered out the window trying to figure out where they were. The 594 bus had just passed Parque da Cidade and was trundling up to Rocinha.

Most of the buses to Rocinha went along low roads like Via Ápia and Largo das Flores. Murilo could get home a lot faster if he took one of those. But the 594 terminated in Leme, right next to the barracks, and he generally preferred taking the circuitous route over walking to Copacabana.

Although the trip was longer, and the traffic on Estrada da Gávea a lot heavier, it was a cool ride. There was the view of Lagoa when the bus went past the RJ-99, girls in spandex streaming in and out of the gym, and billboards for upcoming events and baile headliners. Living where he did put him farther away from what was happening on the hill, which is why Murilo always woke up around that point. He wanted to see what was what.

He only remembered his nightmare when the bus turned into Vila da Miséria. He patted his clothes to make sure he'd changed out of his uniform. Things had been peaceful in Rocinha since Nem took over. Maybe that's why both players and residents started calling him Mestre, because he was the master of the hill. The last major operation they'd had was the one where Fiscal died, trading .30-caliber bullets. Besides that, there'd been no shootouts in years. Cops only went there for their kickbacks, and rival cartels knew that the only way anyone was taking over that hill was with a full-blown coup, so business was smooth sailing. Still, it made Murilo nervous as hell to wear his uniform in the favela.

What was that nightmare about? he wondered, ignoring everything outside the window at every point of the hill: Rua 1, Portão Vermelho, Paula Brito, Dioneia. The 594 gradually emptied out. After Curva do S, Murilo was the only one left. Sitting at the back of the bus, he contemplated his life as a soldier. Sure, he'd been trained, he'd learned to shoot, to take apart a rifle and put it back together. But even though he stood armed guard and called back to military chants, he'd never actually pictured himself in the fray, firing bullets. The truth is, Murilo had considered doing loads of different things since he was a kid, and none of them had involved the military.

It was impossible not to think of everything that'd happened in the last two years. After failing his junior year twice, Murilo dropped out of school and headed straight for the barracks. The plan was to save up some money in the first twelve months, then quit and figure something else out. But then his mom moved out, followed by his sister, and Douglas and Biel moved in. Everything had happened so fast, and in the two years he'd been in the Army, he hadn't managed to save any money. It was like life didn't give him the time he needed to think and make decisions. Like he had no choice but to take things one day at a time and hope for the best.

Murilo nearly missed his stop. Luckily, he spotted Pizza Rio through the window, giving him just enough time to jump out of his seat and yell at the driver to pull over, he was getting off at Via Ápia. Part of his afterwork routine was to hit the boca and cop two bengalinhas, plus the occasional bit of hash, before going home. That night, he went less out of habit than out of necessity.

At the boca, the usual suspects were on shift. Standing not far behind the dealer was Sparks, sporting an MP5 so new it practically shined.

"Sup, man, what's kicking? Throw us a pair of benga."

"Go ahead and pick one." Magic 8-Ball passed Murilo the product.

Every day, he fished out two bengalinhas from that bag. Sometimes, when the stash was nearing the end, he spent ages fishing around for the fuller baggies. If he didn't find any, he hung around and shot the shit until more product came in. But this time, he chose two at random, the first ones he saw, handed over the money, and pocketed the weed. He wanted to go home.

Sparks came up to him. A Botafogo sticker iced up his weapon. Murilo couldn't help picturing how a Flamengo sticker would look on his own rifle.

"How's tricks at the barracks, neguim?"

"Just coming from there."

"Cool. Y'all got heat like this over there?" Sparks showed off his submachine gun.

"Nah, man. All we have there is rifles. FAL and Para FAL."

"My man's rocking that seven-six-two, huh?"

"It's a sweet shot. But sucks for guard duty. Thing's heavy as fuck."

"This girl here's nice and light. Strong in a shootout, and also ace if you gotta bolt." Sparks said this with total confidence, even though he'd never traded shots.

"Cool."

"Give her a try."

Murilo gingerly took the MP5 from Sparks and got the hang of it in no time. He'd never held one in real life, though he was familiar with the weapon from his Counter-Strike days. This reminded Murilo of some good times: his early teens, back when he used to catch waves on São Conrado and then hole up at an internet café until late at night, chatting up girls.

"I used to tear it up with this baby on CS. 10/10 headshot."

After he said this, everybody at the boca, from the players to the junkies, started going on about the weapons they used to fire and the levels they used to beat on the infamous first-person shooter. They all talked over each other, and it was hard to make sense of anything they said.

Not wanting to hang around long, Murilo handed back the machine gun, said goodbye to the pushers, and bounced. The hill still seemed weird. He gazed around at the stores, the botecos, the food stands, the crowds of people on the street . . . Everything was different but also the same. He just hoped the weed he'd bought from the boca was killer. That way, he could wash the day off, hit the sack, and drift into a deep slumber.

RIO—August 17, 2011

It was almost night by the time Wesley made it back to Rocinha. He'd had this weird feeling in his stomach since leaving the precinct. Only when he saw O China did he realize he hadn't eaten all day. The second the pastel hit his hand, Zói was there, asking for money. Wesley pretended he was talking to somebody else. He'd noticed a while ago that Zói only smoked baile cigarettes, and this bugged the hell of out him. Loads of residents had to smoke whatever cancer sticks they could get their hands on. Meanwhile, this panhandler's smoking Gudang Garam? It was a disrespect to the working man.

Zói stuck around, even though he kept striking out. Maybe he was waiting for more customers or hoped people would change their minds once they were full-up. The staff didn't bother trying to throw him out or stop him from asking patrons for money; over time, Zói had become an integral part of that place. On a hill as big as that one, where tons of people were strangers to each other, he was something of a common denominator, a shared interest, from the top of Rocinha all the way to the bottom.

Plenty of folks were convinced Zói only *acted* crazy: never looking you in the eye when he asked for money, never answering your questions, ignoring anyone who cursed him out. It was as if he could say one thing and one thing only: *Gimme some money.* It was a whole different story when you agreed to buy something for him. The baile cigarettes had to be cinnamon. People had tried pushing menthols on him multiple times only to be turned down. He knew his way around the boca too—around eight-balls of coke and dime bags of weed. And he never let dealers get one over on him. Sometimes he slept under a canopy near Curva do S, other times near Valão or Via Ápia. He was always in the area, amassing stories in back alleys, putting fear in little kids' hearts, serving as a conversation piece. There was no helping it—after so many years on the streets of that hill, Zói had won over the vast majority of residents.

Halfway through his pastel, Wesley realized the food wasn't sitting right. He downed the rest of his passion fruit juice and considered throwing away his leftovers, but instead offered them to Zói, who in response just asked for money. Wesley tossed the food at a band of dogs, lit a cigarette, and went looking for a mototaxi.

The mototaxi rank on Via Ápia was empty. It was weird, even at rush hour there were usually half a dozen hanging around. He studied the streets around him. People were walking in every direction, but one crucial thing was missing: the motorcycles. Not one bike zipping up or down, no revving engines, no smell of exhaust.

That's when Wesley noticed the bocas were also deserted. He started tripping. The last thing they needed was for the hill to be hot. He looked down the street, toward Pizza Rio, and saw a mototaxi driver turn a corner with a passenger. They both had helmets on, which happened every now and never, except when the run was to the blacktop. It all seemed so strange to Wesley. Then, all of a sudden, he saw a squad of cops—all Civilian Police—leave Travessa Roma, and spotted several more stepping out of other parts of the hill. With their black shirts and pants and their confidence that no drug dealer would ever dream of messing with them. It made him shudder.

Wesley couldn't remember the last time there were cops in Rocinha. Seeing them there on that day—of all days— made things feel prearranged and creepy as hell. A group of three cops was heading toward the mototaxi stand. When they passed him, Wesley asked on impulse what the reason was for the operation.

"What are you, a journalist?" the cop replied.

Wesley considered saying he was a resident, but then worried they'd think he was giving them lip and ask for his ID, put him through all that grief again on the same day.

"Piracy sweep," the other officer said before moving on.

Wesley glanced around for the mototaxi driver he'd spotted earlier, but the guy was already zipping away with another passenger. Not wanting to stick around any longer than he had to, he decided to walk.

It was business as usual on the hill as he made his way home. Motorcycles, buses, cars, and people jostling for space in the street. The clamor of horns and loudspeakers. Wesley clocked a few mototaxis but decided to keep walking; he was already near Curva do S, anyway. At least he saved himself two reais that way. As he trudged uphill, he couldn't quit thinking about the motorbike his friend was selling. One thousand reais, new, 150 cc engine. Sure, it was hot, meaning he couldn't ride it off the hill, but still worth it. Once he started working as a mototaxi driver, it'd be no time at all before he saved enough money for a bike with the proper documentation. He could even get his license. Okay, so it might mean problems with Dona Marli, but whatever, he'd just come up with some story or other; what he couldn't do was pass up the opportunity. Wesley had wanted to be a mototaxi driver for a while now. Besides keeping his own schedule and working in his neighborhood, he knew chicks went crazy for riders.

When he got home, he found Washington looking very happy. He had no idea there were cops in the area; he was just excited Maranhão had turned up again. True, the guy didn't have the money he owed Washington, but what he did have was a scoop on an over-the-table job—with signed work cards, a hot commodity—a rec from a cousin who'd worked at the joint for a while.

"If menó's so hard up, how come he doesn't want the job for himself?" Wesley asked, a bit skeptical.

"He's got some help right now. Plus, he's trying to see if he can get back up home."

"All right, all right, that's cool. You know, I been meaning to visit Maranhão."

"You know what's crazy? Maranhão wasn't even born there. He's from Piauí or something."

That shit was hilarious. No one knew why nicknames stuck in Cachopa, but they did, and like superglue. They had plenty of friends whose given names they'd never heard in their lives. Maranhão was one of them. The two brothers cracked up, then tried like hell to remember his real name to no success.

"Roll us a joint, menó. Your little brother got certified today," Wesley said, changing the subject. He was dying to tell somebody what he'd been through.

Washington had no idea what Wesley was talking about, but he still had a bit of grass tucked away, so he got down to work. Wesley waited until he'd taken his first long drag on the joint before pulling a citation out of a folder.

"Today was fucking trippy, straight up. Funny too, I guess. Those guys are a goddamn joke. Remember I said I was gonna get my ID straightened out? So, I really did. First thing this morning, I saw the sun coming up and threw on a pair of shorts so I could hit the beach after. Kick back somewhere different, since I was gonna be right near Ipanema anyway. Cool, so, I couldn't be fucked to go up to the boca. Figured I'd swing by the one on Via Ápia instead, seeing as it's on the way and shit. So, check it, I get there and all they got is coke and lança-perfume. I try Valão, same story. Players tell me I'd only find weed up in Cachopa. Fuck, man, what a bitch. I didn't wanna head back up the hill on account of the ID shit at Poupatempo. Then I remembered Chapolha had been on a mission in Cruzada that week, said the dime bags were chronic. You know what he's like, though, you gotta take his word for it cause when that dude gets his hands on grass, he vanishes like a fart in the wind, no joke. Worst of all, mooches like him are a dime a dozen, bumming off us 24/7 and thinking we don't notice. Anyway, there was always the boca in Cantagalo, which is right next to Poupatempo, but, real talk, I'd rather walk around with the sun on my head, beating down, burning hard, than throw money at those opps. Bunch of twitchy assholes. Those dudes are always getting sus around neguins from outside their favela. You know how it is. They ain't got a clue how to make money. They should take a page out of the book of the menós, the shorties, in Jacaré, Manguim, those parts. Now that's serious crime. Those guys don't give a fuck who you are, where you're from. All they care about is moving product, quality stuff. The players at that boca know how to make their clients feel at ease. So who's gonna try anything against them?

"Anyway, I copped some weed in Cruzada and it was like, all right, not great. Should've just gotten bengala in Rocinha. Would've been easier, more low-key. The trouble, the real trouble, came after. I straightened out my ID and shit. True to its name, Poupatempo really does save you time. Took me twenty minutes tops, no joke. If I'd known it'd be so fast, I'd've done this shit sooner. But cool, whatever. A friend and me had agreed to link up in Galo before hitting Arpoador. He got there in no time and pulled out some hash he'd copped in Mangueira. Decent stuff, not gonna lie. When you crumbled that shit, it was brown, but, like, light brown, true Moroccan. Good, strong smell too. I got the itch to hit Mangueira myself and get some for us to smoke at home. But you know how far that place is, and I only been once, with Zeta, not even sure where the boca is located. Plus, it's rough showing up someplace and having to ask around for that kinda intel. Bugs me out.

"So we meet up at the metro entrance. I'd even swung through the South Zone for some cookies, you know, for the eventual munchies. I paid with my last note, this hundred-real bill I'd been holding on to since the last party I worked, the one I didn't wanna break cause, you know how it goes, funds vanish fast once you do. Fuck, the look on the cashier's face. She kept checking if the note was fake. Then she gave me change in five-real bills. Later I told Luan: Shit, if the cops catch me with this, they're gonna think I'm running nickel bags of grass. We laughed about it then, but that's exactly what fucking happened.

"I was pretty zonked by the time we started rolling the joint. After we smoked the hash, I was on another fucking planet. Annihilated. Honest, I didn't even wanna smoke more, but I figured I should contribute or else it'd look like I was holding out on him. So we kicked back there, burning one in a tide pool, right on the edge of the ocean, splashing around, shooting the breeze. That's when the pigs rocked up.

"There were two plainclothes. One was on the phone, fuming cause his car was at the shop or some shit, fuck knows. It sounded like he couldn't get there in time to pick it up. The third cop was in uniform and immediately shoved his gun in my face. The dude on the phone was spitting poison, like he wanted to scare the shit out of us. Asshole wasn't even packing heat either, he just had a nightstick. Fucking moron, I swear. Menó, the second they saw I had money, they let it rip. One of them said they'd been tipped off to some drug deals in the area and that we matched the description. Then another guy wanted to know how old we were and asked to see our IDs. When Luan said he was sixteen . . . shit hit the fucking fan, menó. They started going on about how I'd be going down for possession with intent and corruption of a minor, that kinda crap, I was shitting myself.

"I tried talking my way out of it, right? Showed them the

paperwork from Poupatempo. But it was no use, I was heading to the station, no discussion. For a second I thought all that crap was just an excuse for them to put hands on my money, but they didn't mention it. And I didn't know that once I was at the precinct with all my paperwork and no record, no nothing, they'd have to let me go. Unless the pigs had contraband in their cruiser that they could use to frame us. But whatever, we didn't stand a chance. They put cuffs on us right there on the rock. Folks around us were rubbernecking, wanting to see what was what. We were almost at the cruiser when a reporter from *O Dia*, or *Extra*, or some shit rocks up and asks what the charge is. The cop says we'd been selling drugs in Arpoador, that they'd nabbed us thanks to an anonymous tip. The reporter jotted it all down in his notebook, then got closer to take our picture. Fool thought I'd try and hide my face like Luan, but nah, menó, I stared right at the camera, no joke. I wanna see him try and print my face in the paper tomorrow. I'll sue the motherfucker for all he's got, rake it in.

"They let Luan go the minute we rocked up to the precinct in Leblon. Said they were doing me a solid cause without the rap for corruption of a minor, I'd get four, five years max. I kept my mouth shut. I mean, waste my breath for what? What I wanted was to talk with the chief of police, show him my paperwork and stuff. But first we had to wait for the results of the investigation to come back from Cidade da Polícia, their headquarters in Jacaré. I was raging, I swear. Dudes make a living from shaking down dudes with drugs, and still they have to go to the back of fucking beyond to check if the weed they found really is weed? Fuck them. Those dickrags are always jerking us around.

"So here's the deal: I couldn't even go out for a smoke. I was pissed, bro. Then out of nowhere these three cops come back from some operation and drop a ton of bricks on the desk. They're wrapped in paper, so I can't tell if it's weed, coke, or what. They just drop it all there in a stack on the chief of police's desk, and leave. Then they come back and put a walkie-talkie and a RioCard on the same desk. Another dude walks out of the room and, bam, comes back in with a weed plant and drops it right next to everything else. They start counting out the bricks in front of the boss. Meanwhile, I'm sitting there with fuckall to do, not even trying to act like I'm not peeping. I watch them, wondering if that shit came from a tip-off, where it all went down, if shots were fired . . . There were thirty-six bricks total. The second they stopped counting—you're not gonna believe this—the cop says to me: Bet you've never been so close and so far from this many drugs. Then he and all the other fucks there crack up. I swear, they thought it was the funniest thing on fucking earth. Worst of all, at the time I kinda wanted to laugh too, but I stayed quiet, so they wouldn't get any ideas.

"The dude who put the weed plant on the table stands in front of it, touches one of the leaves and says to his buddy: Man, these guys must be out of their minds to be smoking leaves off this shit. I swear I couldn't help myself, menó. I said to them: Nobody smokes the leaves, man. What we smoke is the bud, which is like the fruit, right? That plant y'all got is worthless. I can tell from over here that it's male, meaning, it's no good for smoking. The other cop, the one who'd made that quip at me, started cracking up: Well, hell. Male, female, bud.

These days you gotta be a professional if you want to smoke cannabis. After that, they left.

"What really pisses me off is that we were around the corner from the boca where I'd bought the weed they'd caught me with. Like, a block away. You know the precinct across from the mall? That's the one. Dudes dealing as usual right there in Cruzada while I'm sitting inside like a dumbass waiting for them to finish the investigation.

"Things went fast after the cop came back with the results. I showed the chief of police my ID, wasn't much else to do. He told me to watch my back cause the officers that had cuffed me were pissed and wouldn't be forgetting my face anytime soon. Fuck that. Like I'm not already watching my back. So I signed the citation. I was sure I was gonna get hit with possession with intent, but then the chief of police decided to charge me with plain possession instead. Plus, the codes have all changed. The old-timers used to go on about article 16 for possession, but now it's 18. And possession with intent isn't article 12 anymore, either. It's 32."

"Fuck, man. This shit only ever happens to you."

Washington was studying the citation. Even though his brother's account of the story was funny, and they'd gotten a good laugh out of it, he couldn't help hating those officers every time he pictured his brother walking down Pedra do Arpoador in handcuffs.

"That's life for you, ain't it, menó? You gave me my first joint, but I got certified before you."

Wesley took the citation back from his brother and looked at the document some more.

"Check it, your boy's a professional pothead now."

RIO—August 19, 2011

After a week of rain, the sun shone with a vengeance. The pharmacy's customers, all from Gávea, kept whining about how there were no real winters in Rio anymore—one week, and it was over, they didn't even get to wear their cold-weather clothes. Douglas could give less of a fuck. Folks always found something to bitch about. After days of riding his bike in a poncho, wheels caked with mud and clothes soaking wet, all he wanted was to feel the sun warming his skin.

He let the wind push his bike down Rua Marquês de São Vicente. Traffic was light, so he zoned out, daydreaming about the future. If he set aside a bit of cash, he could use his year-end bonus to buy himself some tattoo equipment: a machine, grips, needles, a few basic colors. Then, he'd lock down the disposables—gloves, paper towels, plastic wrap—and embrace his new life. It was wild, the more he researched the profession, the more he realized he still had so much to buy, to learn. It wasn't easy getting started, but at the end of the day, it was totally worth it. He knew plenty of tattoo artists on the hill who were making bank.

Thinking about the future inevitably led him to think about the past. When he was a kid, everybody was suspicious of tattoos, claiming only thugs, whores, and junkies had them. That nobody would hire you if you got inked. But it was a nonissue these days. Even his mom rocked a shoulder piece. It was funny, he thought: back then, something as innocent as temporary tats were a no-go. Whenever he tried to talk his family into letting him get one, his grandma would say: You're not cattle, so why get branded?

One time, when he was seven, he'd slapped on a temporary tat without telling anybody. He'd put it on his ribs because that way he could hide it under his shirt and still show it off to his friends in the street. But he hadn't counted on how hellish it'd be to keep his shirt on in the summer heat. At home, everybody was always nagging him to take it off, but Douglas refused. Face dripping with sweat. Cousins splashing around in the garden hose. Before he knew it, he'd forgotten all about the tattoo and started splashing around with them.

His grandpa said nothing when he walked onto the terrace and saw the little rocket on Douglas's rib cage. He just stood there watching the kids play. It didn't take Douglas long to realize he'd better get to the kitchen stat, find some rubbing alcohol, and make that tattoo disappear. Which is exactly what he did. Then he went back to the terrace with no top on and zero guilt, though he was kind of surprised his grandad hadn't mentioned it.

The minute Seu Josias saw his grandson, he stubbed out

his half-smoked cigarette, strode up to him, and smacked him right on the ass. Just the once. Seu Josias had a heavy hand from laying down slabs and throwing up walls. One smack was all it took to make Douglas piss himself. As far as his family was concerned, he'd had it coming; maybe he'd think twice next time before stunting. Funny thing, family.

He was cruising these memories when he smelled some marola. Somebody was burning some loud weed. He wasn't sure if it was because he'd woken up late that morning and not had time to smoke before work, but he was transfixed. Douglas hit the brakes.

The scent was coming from a bakery. A bakery-bar-restaurant right outside PUC, the Catholic university. College kids hung out there before, during, and after class. Douglas quickly found the group with the good stuff; even though loads of people were smoking, the dank his nose picked up was special. He debated sliding up to them and low-key asking for a toke, claiming work was a bitch that day—go on, just one. But he was frozen in place. It wasn't the first time he'd stopped there with the same plan. But when the time came to make things happen, he always chickened out.

Douglas spotted a police car in the distance. Driving past the shopping mall, it was headed in their direction. He figured he'd better dip. Later, he looked back to see if there was any trouble at the bakery—it'd been loud in there—but the police car just cruised past, vanishing into Parque da Cidade.

That scene reminded him of his buddy Renan from Rua 2, a dude with loads of high concepts. Renan was always saying that folks who were born with no disabilities, folks who come into this world with their legs, arms, eyes, ears, and mouths doing what they're supposed to, were born with silver spoons in their mouths. The rest was just a matter of inclination and drive. He was saying that again the other day when a friend cut in:

"If we're born with silver spoons in our mouths, then what're playboys born with?"

"With silver spoons up their asses!"

The crash didn't send Douglas too far. He even managed to turn to avoid banging his head. But his bike . . . The front wheel was twisted into an eight. Only once the shock wore off did Douglas feel his elbow burning, scraped raw by the hot asphalt. Then came the driver.

"Don't you watch where you're going, kid?"

Douglas sized him up. The man was in good shape, but not enough to hide that he was no youngblood.

"If you're going to bike against traffic, then you have to keep an eye out for cars. How am I supposed to know someone's turning the corner?"

Douglas didn't feel like arguing. The less of an issue he made of it, the faster they could settle things and the faster he could get out of there. People stopped to watch them.

"Come on, kid, get up. The cars are starting to honk. It'll be mayhem soon . . . Get up, come on. Are you okay?"

"Fuck if I'm okay. Don't you see my arm? And what about my fucking bike? I need it for work. You gonna pay to get it fixed?"

The argument drew a crowd. The old man seemed daunted, unsure of what to say. After another dozen swear words from

Douglas, the guy said to watch out, because if he acted like that around somebody who turned out to be armed, he could wind up with a bullet in the head. This got Douglas even more riled up. He told the man that if he was packing heat, then he'd best start shooting. But if he pulled out a gun and didn't fire, Douglas would beat his saggy ass to a pulp. The mention of guns attracted some people and scared off others. Around them, tensions mounted. But, in the end, there was no gun. The old man agreed to pay to get the bike fixed but refused to leave his contact details. He said he'd stop by the pharmacy the next day. Douglas didn't believe a word that came out of his mouth but figured he should get going. By now, his colleagues must be thinking he'd cut work to smoke up.

At the pharmacy, he mentioned the accident but not the argument. He knew the manager would lose his shit if he found out one of his employees had cussed someone out in company uniform. Douglas patched up his elbow, left his bike at a shop in the area, and took the rest of the afternoon off.

He was back in Rocinha in a blink. It was crazy how you could walk through a tunnel and enter a whole other world. The altercation with the old man had only underscored how disconnected Douglas felt from the blacktop, which is exactly how he wanted to keep it. He'd gone to school in Rocinha, worked his first jobs there. It had taken him years to step off that hill. Even then, it was mostly for doctors' appointments or administrative errands. That favela was his universe. Douglas had been born and raised in Rua 2. He'd come up stitching every alley together, knew shortcuts nobody could've imagined, remembered stuff that was long gone. Friends who worked or studied off the hill were always trying to get him to link up with them on the blacktop or hit bailes in other favelas. Douglas did go to a couple of shows in Ipanema, some Carnaval blocos in Leblon, even a baile in Vila do João. But the truth is his vibe was Roça Folia, concerts in Curva do S, bailes in Rua 1. The job in Gávea only reinforced his gut feeling: he needed to open a parlor on the hill, find a spot to buy, do his thing in the place he'd always felt most at home.

Douglas swung by the boca on Via Ápia before heading back to the house. It was heated over there. People shouting over each other. Douglas looked around for the dealer while also attempting to piece together what was going on.

"I'd like to see them try. We'll pump those motherfuckers full of lead."

"You're outta your fucking mind. Didn't you see what they did in Complexo do Alemão? Menó, these dudes got tanks, choppers, assault rifles . . . The only option is for Mestre to meet them at the table."

"Word. If UPP really does occupy the hill, those dudes aren't gonna rest till they get their hands on him."

Douglas's head spun from all that talk about cops, UPP, and occupation, so it took him a while to pick out the dealer. When he did, he copped two nickel bags and asked if the police had sent word about an occupation.

"Dudes came by the other day. Talked with the top guns. They just ran it in the paper. Word is shit's going down this year."

Douglas got home raring to light up. He sat on the couch grinding weed, his arm sore. Just the thought of that old man kicking back at home, with no pain or worries, got him all worked up again. Then there was the news about the Pacifying Police Unit, which only made things worse. Douglas had never lived in a UPP-occupied favela, but he couldn't imagine things would end well. He finally finished rolling the first joint. The smoke billowed up and made all that day's problems seem small and far away.

As Douglas lay on the sofa, he felt the high wash over him and his body loosen. Seconds later, though, he got all wound up again over the state of the apartment. Shirts and socks on the floor. Table covered in dirty plates and leftovers. He didn't even want to check the sink. Times like these, he missed living alone. It was a lot easier to clean up after one person. Maybe Coroa kicking them out was the universe telling him it was time to go solo again, to keep an eye out for a room of his own, somewhere a tiny bit bigger than the place he'd lived in before.

He could've let the joint peter out after a few more pulls. Instead, he kept going, just to feel the weed on his palate and the smoke in his lungs. His face was putty. He decided to make the most of the fact that no one was home and draw a little. Recently, he'd been studying old-school tattoos—roses, swallows, skulls. He knew that style wasn't so popular anymore, that if he really wanted to make money, he needed to put some time and energy into tribal and Māori work, into names, stars, butterflies. It's what he saw inked on most people's skin. Still, he was so into those thick lines and color combos that he'd been practicing them for his own enjoyment.

The full force of the couch high hit him when he got up. But he forged ahead and kept smoking while hunting around for pen and paper. He sat at the kitchen table, pushed aside the mess of plates and cups, and faced the blank page. Before drawing, he'd use a pencil to measure the sheet from top to bottom. He'd calculate. Douglas had always enjoyed the sensation of a blank page, of embarking on a new journey. As he placed the pencil tip on the sheet of paper, he heard noise at the front door. Someone was trying to turn the key in the lock, only they couldn't because Douglas's was on the other side. It couldn't be Murilo: he was on duty and wouldn't be back until the next day. For a second, Douglas thought Coroa was breaking into their place in the middle of the afternoon to snoop around. Douglas got up and opened the door. It was Biel. After being MIA for two weeks, he'd shown up unannounced. Even more surprising was that he had his own set of keys.

The sight of Biel at the front door stunned Douglas. He and Murilo had been convinced the guy was never coming back, not after what happened at Coroa's. It made them kind of upset, on account of Biel's antics, but also relieved, since they wouldn't have to kick him out—sure, he was a fuckup, but he was also a decent guy.

Biel walked in all amped up. In just two minutes, he tried to catch Douglas up on everything that'd happened in two weeks. He bounced around, jumped back and forth in time, went on tangents. Biel had probably taken a couple bumps of cocaine on his way home. Douglas stared at him, not really listening. Maybe it was all the weed he'd smoked or some word Biel said, some gesture he made, but Douglas had the sudden feeling that his friend would die young.

They rolled another joint. After passing it around a few times, Biel started mellowing out, though he kept yammering on and on. In his hands, the joint became a microphone. He mentioned a drug run he'd done on the beach, some chick he was chasing in Arpoador, a fight he and these playboys from Ipanema had gotten into with these other playboys from Jardim Botânico. Biel's habit of acting like nothing was a big deal really pissed Douglas off. He tried more than once to raise the issue of Coroa, to get him to cut the crap, but gave up every time. He didn't want to have that conversation without Murilo.

After a while, Douglas managed to relax and get drawn into Biel's stories. Before he knew it, they were both laughing like they used to a couple weeks back. It was Biel who brought up the run-in with Coroa in the end. The way he talked about it, you'd think it was the funniest thing in the world. He listed every detail, mimicked Coroa's expressions. Douglas started seeing red. Not even bengalinha or skunk could've quieted his urge to tell Biel to get the fuck out of the house. While he and Murilo had bent over backward to convince Coroa to let them stay, Biel was laughing it off, treating the whole thing like one big fucking joke.

Douglas was about to hit the roof when Biel interrupted himself and reached for something in his backpack. First he pulled out a bottle of Kovak and said they should game on the PS2 later. Douglas glared, amazed by how oblivious the guy was. But Biel shrugged it off and kept rifling through his bag. Finally, he pulled out a brand-new tattoo gun, two grips, and a power supply—the works. Then, with his zero-fucks-to-give attitude, he placed the machine in Douglas's hands.

RIO—August 26, 2011

Nothing worse than forgetting your cigarettes when you're on duty. Since you can't leave, your only option is to sponge. The thing is, at the barracks, it doesn't matter how much you spot people because the second you're the one asking, everybody pegs you as a freeloader. Murilo knew how it was. At least the other guy on duty with him was Thiago. Good kid, easy to talk to. He actually lived in a command area, but unlike some diehards, he wasn't twitchy around outsiders.

"Sup, man. Spare us a smoke?"

"If I had any, I'd give you two. I quit, though."

"What do you mean you quit, TH? Come on, give it to me straight."

"You heard me right, cuz. I'm done."

"How long?"

"Two days tomorrow."

The two awkwardly shook hands, rifles getting in the way.

"Right on. It's for the best. The worst part of cigarettes is craving them when you run out."

"That said, I do have a spliff we can fire up."

Murilo knew things could go sideways. Wasn't even three months ago he'd gotten in trouble for the same thing and been locked up for a week. But he was dying for a smoke, Bandeira 2 pot was always killer, and going without THC or nicotine all night long was sure to be a shit time.

While they burned grass with an eye on their surroundings, Murilo told Thiago about his dream. It'd been like a premonition. Not two weeks after he had that nightmare, they got news that the UPP was going to occupy Rocinha.

"That's just how it is now, man. With the World Cup and Olympics and shit. They're gonna take over every favela in the South Zone. Just you wait. These dudes will have to show their worth. Folks got their eyes on the city. Tourists everywhere you look. Gringos. You name it. It's over, fam. Soldiers from the South Zone will be assigned to the NZ and WZ. Write this down: Only the militia's gonna catch a break. Cause they're in league with the cops, with the whole goddamn system." Thiago tried to fix the joint, which kept canoeing.

"They better not fucking make me invade Rocinha." Murilo couldn't shake the thought of that happening.

"These assholes are crazy, but they're not insane, menó. They're not gonna force nobody to invade their home turf. They know shit can get ugly."

"But even if they send us somewhere else, it's still whack. You think it's cool if we all rock up to a favela with our rifles and start frisking people, breaking into civilians' houses?"

Murilo thought of the photos he'd seen of the Army invading Complexo do Alemão. He couldn't help thinking that could be any one of them. "I mean, if we're talking about *want*, man, I don't think anybody in here *wants* that shit, you know? Specially since most of these dudes got their own little side hustles. Am I right? Either that, or they enjoy a toke now and then, or a bump, or huffing some lança-perfume at a baile. There's even crackheads up in this joint. That shit's no joke, though. No idea what these dudes are thinking . . . Like, take Oscar, the guy who deserted our squad. So, my buddy saw him in Jaca recently, said he's gone off the deep end, that he's living in cracôlandia and shit. It's fucking crazy. Dude was straight edge when I met him, though he did dabble in grass. Crack's something else, man." Thiago finally got the joint to burn right and passed it to Murilo. "Anyway, where was I? Right, I don't think anybody wants to do that kind of thing. But what choice is there? Our job is to follow orders. Otherwise, we'd have to leave and find some other kind of work, you know? There's this thing my ma's always saying, and she's fucking right, man. What she says is we've all got a part to play. Like doctors, they're here to take care of people. Garbagemen collect garbage. Military police shake us down. Butchers butcher meat. Lawyers defend the rights of their clients. BOPE kills. Bakers bake bread. Drug dealers deal drugs. What can you do? That's just the way of the world, fam, and it's not like shit's gonna change from one day to the next. And you know what soldiers are here to do . . ."

"Soldiers are here to run, do sweeps, and weed out bad

apples. At least that's what everybody's been telling me since I got here," Murilo said. His eyes were still on high alert, scanning his surroundings. "And I was all right with that . . ."

"Listen, Murilo, the truth is that soldiers, we're like cattle, yeah? If they say 'sweep,' we sweep. If they say 'stand guard,' we stand guard. If they tell us to shoot, man, sadly we gotta shoot. Hierarchies are fucked up. That's why I'm quitting next chance I get. I'm not cut out for this crap."

Everything always made sense to Thiago. He had his own internal logic. Dude would probably grow up to be one of those old-timers who's always dropping wisdom bombs on younger generations. Murilo knew he shouldn't push his luck and that he should get back to his post, but the weed and convo were good. They talked about a bunch of things, including their families, some really intimate stuff that Murilo didn't even share with his roommates. Some things were just easier to talk about with people you weren't as close to. Murilo brought up his mom and how she'd moved to Campo Grande, smack in militia turf, how he wished he could've lived with her a bit longer, just until he got on his feet, but there was no way in hell he was moving there. Plus, he hated his stepdad. The guy was weird, always going on about how Brazil's golden era was in the seventies and eighties, when the country was under military rule, and that he was happy as hell that the UPP was taking over. Murilo wound up mentioning Biel too. Ever since he'd rocked up at the house again, he and Douglas hadn't known what to do. Whenever Coroa saw them in the building, he'd ask if they were looking at places, if they'd started packing. It was less than two weeks until their move-out date, and they still hadn't seen any apartments in Rocinha.

Since Thiago seemed interested, Murilo went ahead and told him the whole story, from the Flamengo match to Biel breaking into Coroa's apartment at six a.m. with a half-empty bottle of lança-perfume. He talked about what a bitch it was to hunt for an apartment, to move, all that stuff. The truth was, they'd kind of hoped they could convince the landlord to let them stay, but ever since Biel had come back, Coroa seemed even more unmovable. Murilo wrapped up the story by explaining that Biel was a good kid, ride or die. And at the end of the day, that made everything all the more difficult.

"Bro, let me tell you, I was walking down the street today thinking about something that happened early last year. A buddy and me were headed to the São Cristóvão jam. The two of us had come up together. We used to live on the same street. We went to our first baile together, smoked our first joint together, you know how it is. I had a few paint cans in my backpack, and we were planning on tagging a couple walls in the area after the jam. Anyway. So we're walking past this street, right, when we see a concrete wall across from a school. It's quiet, so my buddy says we should throw our names up there to kick things off. He was just getting started back then, and it was our first time writing together. But there's barely any traffic on that street and no important tags in the area, so I tell him it's not worth the paint. Then my buddy really takes me for a ride. He claims loads of people go to that school and that a Carnaval bloco sets out around the corner. All this shit to get me to believe it's a high-traffic area. Next thing I know, our names are up on the wall. Anyway. So we get to the jam, and everybody's chatting, catching up, when all of a sudden the sky starts coming down. You know, that crazy summer rain that feels like the world's ending? So we didn't bother hitting the streets after. Now, listen to this, I get shivers just thinking about it. A week later, this buddy of mine dies. He gets this stomach thing, and his family takes him to the hospital cause he's in so much pain. The doctor there says it's drugs, that if he just lays off and drinks water, he'll be better in no time. So my buddy goes back home and feels like shit for another three days. Dude's just getting worse and worse. His sister told me later that on the last day, his stomach was so big it looked like it was gonna explode. So they take him to the hospital again and this other doctor sees him and says it's appendicitis, that he needs emergency surgery. Except he dies before they get him on the table. Dude had just turned eighteen. I walked past that street today, menó, and I swear on my little girl's happiness, the best thing I ever did was tag that wall with him."

"Fuck, man," Murilo replied, feeling he had to say something.

"Real talk, though? Nothing better than a cigarette to chase down a spliff."

RIO—August 31, 2011

"Why do you want to work at this restaurant?" the manager asked, seemingly indifferent to the response.

That kind of question always bugged the hell out of Washington. Like, why the fuck does anybody work, if not to pay rent, buy food, subsidize vices? Shit was crazy expensive, and in the favela, bumming around like a playboy just landed you in the streets—the answer was starting to itch up his throat. Worst thing was, he knew that in a place like that he'd have to play their game. Choose his words carefully—no slang or swearing—stand up straight, not drop his endings. Be somebody he's not. Just what he fucking needed.

He'd rolled into the restaurant thinking the job was in the bag. Since he came with a reference, he figured he'd just have a chat with them, fill out some paperwork, hand over his ID, start Monday. Fat chance. There were like ten other guys at the joint. And he didn't even know how many more had been through there the past few days.

The minute he saw the competition, he thanked God his mom was uptight. He'd been feeling so confident, he nearly walked down the hill in a shirt and cargo shorts. But Dona Marli was having none of it and made sure to set him straight. So there he was, in jeans and a polo shirt. It was a bitch walking down the hill in those clothes, under the beating sun, which had been shining fierce since morning, but it was worth it in the end: looking around at the other guys, he felt no worse than anybody else.

"I'd like to work here because I know it's an amazing opportunity. I've been studying up on cocktails for a while and even did a bartending course. I've always had a way with drinks, so I decided to take a chance . . . Getting a start here, even washing dishes, would be an opportunity for me to see how the business works, especially at an important establishment like this one. It would definitely help me achieve my goals."

The truth was, Washington had never considered taking a bartending course, nor was he any good at mixing caipirinhas, the only drink on his roster. What he had was a knack for making any old bullshit sound legit. And the advantage of living in Rocinha. From what he'd heard before being called in for the interview, most of the other candidates lived in the West or North Zones. The restaurant being in São Conrado, it made a lot more sense for them to hire a local who could walk there. That way, they not only saved on bus fare, but their future employee was also less likely to be late.

"You must be happy, huh? Things are going to get better once the UPP is in Rocinha . . . I've always worried about our employees who live up there. They're all such hard workers.

There's Aloísio, our server. Do you know him? Our kitchen staff. There's Rose, our cleaner, she lives there too . . . Things will look up. That's the hope, right? No one deserves to live in the crossfire."

Washington had no way of knowing what would happen once the UPP occupied Rocinha. All he knew for sure was that there hadn't been any shootouts in a long time. Ever since Mestre took over, the hill had been at peace, and the guy had paid out of pocket for it too.

As a result, bailes went down without a hitch, residents and users didn't have to worry about bribing cops at the entrance, and there were still shows promoted by the organization. Even gringo artists performed in there. This way, bocas could make back the money they paid in bribes. Dudes well-versed in crime would rather lose out now if it meant making bank later. More importantly, they knew it was better to lose money than their lives, or their freedom.

"I just hope it's good for the residents," Washington said, trying to put an end to the subject.

"It'll get a lot better. Down here too, the apartments and hotels are going to appreciate. It'll be good for everybody."

After the one-on-one interviews, the candidates were taken to the main room for the group interview with a woman from HR.

Washington left the restaurant with the other guys in his group. Even though they were hungry—it was way past lunchtime— they decided to take a spin around São Conrado beach. Less than five minutes later, they were facing the ocean.

The sun blistered on the sand. Washington was pissed he hadn't brought trunks, or shorts, or anything. He couldn't remember the last time he'd been swimming. The others were prepared. The minute they set foot on the sand, they dropped trou and made a mad dash for the water. It was funny seeing them in the ocean. Zero duckdiving skills, getting their asses handed to them by the puniest waves. Nothing like the other kids splashing around. All Rocinha born-and-raised, like they'd come into the world knowing how to swim.

People started getting better acquainted during 420. Of course, none of them were anything like the front they'd put on for the interviews.

"So, like, the company wants to get to know me, sure. But what the fuck is with those games? I mean, imagine if it was always like that: you introduce someone to your mom, or another friend, or whoever the fuck, and you make them, like, hold hands and chase fucking balloons together or some shit. These people are playing . . ." The guy from Praça Seca was called Estevão but went by Jamaica.

"The worst fucking part was when she told us not to be discouraged. Bitch, please. You're not the one that hauled ass here from Camará." Vinícius had been quiet and mild-mannered throughout the interview process. But as soon as they started walking, he cursed out the HR woman more than anybody else.

"It's fucking crazy. There I was thinking the job was washing dishes, and this bitch wants to play games so she can evaluate my skills. Fuck. Like, just hand me a pot and sponge already!"

The oldest guy in the group, from Mangueira, was called

Jorge. Washington only noticed the ankle monitor on his right leg when they got out of the water.

Since they were all from different parts of the city, various qualities of weed were passed around. Every hill brought a different strain to the blacktop, and that year's harvest had been a good one. In Rocinha, there was bengalinha; famous among potheads, it was almost as good as the stuff playboys smoked. Though Mangueira weed had seen better days, their hash was still killer. Camará was known for selling one-real weed; sometimes it was top-shelf, sometimes not, but it was always cheap. In Praça Seca, there was Morro da Barão and a load of other favelas; even under militia rule, there was always somewhere to cop a drug. Junkies just had to stay on their toes because the militia had no mercy.

Jamaica was there to start at the bottom, move up to waiting tables, set aside some money for a cooking course, then work in the kitchen. His dream was to open a restaurant where customers were served a joint instead of bread.

"To whet the appetite," he said and laughed.

Vinícius had found out recently that he was going to be a dad. Which is why he started sending out CVs. The interview at the restaurant was his third that week. It made his mom happy as hell to see her son putting himself out there, though she had no idea about the news that awaited her. Vinícius wasn't sure whether or not she'd be happy, only that there was no chance in hell he was telling her while he was still unemployed.

After chopping it up awhile, Washington started feeling annoyed about only one of them getting that job. Especially after Jorge explained the ankle monitor. He said he'd gone down on his own, slinging drugs in Mangueira. They'd caught him with a stash of weed and a semiautomatic. He made a point of repeating that he never snitched on anybody in the four years he spent waiting for The Out.

"Comando Vermelho had my back in there, brother. Things could've been a lot worse. I'm not saying this outta distrust or nothing. I know y'all tight with Adelaide in Roça, that dudes in Camará are in with Terceiro, but none of that means shit at the end of the day. If I was born in Rocinha, I'd be standing with Nenzão too. It's 'tudo A.' Isn't that what y'all say? And if I was born in any of the favelas under Terceiro's command, well, hell, same shit. Cause, real talk, this stuff about factions is no different than pulling for a soccer team. It all depends on where you're born, who you know. Amirite?"

"Users gotta go where the grass is greenest," Jamaica said.

"Been hearing this stuff since I was a kid, and real talk," Jorge continued, ". . . it's always *nós*, or *a gente*, just can't be *eles*. Us versus them. You know what I'm saying? That's the thinking of the guy who knows his boss doesn't give a rat's ass about all this 'tudo 2,' 'tudo 3' bullshit. When the Army invaded Complexo Alemão, didn't FB hole up in Rocinha? You think the bosses worry about factions? Bitch, please. All they care about is making money. That's it, that's the goal. One thing I learned is that criminals gotta be cold and calculating, cause diehards die young."

"That's right. Plenty of radicals didn't live to tell the tale," Vinícius said while rolling another spliff.

"So, that's the story. The guys really took care of me in there. Even helped my ma out when she needed it. I appreciate it and all, but it's each to his own now, brother, no sweat.

I took the interview cause it's a condition of my parole. And here we are. I know nobody's gonna hire me, but what else can I do? It's all rich folks in the South Zone, you think they're gonna want someone who's done time? But it's different around here. And I gotta show up, right? Prove that I'm trying. That's just how it is. Soon I'll be working some construction site, taking it easy. All I know is I'm never going back into the system. It's hot as fuck behind those walls. All you want is to hit the beach but instead you're trapped inside, packed in with a ton of other dudes. That's no way to live. My dad died when I was locked up . . . You can't know what that's like. Your dad keels over one day while you're trapped in there, and there's nothing you can do. What if it was my mom? You tell me. I don't even wanna think on it."

As Washington listened, he couldn't stop picturing how happy Jorge's mom would be if he got the job.

All that grass had them faded.

The munchies took hold, and the others figured they'd better get a move on. It was a long way home, and none of them could afford to eat out. They walked to the bus stop together, laughing like crazy at their stories. Then Washington went home. But not before they all linked on Facebook. They said goodbye, promising to hit a baile someday. Everybody wanted to see if Rocinha was as lit as people said.

That afternoon, Wesley got to the party hall early. He wanted
to meet Talia before work so they could hang out a little, chat.
But she wasn't there at the time they'd texted about. Wesley
was fooling around in the hall before the party started when
Ângela made an offer he couldn't refuse. One of the people on
the entertainment team was blowing chunks in the bathroom,
and Alex, the team leader, had suggested Wesley could fill in
for him.

Not long after Wesley started working at the party hall,
he heard the entertainment team made twice as much as the
stewards and waitstaff. The day he found that out, he went
straight to management to see about learning the ropes. Apparently, the venue offered training courses for entertainers. For a whole week, Wesley played with a gaggle of brats,
learned dance moves to Xuxa's greatest hits, and did puppet
theater for no pay while losing money on bus fare. That's what
passed for training. With his eyes on the cash he could make

down the line, he gave every activity his all. Still, they never called him up. Until then. Not that Wesley wanted to make a career out of it. Truth be told, there were plenty of times when he'd looked at the entertainers and felt so deeply embarrassed he was thankful he'd never been asked. It was the money that swayed him. He could make the same in half the hours.

He hesitated over Ângela's offer, especially once Talia walked into the venue. They'd been texting a lot, trying to schedule a hang. Wesley didn't want to cut his chances with her, but he didn't have much of a choice. As much as he was scared of wasting the energy he'd invested in Talia, he had to say yes. That's how things rolled there: they didn't make noise if you said no, just low-key took you off the roster without explanation. Wesley didn't want to come away with nothing; his plans of becoming a mototaxi driver had gotten a lot more complicated since the news of UPP's arrival. Now he was going to have to get a driver's license, a motorcycle with up-to-date paperwork, that kind of thing. His new goal was to pay for driving lessons with the money he made at the venue while looking for a formal job. That way, he could apply for a loan.

The birthday party was for a six-year-old called Valentina who glommed onto Wesley the second she set foot in the venue. It was all so weird, he couldn't wrap his head around it. Used to being the center of attention, Alex got jealous. To the point that he tried even harder than usual to get the children all excited and playing games together. It didn't matter. All the birthday girl cared about was Wesley.

Valentina liked painting and took her sweet time at the art station. Wesley was fine with this as it meant he could sneak food in the bathroom where they rinsed the paintbrushes. The place was a blind spot, and the nannies sometimes hid there to eat, when they didn't count as regular guests.

"Her mom thinks she's gonna be an artist . . . that she has a strong personality."

"And does she?"

"Pfft. What she's got is attitude. Not saying hello to anyone, at her age . . . If she was my kid, you bet your ass I'd set her straight."

A bored Wesley listened to the nanny's chatter while waiting for Valentina to finish painting. He wanted to go to the dollhouse, where Talia was working. But no matter how adamant Valentina was about not leaving Wesley's side, she still only did whatever she wanted to. No point pushing it. She finished her painting but instead of handing it to a chaperone to hang on the clothesline, she turned it upside down and rubbed it all over the white table until the sheet ripped. The table was covered in paint and shreds of paper. The nannies in the area just shook their heads like they'd seen it all before.

Wesley helped one of his colleagues clean up while Valentina went around touching everything. He was the only one who saw her pull the glue gun out of the drawer. Instead of taking it from her, Wesley prayed she found an outlet, and fast. If she burned her hand on the gun, she'd probably cry long enough to forget all about how much she loved Wesley. The girl wandered around a bit more before finding an outlet and plugging in the gun. Wesley watched Valentina out of the corner of his eye. He saw one of the guests approach her.

"Where in God's name is her nanny? Can't she see what's happening? This is a safety hazard!"

After the art station, the two spent a long time in the ball pit. Wesley would close his eyes while she found a hiding place, then dive in after her. Except he never reached her in time, and she always leaped out of the ball pit victorious. After a while, Wesley started feeling thirsty. He tried to go get a drink of water, but the birthday girl threw a tantrum and made him jump back in the ball pit.

"Not now. I'm thirsty. We'll play again later."

"No. Jump now."

"I'll be back in a second."

"My daddy's paying for you to play with me. Jump!"

Wesley glanced around him and saw that Talia was busy with another girl. He jumped in the ball pit, laughing and making Valentina laugh as well.

He only stopped when the nanny took the birthday girl to the bathroom. Instead of grabbing a cup of water from one of the waiters, he went to the kitchen for a breather. It was almost time to sing "Happy Birthday."

He drank two glasses of water, then went to the bathroom and back to the kitchen, where he chatted with his colleagues and snacked on the tray of leftovers. Ângela walked in.

"Great job, Wesley! The birthday girl adores you. Her mother just told me she's never seen her become so attached to someone right off the bat."

"I took the training course when I started working here. You're the ones who never called me up."

"How's Washington doing?"

"He's cool, pô. Got a job with a signed work card and stuff . . ."

"Amazing! I hope he cleans up his act . . ."

After that comment, Wesley went back to the hall. The birthday girl was frantically searching for him. As soon as she laid eyes on Wesley, she ran up to him and hugged him so hard you'd think they were related.

It was time for "Happy Birthday," and Valentina wanted Wesley to stand with her and the family by the cake. Her parents thought it was ridiculous, but she wouldn't stop crying, so they were forced to agree. The staff sang from the sidelines while Wesley stood with the family, as if he were one of them, and felt like digging a hole in the ground to stick his head in.

After the party ended, several of his colleagues came up to chat with him, impressed by how he'd won over the birthday girl. But Alex refused to sing his praises. Instead, he said that while it was always good to charm the birthday girl, it was even more important to make sure the kids—especially the guest of honor—were playing together and taking part in games. Because later, when the family looked through the pictures and saw none of their little girl enjoying herself, they'd think the entertainment team had failed at their job. Wesley, who after all the humiliation, was finally savoring a victory, was furious.

"Whatever, menó. You really think I give a shit? I just want the money. The birthday girl, the family, the whole damn guest list can kiss my fucking ass."

Although Talia didn't usually stay for the meal, she stuck around that day, then left for the bus stop with everyone else. She and Wesley walked slower and slower, letting their co-workers get ahead of them. Until it was just them two. Neither mentioned the party. Talia told Wesley that her relationship was on the rocks, that this time she knew for a fact that her boyfriend was cheating on her. Wesley listened attentively. He didn't know what to make of what she was saying. On the one hand, it sounded like good news; she was fair game. On the other, it could mean that she just wanted somebody to talk to, and he was already in the friend zone.

"That's messed up, Talia. I'd dump his ass if I was you. Once trust is broken, there's no going back."

"I know . . . I'm just working up the nerve. We've been together a long time."

Wesley was about to say that if a guy couldn't appreciate a girl like her, he deserved to be kicked to the curb. But then he stopped himself. He didn't want to come on too strong. The 557 was rolling down the other side of the street. They'd better cross if they didn't want to miss it. It could be another half hour before the next one.

"Stay a bit longer. I'll wait with you," Talia said.

It was the perfect moment to go in for a kiss. Wesley knew this. He leaned in but then stopped himself and just stared into her eyes. Talia stared back. He was suddenly daunted. He got the feeling he liked her more than he realized.

"Okay, let's cross, though," Wesley said, pointing at the empty benches at the bus stop.

They sat in silence for a long time, staring in opposite directions, speechless. Wesley regretted not leaving. He worried the rest of the crew had seen her ask him to stay. The last thing he needed was to get a rap for no reason. That kind of shit always made trouble. Next thing he knew, dudes would be finding out and pegging him for one of those guys who's all talk no action. Like a two-pump chump.

"Did you have fun on entertainment today?"

"Uh, I dunno, sort of. It's nice to make more money, but the work's kinda a lot . . ."

Wesley wanted to tell Talia about the ball pit. About how he'd had the urge to drown the birthday girl in all that plastic. About how he'd prayed she got burned on the glue gun. But he was too embarrassed, and instead he just stared across the street.

"Oh, shit, hurry up. The bus."

The 557 was coming toward them. Wesley raised his arm way ahead of time and waited. Before the bus pulled over, he leaned over to kiss Talia goodbye on the cheek, but she turned her face and gave him her lips. The number 557 rolled right past them again.

"Nah, man. The swell at Arpoador is weak sauce. I was there earlier. It's super weird. The good surf is in Grumari, Prainha, those parts."

Biel's head pounded harder and harder as he listened to the guys at Bibi Lanches talk out of their asses. He and his roomies had blown past their move-out date, and last night Coroa had stormed down to their apartment and asked them if he looked like a clown. He told them that if they didn't move out A-S-A-P, he'd have to take a stance. Though he may not have said it explicitly, they all knew he meant he was ready to kick the issue up to the boca.

The month had flown by, and they'd barely seen any rentals. There was a place in Rua 2 with moldy walls and no ventilation. And one near Vila Verde that looked out over an open sewer—the smell was criminal. Truth told, they'd been spoiled by Via Ápia. Life there was easier, cleaner. It'd be hard to find somewhere else that met their standards.

That was the first time Biel realized how royally he'd fucked up. Up until then, he'd assumed Coroa was just trying to scare some sense into them. But no, from what Biel saw the night before, Coroa was on a mission to get them out of there for good. The other thing was that he couldn't make up his mind about whether to stay in Roça or move somewhere else. Once the residents got confirmation that the UPP would be occupying the hill before the year was up, it was all anyone talked about. The situation was like a ticking time bomb. Plus, Biel knew that as the police took over every inch of Rocinha, it'd be harder and harder for him to transport gear on and off the hill to sell at the beach. Even if he decided to try his luck somewhere else in the city, he still had to scare up some money to help his buddies with moving costs. He wasn't about to leave them in the lurch.

In all the time Biel had spent hanging around those playboys, the only true friends he'd made were Douglas and Murilo. They'd taken him in when he most needed it. In that apartment on Via Ápia, Biel had been allowed to be himself, to talk to them about what it was like coming up in Cruzada and going to school at Santos Anjos.

He checked his cell again—nothing in over an hour. The guy wasn't picking up his phone or replying to texts. Meanwhile, Biel was sure there were tons of people on the beach waiting for their grass. It didn't take much to make a whole day go to waste. There was no shortage of dealers on that beach: between the playboys, the hawkers, and the handicrafts vendors, competition was fierce.

He couldn't just do nothing, not after all the trouble he'd gone through to infiltrate Ipanema. His first couple tries, he'd been ignored. The fact that he was from Cruzada São Sebastião, a microfavela between Leblon and Ipanema, hadn't helped breach the distance between him and the group he wanted to belong to. At first he tried using surf to get close to them. But the equipment was pricey, and the competitive atmosphere in the water not exactly conducive to making friends. So, he decided to hone his skills at altinha, which was like keep-ups but on the beach. He went to São Conrado every day and played with his school friends, who were mostly from Rocinha and Vidigal. After a while, he got pretty good at keeping that ball in the air. That's when he started joining altinha circles at Posto 9 in Ipanema. It wasn't long before he realized that if he wanted to be accepted by the playboys, he'd have to dress and talk like them. It was hard work, but it paid off. His skills in the game helped him cement a friendship with the beach crew. Andrei died and out of his ashes rose Biel, or Gabriel Moscovoci, as he called himself on social media.

But it wasn't cheap being friends with those people. Cover charges for clubs were a fortune, the bars were a lot more expensive than the ones in Cruzada, and the price of a juice and snack combo at Bibi was the same as a full meal in any favela in the city. So Biel started selling drugs. That way, he could kill two birds with one stone. Dealing earned him money and popularity. A few days in, he already felt he was part of the crew.

Tired of waiting, Biel started walking toward the guy's house. He couldn't show up at the beach empty-handed, not on a

Saturday like that one. After a string of cloudy, overcast days and indecisive weather, the sun had finally made an appearance on the weekend. It was time to make some money.

As Biel passed more diners and the playboys' favorite haunts, it dawned on him that if he wanted to stay in the game, he would have to find a new connect. His current supplier gave him a good price, and he could turn a decent profit. But the kid was out of control. When he wasn't rolling on E or tripping balls on a random school night, he was fucking with even heavier stuff. Every now and then, his family sent him to rehab and told everyone he was doing a semester in the U.S. or Europe. Which was the same tactic rich people used when one of their little princesses needed an abortion: an unexpected trip abroad.

After walking around a while, Biel realized he was out of options. He'd have to hit the beach and inform his clients that his re-up had ghosted him. Then he could go back to his previous supplier. Sure, the gear was pricier but at least the guy could be counted on. He was a police officer, a family man. A lot more responsible.

Biel was walking toward the beach on Rua Joana Angélica when he saw this street kid being chased by some six or seven guys, including a couple he knew. By that point, his head was on the verge of exploding. The lynch mob recognized Biel and hollered at him to grab the kid. As the street rat sprinted past him on the sidewalk, Biel reflexively stuck out his foot. The kid tripped and fell. Seeing him there with his face on the ground, playboys hoofing toward him, Biel felt a pang of regret. But it was too late.

RIO—September 12, 2011

She was even better in real life, which had Washington thinking his luck had finally changed. Everything was beginning to make sense: things only started working out for him once he had the courage to turn down what he didn't want and risk what little he had. As this thought knocked around his head, Washington's every gesture oozed confidence. When Gleyce came up to him, he didn't hesitate before going in for a hug.

"Pleasure," he said, slowly, looking her in the eyes.

Gleyce gave a casual reply and headed into the mall.

"Jesus Christ, this heat's like a preview of hell or something. Can you even imagine what summer's gonna be like?"

She'd been so nonchalant introducing herself that Washington instantly felt intimidated. It wasn't what he'd expected.

"At least there's AC in here."

After recovering from the swelter, Gleyce finally turned her attention to Washington.

"How did you not die walking here in those pants?"

Washington had debated wearing shorts. He had these new Kenner flip-flops that, paired with the right shorts, could really hit the sweet spot that drove girls wild. He only wore pants so he wouldn't draw attention. From experience, he knew that if you wanted to avoid a headache at a place like Fashion Mall, you were better off wearing pants. Mall cops were always side-eyeing dudes in shorts.

"Movie theaters are freezing. My legs get crazy cold!"

After the movie, they wandered around the mall and got to know each other while absently scanning window displays. Until Gleyce came across a golden top. She stared at it a long time, listing off some of the clothes she could wear it with. Washington was convinced the price was a typo, but he was wrong. The top cost 298 reais. More than half a month's minimum wage.

"I'm gonna try it on."

She went straight to the sales associate. Figuring he didn't have much of a choice, Washington followed. The staff seemed bored in the empty store. The sales associate flippantly passed her the top, illustrating her certainty that Gleyce would never buy anything from that store. Gleyce went into the changing room. Washington couldn't figure out what to do, surrounded by all those skirts and dresses. He tried to relax in an armchair, staring up at the weird ceiling decorations.

Gleyce walked out of the changing room wearing the top. The gold color of the clothing highlighted her brown skin. It was like she was all aglow.

"So, how does it look?"

"Perfect." Washington couldn't have been more sincere.

"I know. But there's no way in hell I'd ever pay that much for a top," she said, right in front of the sales associate, without batting an eye.

After they left the store, Gleyce explained that she liked trying on clothes in window displays. I mean, why else did they put them there?

"Plenty of rich people are always trying on loads of clothes they don't buy. So who cares if I try on something I wind up not getting? I just like putting them on, you know? Seeing how they look on me, picturing myself wearing them out. I can always take a photo to a seamstress and have her make me one just like it."

Washington was impressed by how Gleyce acted in that place. Most of the people he knew in Rocinha tended to behave more or less the same when they went to Fashion Mall: either they were unnerved by all the marble and designer clothes, and the customers who could afford them, or they immediately adopted a fuck-you attitude, a heavy gait, fire in the eyes, as though saying I know you don't want me here but I could give less of a shit. Washington himself wavered between those two stances whenever he walked down those corridors. But not Gleyce. She strolled, checked stuff out, and chatted about the actors in the movie with the level head of someone who knew that place had been designed for her to walk through, that all those air conditioners had been put there to spare *her* from the heat.

They went to McDonald's for something to eat. Washington hadn't been in years, so it took him a minute to order. All his memories of that place involved Happy Meals, but he was too old for that now. As he stood in front of the impatient cashier, he remembered the ad on TV, the jingle for the two hamburger patties, lettuce, cheese, special sauce, onion, pickles, and sesame seed buns.

"One Big Mac, please."

Gleyce was more familiar with the menu, so it took her only a couple seconds to reel off her order. No surprise there. By then, Washington was kind of banking on it. What he wasn't banking on was that she would pay with a credit card. Not long ago, credit cards had felt completely out of his reach, something only grown-ups with kids had. Then he remembered the bank account he'd had to open to work at the restaurant. Soon enough, he'd be the one flashing plastic, buying tons of stuff, paying in installments.

The burger was way smaller than it looked on TV. He could easily polish off the whole thing in three generous bites. Washington took the first one, then set the burger aside to work on the fries. Time to get serious, he decided. During the movie, and after, when they'd wandered around the mall, he'd tried to lay on his game—putting out feelers, filling his eyes and words with intention—but Gleyce didn't seem to be catching on.

"All right, be honest, all that stuff about mixing me up with somebody else is bullshit, right?"

"I swear, there was this boy called Washington in my sixth-grade class. Only one I ever met. Kids called him Wosheeto, it was hilarious. Anyway, he left school, and I never saw him again. When I saw your profile, I thought for sure you were him."

"Oh, please. Act like you got me fooled, and I'll act like I believe you."

"You think you're something else, don't you? Must be in the name. That other kid was like that too. He thought he was a dreamboat, but boy couldn't catch a cold, let alone a girl."

"C'mon, you can tell me. I won't hold it against you."

"I swear. On second thought, it makes sense. You kids with gringo names all think you're hot shit."

"And nobody blinks when they hear *your* name, do they?"

"Whatever, man. That gringa princess's name was Grace Kelly. My name's G-L-E-Y-C-E, with an L and a Y. You know there's nothing more Brazilian than sticking a Y in a person's name."

The two of them spent a while chopping it up about funny names and reminiscing about their schooldays. Then Washington told Gleyce the story of his own name. How his dad used to work as a projectionist right there at Fashion Mall, and his mom practically lived at the movies before and during her first pregnancy. Back then, Denzel Washington and Wesley Snipes were her favorite actors.

"What does your dad do now that movies are all digital, HD, and whatever?"

"No idea. Haven't seen him in years." Washington took another bite of his burger, which was starting to get cold. He swallowed, then said: "I wasn't even three years old when they split. Dona Marli's always telling us about how Wesley was still nursing. After that, we linked up a couple of times.

Back when I was a kid. He lives over near Caju, Barreira do Vasco, or something, can't remember where exactly."

Washington wasn't sure why he'd started telling her that stuff. He almost never talked about his dad. It wasn't the first nor the last time that Gleyce would hear about absent fathers. Still, she was listening so intently that Washington decided to keep going.

"There was this time when I got, like, obsessed with looking him up. I was fourteen or something. I bugged my mom about it forever. Accused her of not wanting me to have a father. Some really nasty shit. Teenagers are fucking assholes. Anyway, one day she gets hold of his address, buys me a ticket, and I go all the way to Tuiuti on my own. Wesley wasn't interested in seeing him. After that first trip, I visited a couple more times. It was always the same bullshit. I'd show up, and we'd get drunk with this juicer he was friends with. Those guys did not fuck around. They downed Ypióca like it was beer, no joke. My old man would get wasted and start rambling, saying he missed us like crazy, that my mom was a bitch for not letting us visit, you know the drill. One day he was on his usual bullshit when he started crying, and I thought it was so fucking funny. He promised never to fall outta touch with me again, said I could count on him for anything, blah blah. After that, I left and never looked back."

Washington turned his attention back to his burger and polished the rest off with a third bite. As soon as he was done with the meal, he started craving a smoke.

"Does your mom still like going to the movies?"

"Honest, I don't think she ever went back after Wesley was born. Mostly watches whatever's on TV."

As they left the mall, Washington was still trying to figure out how to show Gleyce he was interested. Several times, he almost came out with: *So, babe, what's good? We in or out?* But something always got in the way. Gleyce was different. He'd have to let things happen naturally.

"Down to smoke?"

It sounded like a cop-out, but Washington had left his stash at home that day. Sure, he'd thought of bringing it with him, but since it was their first time out together, he figured he should probably suss out how Gleyce felt about pot first. Plus, he didn't want to be carrying contraband around the blacktop—the last thing he needed was to get busted on their first hangout.

"My stash is at home. I forgot to bring it with me."

"I've got some, pô. Don't sweat it. I almost suggested lighting up before the movie, but there wasn't enough time."

They started walking toward the beach. There wasn't a single cloud in the sky. Surrounded by those big trees, under that golden-hour light, Washington felt once again that he just might have a chance with her.

"You know what my favorite part of Fashion Mall is? The restrooms. Those restrooms, damn. You could live inside them," Gleyce said, dispelling the silence.

"I bet cokeheads love it in there. All that marble. For fools that like white, those restrooms must be heaven."

"And do you?" she asked out of the blue, not seeming to care much what he answered.

"Snort cocaine? Nah, never. That shit is for people with deep pockets."

"Totally."

"I had a laced joint a couple times. Not gonna lie, it's a pretty nice buzz. But a buddy told me it messes up your enamel. So I stopped. If there's one thing I hate, it's fucking dentists."

At the beach, they sat together on the sand. It was more night than day, and a couple of stars dotted the sky. Washington was surprised by how big Pedra da Gávea looked. Something about that moment made him feel like it was his first time seeing that mountain, and this really threw him off-balance. Gleyce finally pulled a crumpled joint out of her wallet and tried fixing it up a little before fishing out her lighter. Washington usually clowned with friends who broke out joints as janky as that one, but he decided to keep quiet. At the end of the day, she was the one spotting.

"It's a bit sad-looking, but I'm pretty sure it's smokable."

"Roll it yourself?" Washington pretended he only noticed the joint after she said that.

It caught fire after a few tries. Gleyce took a couple long pulls and tried to get it to burn right before finally passing it on.

"I rolled it earlier. I think it got beat up in my wallet, though it wasn't all that to begin with. Been smoking a while, but I'm still no good at rolling. I'm used to other people doing it for me."

Washington wondered who she'd started smoking with. A boyfriend, maybe? Some guy who liked rolling blunts and threw her a couple now and then to smoke with her friends on the beach? Now Gleyce had to work it out on her own. Did she go to the boca herself? It made most girls nervous.

"Release the prisoner, officer," she said when she saw him hogging the joint.

"Speaking of officers, I just remembered this hilarious thing that happened the other day."

"Cool, but pass the joint first. It's not a microphone."

Washington took a few more pulls before passing it on.

"This was a year ago. I'd lost my ID and been dragging my feet about getting it replaced. Dona Marli was on my case, cause she gets all paranoid about people not having their IDs. But then somebody, I can't remember who, told me that if you report it stolen at the precinct, you don't have to pay a fine. I was hung up about doing that cause I hate talking to cops, but thirty bucks is thirty bucks, right, so I head down to the station in Gávea. At first the dude there, the officer, makes things hot for me. I have to tell him I've been robbed like three fucking times because the asshole keeps trying to catch me out. But it's cool cause on the way there, I'd been visualizing exactly how everything went down. I swear, there was times I was telling him the story that I felt like I was running back something that actually happened in real life. It was fucking weird. Anyway, I think the officer got kind of sus when I said the guy that robbed me was blond. He was like, You sure about that? Dude had blue eyes, I told him. Then, out of nowhere, he asks if I smoke weed. Don't know what got into me then, but I say, Yeah, I do. Dude starts cracking up. He turns to his partner and says: Yo, Miranda, listen to this. This guy here just told a cop that he smokes grass. I get all kinds of people coming through here . . . Then he asks if I have any weed on me and obviously I say no. So he's like: I can't believe you just told a law enforcement officer that you smoke pot. Are you crazy, or retarded, or something? I swear he was laughing so hard he couldn't even type. I said to him: You asked, sir. What was I supposed to do? Now that I think of it, I'm pretty sure I told him I smoked weed so that he'd believe I'd actually been robbed, you know? Like, that way he'd see he was dealing with somebody who was on the level. Then he tells me: Listen, next time, you got to lie to the police, man. Tell him, Miranda, tell him what he has to do. Cops love a well-crafted lie, and I dunno what else. He only starts filling out the report after he's done laughing. Then he asks where I live. When I say Rocinha, he starts razzing me again. He's like: So I guess that means you're friends with Nem? And I say: Friends with who? Nem, fuck's sake, Antônio Bonfim Lopes. The two of you friends or not? Never heard of him, I say, straight-faced. The dude couldn't believe it: How can you live in Rocinha and not know who Nem is? The guy runs the place. Officer, sir, you just told me to lie to the police . . . That's what I said, straight up. Dude started banging his fist on the table, laughing so hard he was wheezing. Everybody at the precinct stared at him. Even Miranda laughed. Those cops are a fucking joke."

A guy appeared with his dog, interrupting their conversation.

"Y'all got a light?" he asked.

They stood there awkwardly, not knowing what to say while the man kept trying to spark up. Then he handed back the lighter, walked away, and left the awkwardness with them.

"What do you think's gonna happen?"

"With what?" Washington pretended not to know what she meant. He wanted to forget the subject that had taken hold of Rocinha, just for a minute.

"When UPP invades the hill."

"Fuck knows. It'll probably be rough."

They hung out on the beach a while longer, relishing the high. Gleyce told Washington about her life too. About how she started smoking with her aunt, who was only five years older than her. About working the register at a small grocery store near Curva do S. About ENEM, the national high-school exam she was taking next month, though she didn't think she would pass; she hadn't really studied, just wanted to see what the deal was. About how she was going to enroll in a cram school next year so she could take the college entry exam. Gleyce's confidence as she spoke about her life, and all her plans, made Washington jealous, but also a little sorry, because then he remembered just how much shit could go wrong in life.

They walked back to Rocinha together. Anyone who saw how lively and intimate their conversation was would assume the two of them had known each other forever. Washington was ready to walk Gleyce up to Paula Brito, but she fed him some line about needing to stop by the grocery store or something. So they said goodbye on Ladeira da Cachopa, leaving Washington confused about their last few hours together.

"Let's hang again soon. Today was fun," Gleyce said after they hugged.

RIO—September 15, 2011

Douglas stepped off the bus cranked up. After running around all day, he couldn't wait to get home. He was in such a hurry, he hadn't even swung by the boca. It was only as he walked up the stairs in his building that he realized he didn't have any grass to burn at home. Luckily, the second he stuck his head in the door, he smelled the marola.

"You install a nanny cam or something?" Murilo cracked that joke every time somebody showed up right when a joint was being lit.

Douglas ignored him and started emptying out his backpack. Ink, needles, gloves, grips, a huge roll of plastic wrap, plus some small cups and other bits and pieces. Douglas knew he'd be broke for the rest of the month, and he'd never felt happier about it.

"Yo, menó, you think the butcher's still open? The one over on Largo do Boiadeiro?"

The way he arranged everything on the table made him

seem like a completely different person. The messiness of the apartment was a funny contrast with how Douglas arranged his equipment.

"They close at ten p.m., I think."

"Cool. Gonna head over there, see if they'll comp me some pigskin."

Murilo looked confused.

"Pigskin's supposed to be good for practice. Cause it's a lot like human skin." Douglas had a new glimmer in his eyes, a different energy in his body.

"They sold fake skin at the store where I bought all this stuff, but then I heard pigskin's where it's at."

"Sit down, dude. Have a toke before you run out again."

Douglas sat on the sofa, inhaled some smoke, and felt his body finally loosen up. He told Murilo about all the places he'd gone for the equipment, about the parlor on Rua Buenos Aires that sold tattoo supplies for a reasonable price. The owner, a dinosaur who'd been inking people for over twenty years, had shared some wisdom. It was the first time Douglas had anything resembling a lesson, unless you counted the stuff he learned from magazines and YouTube.

"Dude's fucking awesome, said I could come through sometime to shadow one of his sessions, see how it's done. I swear, neguim, if this guy ever offers me a job, I'm taking it on the spot, no questions asked."

Murilo's head was somewhere else. He let the joint peter out between his fingers, making no effort to relight it. Murilo didn't even nod along or look at Douglas as he ran his mouth. Instead, he stared up at the ceiling, watching a fly trapped in a spiderweb.

"Where you at, neguim?"

"Real talk? I'm thinking of leaving the Army. There's no future there."

Murilo had never mentioned how terrified he was of being deployed to a favela. As much as he wanted to talk to his roommates about it, every time he tried, he got the sense opening his mouth would only make it more real and therefore more likely to happen. So he didn't.

"I'm sitting here listening to you talk about all the shit you wanna do, about the stuff you're already learning, and I keep thinking: cool, so I wanna leave the Army, right, but for what? And, honest, I've got no idea what I'd do instead. That's what really stresses me out. It's fucking weird, not knowing what comes next. It's rough, you know? My sister, she took the ENEM the other day, and the admissions exams for UERJ. Now, she's waiting for her results. You, you're saving up money to become a tattoo artist . . . I'm happy for the two of you, menó, I mean it. Don't think I'm jealous of your success and shit. It's not like that. It's just that sometimes I get anxious that I'm being left behind, right? That ten, twenty years from now, I'm still gonna be stuck here. That I won't have done shit with my life."

Douglas didn't know what to say.

"Anyway, never mind. You should hit the butcher's before it closes. I didn't mean to cramp your style or nothing. I just brought it up cause it was on my mind."

Douglas racked his brains for something he could say to cheer Murilo up. But nothing came to mind. The truth was, all he could think about was tattoos. He'd been so wired the night before, he could barely sleep. And now, it was all there, it was really happening, right in front of his eyes.

"All right, I'm gonna head out then, before they close for the night."

"Cool, I'm just gonna lie down here a bit. That weed gave me a bitch of a headache."

Douglas glanced again at the equipment on the table. He couldn't stop picturing it in action. The machine humming, the ink sorted into cups on his workstation, the needle breaking skin and leaving a mark.

"Yo, Mu. Once I'm holding my own on the pigskin, what're you gonna get?"

"Easy there, DG. I'm not ready for any ink yet."

"Something simple, pô."

"Nah, man, I'm good, for real. I'd rather wait until you're pro and then get something hardcore."

"C'mon, neguim. If *you* don't trust me when I'm just starting out, then who will?"

Coroa knocked on the door. He'd been doing that so often, they could always tell when it was him. They tried playing possum, pretending nobody was home, but between the lights being on and the noise, it didn't work. The fact that Coroa got a face-full of marola when they opened the door only riled him up more.

Murilo decided to cut to the chase. They'd looked at some places in the neighborhood, but most of them were shit, and the only ones good enough were through brokers and involved a ton of bureaucracy, plus a deposit, a guarantor, the works. He told Coroa they'd keep looking but that the UPP news was making it harder to find a place, that it was like everything in Rocinha was on hold, just waiting for the other shoe to drop. Things would get a lot easier once it did, and they'd be out of his hair in no time.

Coroa gave them the usual spiel, saying he'd take the matter to the boca. But they all knew it was a hollow threat: now that a date had been set for the next police operation, the dealers weren't about to get involved in landlord-tenant disputes. At times of crisis, it was each to his own.

Even though Coroa's scare tactics had no effect on them, they'd accepted that his mind was made up: they were going to have to move. There was no point staying there, at war with the landlord. They really did just want to wait for the UPP. It was harder for cops to start shit in the lower part of the favela, and when they did, they tended to be less aggressive than they were farther up the hill, deeper in the alleys.

"Relax, Coroa. We're trying," Murilo said before shutting the door.

Luckily, Biel only came back after Coroa had left. Otherwise, the old geezer would've hung around another two hours, making their ears bleed. Biel was happy as hell. He'd copped 200 grams of Colombia Gold on the cheap, which meant he'd make good returns. To celebrate, he set aside twenty g for personal use. It took him under two minutes to roll a joint fatter than his fingers. He lit up.

"Yo, I was thinking. Seeing as we got no choice but to move, why not try someplace new? Parque da Cidade, Vidigal, Chacrinha? Those hoods are dope too. The cops are gonna be breathing down our necks here."

"You think those fools are gonna occupy this favela and

leave the rest alone? Dream on, bro." On the issue of the UPP, Murilo was the most pessimistic of the three.

"You do you, Biel, but there's no way I'm letting some blue-assed pigs push me off this hill. That's exactly what they want." Douglas seemed offended at the thought of leaving Rocinha.

"Listen, you know this shit's just a front for the World Cup and the Olympics, right? It's all going back to normal after." This was one of the most popular beliefs in Rocinha, one Murilo loved to repeat.

"By the time the Olympics comes around, I'll be living it up in Ipanema, my dudes," Biel said. Douglas and Murilo laughed about it, but Biel had a building picked out and everything.

"Y'all talk too much, neguim. No way is Mestre handing over this hill without a fight."

"DG, you're being as twitchy as Murilo. Y'all seem to think we're getting a full-blown war, that the players are gonna rain missiles on the cops, that it'll be a week of nonstop shootouts. Wake up, man. What exactly do you think Mestre is planning? There's gonna be riot police, military police, and BOPE all up in here. For all we know, the Army too. I mean, come on."

They passed around the rest of the joint in silence. Those days, all anybody talked about in Rocinha was the UPP. It was the topic of conversation at every bakery, church, boteco, diner, and market stall. Every resident had a theory, ranging from deeply tragic to highly optimistic, but the truth is nobody really knew anything.

Changing the subject, Douglas showed Biel his equipment. The shadow of UPP had actually made him forget about it for a while. He showed him each piece one by one, as though accounting to a sponsor. At some point, he remembered he had to buy pigskin from the butcher. There was nothing he wanted more than to switch his machine on that night. He checked his watch. It was 9:45 p.m.

"Yo, Biel. Wanna hit the butcher's with me?"

"You making us all dinner or something?"

"Nah, I just gotta buy something there. I wanna put this machine to work stat, and this dude I met today said to practice on pigskin."

"Nah, man, forget pigskin. That shit fucking reeks. If you really wanna put that machine to work, then let's do this shit right."

Douglas thought Biel was kidding when he asked to see the drawings. He leafed through the Māori designs, the swallows, butterflies, anchors, and other stock tattoos before finally settling on a red swallow holding a ribbon with the word "Peace."

"This one."

Douglas liked drawing swallows. At first, he copied out images he'd found online, but now he was doing his own old-school swallows. The one Biel had picked out was his creation. But things are different in theory than they are in practice.

"Pô, neguim. Real talk? I think we should start with something easier."

"C'mon, cuz. This one's perfect. Check out that line. Not too thick, not too thin."

"What about a name? I can look up a font right now. Honest, it makes more sense. I'll do that bird on you some other time."

Even though he never talked about her, Biel decided to get a tattoo in honor of his mother: the word "Mom" on his right shoulder. He picked a font. Douglas suggested adding a crown over it. Murilo stared at the two of them. He never felt more certain that Biel was out of his mind, straight-up certifiable.

"Gonna want that swallow once you're pro, though. Dunno why. I just know that shit will look dope on me."

Douglas copied the font he'd found online, did a clean pass onto another sheet, added the crown, then put transfer paper over the drawing. Then he wrapped his makeshift workstation in plastic, laid out the equipment, cleaned Biel's shoulder with rubbing alcohol, and pressed the drawing onto his skin. He tried to do everything exactly as he'd seen it done online, though he hadn't counted on his whole body trembling along with the tattoo gun.

As he geared up to make his first mark, Douglas finally grasped the sheer magnitude of what he was doing. Every tattoo was a path of no return. Taking a deep breath, he stretched out Biel's skin as tight as it went, lowered the needle, and saw his friend's flesh tear.

RIO—September 27, 2011

No matter how much they tried, they couldn't remember the last time Dona Marli had made them dinner. She was always tired when she got home from work and couldn't be bothered to cook for two grown-ass men on top of everything else. The truth was, the brothers had learned their way around the kitchen pretty early on. At first, they just heated up the food their mom cooked and froze every Sunday. With time, they got acquainted with the stove and the pots and pans, and had a go at making recipes of their own. Stroganoff, pasta with wieners, and rice and beans with fried eggs were specialties of the house.

Earlier that month, Dona Marli had decided to switch up her routine. She started coming home for dinner and made a point of rustling up a nice meal, sometimes even preparing the same dishes she cooked for her employers.

Things at work were going well for Washington. He was never late, had quickly won over his colleagues and superiors, and made a real effort to excel in the role. It was starting to feel like it was only a matter of time before they signed his work card. And ever since Wesley had joined the entertainment team, he'd started helping out more at home. He even managed to set aside some money for driver's ed.

As Washington served himself food at the kitchen table, he noticed Dona Marli's satisfied smile. His mother, a woman who'd pulled off raising two kids on her own while working ten-, eleven-, twelve-hour days, only to have just enough money to pay rent and put food on the table. A woman who, in her little spare time, still managed to make it terrifyingly clear that if either of them ever got involved in crime, she would not visit them in prison, let alone cry at their funeral. Who told them every day, before they even knew how to jerk off, that she wasn't raising anybody's kids. But she'd managed. Washington finished serving himself dinner and had the urge to thank Dona Marli for all she'd done, for riding them, chewing them out, loving them. But instead he just shoveled food into his mouth and said nothing.

"Remember that time I gave your bare asses a lashing?"

Like they could forget: Dona Marli never passed up a chance to tell the story about the day she made her kids strip and hug while she brought the belt down on them.

"And Washington even pulled a fast one. Remember, Wesley, how he kept trying to turn you round when it was his turn to take it? Except, when I noticed, I started aiming only at him so he'd quit messing around."

"You remember why?" No matter how many times Washington heard that story, he could never remember the reason.

"I think you all were throwing shit around and broke Ne-ném's window or something."

"Nah, it wasn't that, Ma. I think it had to do with us and the other kids shooting balloon guns with shirts tied round our faces, right? You were so mad." He was doing his best to remember.

"That was another time, bro. The day we stripped down had to do with us throwing hands in the living room. Something about the TV, I think. I wanted to watch something, you wanted to watch something else. Then, mid-dustup, a frame broke, the TV almost tipped over. It was a huge fucking mess." Wesley never forgot the reason behind anything.

"Yeah, that's it. That's why I was thinking about it just now. I made y'all hug to teach you that brothers have to stick together. Play together, pull shit together, get beat together."

"For real." Washington felt the relief that comes from re-membering something that's on the tip of your tongue.

"All I know is it worked. There was no more fighting at home after that."

Washington polished off his plate in record time and went in for seconds. He'd missed those ground beef crepes. But the joy he felt that evening was about more than just food. It was different, both old and new at the same time. When they were younger, in their teens, they'd get annoyed whenever their mom tried to make them sit down to dinner together. Over time, they did it less and less, and Washington was only now realizing how much he'd missed these moments at home—sharing food, telling stories.

"Honest, Dona Marli, I think it was the TV stand that brought us together."

"For sure, I still don't know how it took you so long to notice." Wesley served himself more food as well. It had all started with the two brothers duking it out at home while Dona Marli was at work. The reason for the fight was a Flamengo jersey that Wesley had borrowed without permission and accidentally torn when he was out. Washington was chasing Wesley and threw a hairbrush at him. Wesley ducked, and the hairbrush crashed right into the TV stand their mom had just bought at Casas Bahia. The two instantly forgot why they were fighting and teamed up, their sole purpose ensuring their survival. For over two weeks, they acted like nothing had happened and even pretended to open the glass door when they had to grab something from that section of the TV stand.

"That's the day we really became tight. Dunno, it's like we panicked. I think we realized things could turn out bad unless we had each other's backs." Washington smiled at his mom, knowing how happy it made her to hear those words.

"And I didn't even smack you that day."

"That's right. And me thinking you were gonna kill us. I had nightmares and stuff." Wesley laughed at the memory.

"We talk like this, but you know I was never the kind of mom to be beating her kids. Considering the crap you two got up to, you're lucky you weren't born in a different family. Plus, I never liked the idea of spanking my kids after the fact. Once the rage leaves my body, I'm done teaching lessons."

They finished up dinner. Washington took his plate to the sink, but Dona Marli made a point of doing the dishes. The two brothers went into the hallway outside the apartment for a cigarette.

"Dona Marli's a trip, man. She gave me a hard time the other day about the dishes in the sink. Now look at her," Washington said while tearing the plastic wrap off a pack of Hollywoods. Since he'd started working at the restaurant, loosies had become a thing of the past.

"She's always been like that, menó. This job stuff's no joke to her. Makes her happy as hell."

"Yeah. I like seeing her like this, for real. I actually wanted to talk to you about this idea I had. You know, now that I've got formal work, and you're on your way to getting your driver's license, a steadier job, regular pay, et cetera, I think that if the three of us join forces, we could for sure get a loan." After the bank rejected his mother's request, Washington had become obsessed with the idea of helping her buy a house.

"Forget it, menó. We can put in a thousand loan requests, they're never gonna get approved."

It had been hard to buy houses before the UPP occupation was announced. Now, with prices skyrocketing, it seemed close to impossible. As much as Wesley also wanted to help his mother attain her goal, he didn't think they should indulge any fantasies.

"C'mon, man. Hear me out before you start shitting on my plan. Me and you, working full-time, bringing in six hundred, seven hundred reais a month, aboveboard. If Mom gets a job with a signed work card and all, there's no way they don't give us the loan. We could pay a thousand a month, easy. Then if I get promoted to waitstaff, start bringing home tips . . ."

Washington had been wanting to talk to his brother for a few days. The idea seemed fail-proof, but it'd only work if the three of them pooled resources.

"Listen, no way Dona Marli's ever leaving that woman's house."

"I'm gonna talk to Mom as well. She's gotta pressure them, tell them that if they don't get her paperwork straightened out, she's leaving."

"C'mon, Washington. She's been cooking for them for three years, and it's always the same shit. Her boss gives her PTO once in a million years, gets her some clothes, all to buy her more time with Dona Marli. It's fucked up."

Wesley wanted to help his brother. He knew Washington's heart was in the right place, and he wanted to do his part. But he just didn't believe it was possible. When he looked ahead, everything was even hazier and more confusing than Washington seemed to think it was.

"Bro, all we need is some focus, okay?"

After finishing their cigarette, they went back in the house to roll a joint. Time to burn the real digestif. The kitchen was clean, and Dona Marli was waiting for her sons.

"Hold on, I wanna say something before you go out." Each brother stood in a corner of the kitchen. "Everybody's talking about the UPP. About how hard they came down on residents at Complexo Alemão. So, I was thinking . . . I realize there's no use trying to get you to stop smoking that garbage. You love that stuff like nothing I ever seen. And I . . . well, I'm your mom. I worry. About somebody catching you smoking in an alley. About you getting smacked by the police. I don't know. You hear all kinds of things. I think that, from now on, if the UPP really does occupy Rocinha . . . I think I want you smoking inside the apartment."

The two brothers were stunned. Dona Marli was always

complaining about the smell. If she ever came home and caught a whiff of the marola, she flipped out, yelled at them to go smoke that shit far the fuck away from her. The truth is, she'd always been of the opinion that people ought to face the consequences of their vices. She must be really scared to be saying what she just did.

"So, like, is that after UPP shows up or can we start now?" Wesley joked.

She nodded and moved her hands in agreement. It was enough to make Washington run off to grab the weed. The two brothers sat on the living room sofa. Dona Marli watched the rolling ritual from the door between the living room and the kitchen.

"Are we allowed to light up?" Washington held the joint between his fingers, still disbelieving.

"Didn't I already say so?"

Washington sparked up and the scent of bengala took over the entire apartment. Dona Marli grabbed the remote, sat on a chair near the sofa, and started zipping through channels, trying to act natural.

"You know, this weed doesn't smell half as bad as some of the shit people smoke on the street."

RIO—October 7, 2011

As Washington left the bathroom, he could still taste puke in his mouth. He stumbled into the bar and saw that it was starting to empty out. By the time he was at his table, his buddies were already on another bottle of Contini. The sight of booze was enough to make Washington shudder and choke back the urge to heave.

It was his first time out with his co-workers. His paycheck had just hit his bank account, and he was over the fucking moon. He mixed caipirinha with tequila and beer with whiskey and Red Bull until he found himself face-first in a toilet bowl. The last thing he wanted to lay eyes on when he got back to the table was more liquor. To make matters worse, neither Adriano, nor Rubinho, much less Chico, seemed to be affected by the booze. Washington took the drink he was handed so that he wouldn't have to explain he'd just been sick. He toasted with his friends, pretended to take a sip, and went outside for a cigarette. He was surprised by the foot traffic on Travessa Roma. Crowds of people walking, talking, and zipping by on their motorbikes.

He found a crooked joint tucked in his cigarette pack, considered lighting up, then backtracked. The last time he'd smoked pot after having that much to drink had sucked big-time. He'd blacked out on the dance floor of Emoções, everybody staring at him. The friends he was with were all shit-faced as well, and they still had to take him to urgent care to get a glucose shot. What a mess. Truth is, weed was better the day after. Forget Engov, Sonrisal, all that stuff. The best hangover cure was a joint.

"Hey, did you clock that guy at the end of the alley?" Rubinho popped up out of nowhere and pointed toward Largo do Boiadeiro.

"What're you talking about, man? You high or something?"

"That motherfucker over there. Wait, he's gone again. Keep watching. Keep watching. He'll be back."

"You tripping? Ain't nobody there."

"Whatever . . . You think those fools are gonna storm the hill without scoping it out first? Gimme a break." Rubinho started whispering, like he was sharing a secret: "There's probably moles all over this joint, passing on intel. You don't think so? Wake up, cuz. Read the news. The police are knocking on our front door. Word is they're gonna be here in less than a month."

It wasn't hard to believe the military police had sent a bunch of undercover cops into Rocinha to map out bocas, catalog snitches, find the best ways in and out of the favela. But wasted or not, Washington was sure no one was hiding at the end of the alley. In part because moles needed to lay low, not draw attention. At least if they had any hope of surviving. A good step in that direction was not posting up at the end of a deserted alley at three in the morning.

"My nose white?" Rubinho raised his head, flaring his nostrils. "I don't want that dude noticing if he shows up again."

"You're cool." That's when he caught on: of course, they were doing lines. Nobody could drink like that and be okay.

"Wanna smoke?" Washington slipped the joint out of his cigarette pack and tried to make it look less wonky.

"Nah, I'm not smoking that. It fucks me up."

Rubinho lit up a Gudang Garam. He took such a long drag you'd think it was a Free or a Marlboro Light.

"I'm feeling kinda off today, man. Maybe it was something I ate. Weed helps with digestion, for real."

"Ingestion too. Shit always makes me ravenous."

Washington sparked the joint.

"Yo, smoke that someplace else. If that mole comes this way, you're not the only one getting busted." Rubinho tossed out his half-smoked cigarette and went back to the bar seeming pissed.

Even though Washington knew there was no one there, he walked in the opposite direction of the so-called hideout for the sake of his buddy's peace of mind and wound up on Via Ápia.

It was crazy how that street was always popping, no matter the time of day. Naturally, since it was late at night, the place was crawling with wasteoids: the usual drunks, cokeheads on the lookout for their next bump. But it wasn't only them. Some folks were on their way in or out of work while others grabbed a bite or just chopped it up with their friends.

A couple and their two kids waited in line for hot dogs. Three a.m. That was Rocinha for you, the hill that never sleeps.

Not that this was news to Washington, but, just then, as he looked around him, he felt proud of his birthplace. The largest favela in Latin America. A city within a city. So big not even people born and bred in Rocinha knew every alley. So big no census poll could account for every resident.

Halfway through his joint, Washington felt queasy. He put it out and started heading back to the bar. When he got there, he'd order a soda to close out the night. He was having such a good time wandering the side streets that he decided to go around Valão, and take Largo do Boiadeiro to Travessa Roma. That way he could reassure Rubinho that the dude at the end of the alley had moved on.

From the footbridge, Washington watched the cars on the highway below him. He was stunned to see the barbershop was open. Twenty-four-hour bakeries, grocery stores, diners, bocas . . . but a barbershop? Why would anyone get their hair cut so late at night? Washington stood outside the window tripping about that while the barber, the customer in the chair, and the two people waiting their turn stared right back at him, just as confused as he was.

Right then, Washington felt so dizzy he had to sit on the stoop outside the store next door. He was scared he'd be sick. Things got more intense around him. Different styles of music mixed together. Forró, pagode, and Brazilian funk and rock streamed out of bars. The chaos didn't seem to weird him out so much as calm him down. At the end of the day, this was home. He lowered his head and puked a second time.

Back at the bar, Adriano and Rubinho were the only ones talking.

"I'm telling you, man, my girl is not to be fucked with. Hand to God. To give you an idea: We've got this dog, right? A puppy. You know what they're like, shitting everywhere, barking all the time, that kinda stuff. So the dog was yapping non-fucking-stop, I swear. Night, day, it didn't matter. Then one morning, our neighbor knocks on the door to complain: Blah blah, the dog won't shut up, blah blah. I'm giving my daughter breakfast, and all I hear is my wife say: Dog barking too much, is he? Funny that. You know why my dog barks so much? The neighbor says she doesn't know. And my wife goes: Because he doesn't know how to tell you to go fuck yourself. Because if he knew . . . bitch, you bet he would! Then she slams the door in the woman's face. That's my girl for you, Rubinho. Straight up."

"So what're you gonna tell her tonight when you drag your drunk ass home?"

"Uh, I . . . I'll tell her . . . Honest, no idea. If I thought about it too much, I wouldn't be here, pô."

"Hey, did Chico bounce?" Washington cracked open a can of Coke.

"Nah, he just went to grab something. Be back soon." Adriano filled another glass with beer to toast Washington's return.

Washington both wanted and didn't want to leave. He was doing a lot better after throwing up. The exhaustion he felt after a full-day's work was just as strong as his desire to celebrate his first paycheck. He'd waited so long, he wasn't ready to throw in the towel just yet. So he poured some beer into his glass and toasted with his two friends.

Adriano ran his mouth while they waited for Chico to come back. He talked about work, about how smart his daughter was, about his mom up in Ceará who he hadn't seen in over seven years. Washington took a seat, leaned against the wall, and zoned out. After a hard month of work, he deserved to be there, to take it easy. Soon enough, he'd get to start buying things. A pair of cool kicks—he was in need of new shoes. An official Flamengo jersey. Importantly, he'd get to pay his mom back the money she'd fronted him last month. Washington knew Dona Marli would never ask for it, but he also knew it would make her happy to see her son honoring his word.

Adriano only stopped talking when Chico came back with the powder. The three discussed the state of the bar bathroom. Reeking of piss, smeared in puke, no toilet lid. They couldn't keep snorting lines in there. They'd need to pick an alley, even if they risked being seen by someone they knew. Before leaving the bar, they asked Washington to keep an eye on their stuff.

"I was thinking of joining you."

The bar owner was put in charge of their bags, and they set off in search of a deserted alley. They finally found one they agreed on, and Chico got down to work. He took Rubinho's ID card and Adriano's credit card, and started cutting lines.

"Finally, a fat sack. Last time, I got scammed. It's dead disrespectful to users, for real. We stick our necks out with family, police, fucking everybody. The least they could do is sell us decent drugs." Rubinho was truly outraged at the local operation.

"If you're so upset about it, Rubinho, maybe you should put that pretty mouth of yours to work," Chico said without taking his eyes off the lines, and choking back his laughter so he wouldn't blow away the powder.

"Think about it, though. It's a way better deal for them to mix shit up, toss in some glass, cement, whatever the fuck. Good or bad, they know we're buying their product no matter what. I'm telling you, dudes buy even more of the stuff when it's bad, chasing that good high," Adriano said.

"Somebody roll a straw."

Washington tried to give Rubinho a two-real note, but he said those were the worst straws because they got passed around too much—they were old, soft. The best straw was a hundo. But half that would do the trick. Washington pulled a fifty out of his wallet. As Chico finished up the lines, he asked:

"So you doing a bump with us or what?"

"Leave a rail for me at the end." Washington was trying to hide the shakes he'd had since they'd set foot in that alley.

Adriano took back his credit card, licked it, and slid it in his wallet. Rubinho went first, snorting the whole thing in one go, careful not to blow the other lines. Adriano went second and took his sweet time choosing the most bountiful rail. Chico was third. Then came Washington's turn. He took a deep breath, grabbed the straw from his friend, and dove right in.

RIO—November 12, 2011

São Conrado was lit, especially near Cantão. It was as if all of Rocinha had conspired to hit the beach on the same day, just like they did every December 31, for that final dip of the year.

Douglas staggered out of the water after getting dragged under by a wave. He caught his breath, then said hello to some acquaintances who were smoking grass, playing altinha, and sunbathing. The sky was cloudless, and Douglas's eyes rested on a hang glider in the blue expanse. He followed it for a while, wondering how it felt to see everything from way up high. The beach, the hill, all those dozens of people.

"Yo, DG!" Biel said while pointing at the spot they'd picked on the sand.

They moved awkwardly under the weight of the chairs and the beer. Douglas went over to give them a hand. Then the three of them sat facing the ocean and finally cracked open a cold one.

"Neguim, it's bad enough you're white. You gotta lotion that shit."

Douglas was feeling salty because Biel's tattoo had faded during the healing process. Worst of all, he had no way of knowing whose fault it was. If it was on him for being inexperienced and too chicken to push the needle deeper, or if it was on Biel for eating a ton of fatty foods, chocolate, and shrimp—everything tattoo artists beg their clients to stay away from for the first two weeks of the healing process.

"We'll touch it up, pô. It's gonna look great. Trust." Biel always spoke with the confidence of someone who knew who was at fault: never him.

"Hey, Biel, see that girl over there playing altinha?" Murilo pointed at a circle of people, making no attempt to be discreet.

"That chick surfs mad waves. I'm always seeing her at Arpoador," Biel replied as he started rolling a joint.

"Cool. She looks like a surfer, too. She's got that nice tan. Like those gringas on Canal OFF. The Californian ones."

"She's a ten, not gonna lie." Biel watched her trying to keep the ball from touching the ground.

"What's her name?"

"Chicks like her only date other surfers, bro. Beefy health nuts. You really think she'd be into a pothead like you?" Biel carefully sprinkled weed into the rolling paper.

"You wouldn't be saying that shit if you were from here. Everybody knows I used to shred epic waves on my board. I can ride a ripple like a beast."

"Yeah, whatever. You talk a big game, but I never even

seen you bodysurf." Biel finished rolling the joint so perfectly he didn't even need to pack it.

"It's cause of work, neguim. Before I joined the barracks, I basically lived on the sand."

Biel lit up. The marola hit him immediately. He wasted a minute or so blowing smoke rings.

"C'mon, DG, speak up. Can you picture this dude on a surfboard or what?"

Douglas looked at his friends weirdly, like he wasn't sure how he'd ended up there. Then, he cast the same weird gaze on everything around him, took a sip of his beer, and lit a cigarette.

"Dude, I was on this journey just now. Staring out at Pedra da Gávea and wondering, like, damn, how long has that rock been sitting there? Three hundred, fifteen hundred years? It's fucking wild. I was tripping, thinking about how, like, dinosaurs used to walk this place, you know? Can you even imagine? These huge-ass creatures, bigger than fucking trees. So, catch this: dinosaurs walked there, and Indians, and now, bro, all you gotta do is hike a trail to walk in the same place as them. See what I'm saying? Like, everything's fucking changed. Humans invented cars, guns, planes, whatever. But that chunk of land over there, menó, that land's just the same. Isn't that wild? It's like Rocinha, right? We live there and all, but if you think about it, we got no clue what went down there, like, before. We don't know shit about the animals, the rivers, whether or not there were any Indians, and if so, from what tribe. I mean, c'mon, there must've been hundreds of Indians living up there. But then a load of stuff went down, some major shit, these crazy-ass wars, and we know nothing about any of it. And it's all happening again, right? Let that sink in. Years from now, nobody's gonna know about our troubles. Or our bliss. Nobody, man. But this place doesn't change. And fuck it. We were here, right? And *we* know that."

The three friends sat there, the only sound the roar of the ocean. They were stumped. Finally, Biel couldn't help himself: "What did I tell you? The acid's rewiring your mother-fucking brain!"

They burst out laughing. Then they ran into the water and spent a while bodysurfing. The temperature was on point, not too hot, not too cold. Murilo watched surfers catching waves on their boards and spotted some people he knew. The thought of surfing again seemed to help him reconnect with the kid he'd been a few years back, when he still believed he could do anything.

They headed to the beach again and spent the next few hours smoking. The afternoon disappeared without a trace, each of them on their own personal journey. Douglas with his dinosaurs, Biel doodling in the sand on his legs, and at some point, Murilo started begging his friends to explain stuff to him, anything; he had no idea what was going on.

"What do you think? Should we save this J for home or burn it here?" Biel asked after the sun had set.

"Home!" Douglas and Murilo said, almost at the same time.

One thing was for sure, they either had to smoke that joint or dump it because there was no keeping weed in the house that evening. The UPP was gearing up to occupy Rocinha.

Dona Marli wouldn't be sleeping at home. The family she worked for had decided to throw a big lunch, and since nobody ever knows what tomorrow will bring, they had her stay overnight. Washington was also of the mind she should steer clear of the hill, even though her being there would've eased things if the cops came knocking on their door. Still, picturing their mom in that situation—all her things turned over, her sons treated like criminals—sounded a lot worse.

Like other users in Rocinha, the two brothers knew they needed to polish off their drugs before hitting the sack. What Wesley didn't realize, though, was that his brother had a dime bag of coke in his shorts pocket. Leftovers from the first time he'd purchased coke.

It'd all gone down a few days ago. He'd been kicking back at a baile in Rua 1 when his workmates busted out some rails and the evening got wild. It was Washington's third time bumming lines from them. Figuring he should probably start pulling his own weight, he headed to the boca to cop five dime bags. He couldn't stop thinking about how weird it all felt. He'd started shaking, his voice barely made a sound, and he had the feeling all eyes were on him. Of course, he'd gophered before for hopheads too scared to hit the boca themselves, using his commission to cop joints, go halves on cigarettes, the uzh. But now that the gear was for him, it was something else. He bugged out, convinced everyone who saw him knew that, this time, he was the one snorting the stuff.

His buddies dipped out before finishing the last bag: the baile had gotten to the point where the soundtrack was Legião Urbana and church songs. Washington took the leftover powder home but never found the right moment to use it. Now, there he was, hours before a major operation, with no idea what to do with the contraband. It seemed wasteful to throw it away. Plus, he had the itch to do a line, to feel something different. He was both ashamed to tell his brother and scared to snort on the DL, then mess up the explanation.

"Thank fuck I'm not on shift tomorrow morning. It's crazy out there right now."

Every time Washington thought about the following day, he panicked. That weird thing that had the whole hill on edge the past few months was getting closer and closer by the minute.

"That's if we can leave, right, menó?" Wesley burned another joint, intent on finishing his weed.

"You really think there's gonna be a shootout?" They'd had that same conversation a thousand times, but it hit different that night.

"Dudes would have to be outta their minds to pull a stunt like that, bro. But then pushers *got to* be outta their minds, right? So I dunno, menó. Anything's possible."

After a couple more tokes, Washington was hit by a serious case of the munchies. He'd been hungry all day, actually, from the family meal at work to the second he got home. No matter how much he ate, he was never sated—it was like having a hole in his stomach. The hunger was almost painful. So, when he felt that pang again, he dropped the unlit joint in the ashtray and went to the kitchen to see what was what. He found some stale bread; there was cheese and tomato sauce in the fridge. All he needed to make one of his favorite snacks for the munchies.

"Yo, Wesley. Want some pizzawich?"

"Definitely. Throw one in for me."

Wesley walked into the kitchen with the joint. He made the requisite complaint about Washington letting the cherry go out like that, claiming he'd been waiting his turn. Only after finishing his sermon did he toke up. Washington covered the bread in mozzarella, then popped it in the oven.

"Bro, real talk. You ever consider trying coke?"

Wesley was taken aback by the abruptness of the question. People must be talking about him, raising suspicions.

"The fuck, man. Did somebody tell you I'm doing blow?"

"Nobody said nothing, man. I'm just curious is all."

There was something weird about that convo, and Wesley was still convinced he'd been the subject of some he-said-she-said. Maybe it all started when he went to Bee's one day while the crew was speedballing. He'd even pitched in five to help out, though he didn't partake. He stuck to weed.

"Pô, menó, when it comes to blow, I get the inclination sometimes, like I wanna know what the deal is, right? People fucking love that stuff, bro. More than lasagna, churrasco, whatever. Then you think: it's gotta be fucking *dope*. And that's the thing that wigs me out. Shit that's too good always ends bad. Loads of guys go off the deep end."

Then Washington started talking about his first time using. He spoke about his workmates, a whole crew who'd been at it for a while with no issues, about how they had kids, families, and stuff. Seeing the interest in his brother's eyes, he mentioned he had a dime bag in his pocket, that his friend had left it with him. Eventually, the two of them agreed it only became a problem when folks started buying it for themselves, especially to use in private.

Washington never imagined he'd be doing lines inside his own home one day, but that didn't stop him from reaching for a plate in the kitchen cupboard. Wesley wasn't sure why, but as he watched his brother cut lines with his RioCard, he sweated bullets.

They could smell the pizzawich now. Washington finished the prep work, ran his tongue down his card, and went to scope out the food. It was ready. The bread golden-brown on the bottom, the cheese melted through. He left the baking tray on the stovetop to cool, pulled a ten-real note out of his wallet, and rolled a straw.

"You first."

They couldn't sit on their hands; even high on acid and tired from the sun, they needed to hit the grocery store. In part because nothing motivates like the fear of running out of food. Proof of this was that everybody on that hill seemed to be on Largo do Boiadeiro too, having obviously had the same idea: all the stores were packed with people elbowing each other and raising hell as they stood in line for the cash register.

Douglas wanted to smoke a cigarette before going in. It was like he was trying to delay the inevitable. While they stood outside smoking, they peeped other people's groceries. An older man had stocked up on rice, beans, pasta, and several heads of garlic, and also thrown in a special treat: two Ana Maria snack cakes. Another guy had bought multiple bottles of oil. Like fifteen. Then there were the people doing their monthly supermarket runs: meat, chicken, rice, cookies, that kind of thing. The three of them stood out there, observing in silence. It was a different vibe from the one on the beach. Right then, it was clear, beyond the shadow of a doubt: the UPP was there to stay.

They brought home chicken nuggets, instant noodles, and frozen potatoes. Stuff that was easy to cook and lasted forever. The apartment was a shitshow, much worse than they remembered. The dirty dishes were about to swallow up the whole sink, and there were a load of glasses scattered around, some filled to the brim with ash. Dirty laundry everywhere you looked. They stood in the middle of their pigsty and began putting away the groceries.

"That shit that went down with Mestre is *fucked up*. The guys at the boca in Via Ápia were bummed the fuck out. I felt kinda sorry for them," Murilo said while trying to shove things in the freezer.

"Say less, neguim. They're like chickens with their heads cut off, no clue where to run. Mestre was more than just the kingpin. He was their role model, you know? Then, outta nowhere, the guy gets busted while he's on the lam. It's crazy."

"You think they didn't know he was gonna run? Please."

Murilo got worked up whenever he thought someone was talking smack about Nem. He was Rocinha born-and-bred. Had lived through wars, coups, new factions, new kingpins. As far as Murilo was concerned, nobody had done a better job at the helm than Nem.

"Dunno, neguim. So maybe some people knew and some didn't. Whatever. All I know for sure is that a lot of folks, even residents like us, were counting on Mestre." Douglas couldn't hide his disappointment.

"For sure. Mestre was a lot of people's only hope to stop a war from happening."

As soon as they were done putting away the groceries, Douglas grabbed a towel and jumped in the shower. He was dying to rinse the salt off his body. Biel could care less. He slumped onto the sofa, legs caked in sand. It drove Murilo crazy when he did shit like that.

"Goddamnit. Now I'm really fucking pissed. My weed connect just texted to say that if it wasn't for these UPP shit-bags, I'd have copped half a kilo for a good price," Biel said without taking his eyes off his phone.

"So, I wanted to talk to you about that," Murilo said and lit a cigarette at the window. "Now that the hill's gonna be hot like 24/7, what's the deal with holding contraband in the house?"

"Dunno, bro, we just have to wait a beat, see how things shake out, find the best way in again."

"You realize the police are gonna be breathing down our necks, right? They're gonna want to show everyone they're putting in the hours, and I'm not interested in being turned into an example. Especially for something I got no business with."

This didn't sit well with Biel, who dropped his phone and leaped off the sofa in a rage.

"Listen, Murilo. None of us kids here. If shit hits the fan, you know I'm good for it."

Murilo took one last drag on his cigarette before flicking it out the window.

"Whatever, man. You gonna be good for it like you were with Coroa?"

Biel flew off the handle and stepped up to Murilo.

"Fuck you, asshole. Didn't hear you complaining when you were smoking the stuff," Biel spat out while pointing his finger in Murilo's face. Murilo reacted by pushing him away.

Things got serious. Biel shoved Murilo back, and the two of them squared up. They stood there in silence, just waiting for the next move. That's when Douglas came into the living room with a towel wrapped around his waist. He separated them and planted himself in the middle.

"Y'all cool it. Let's clean this place so we can light one up and bed down, okay?"

––––––––––––––

Wesley would never forget the bitter taste that crawled up his nose and down his throat. Strong, not good or bad, kind of rusty. Everything sped up after that; his heart pounded so hard he could hear it. Then there was this mad rush of energy, all through his body, a sudden drive, the itch to do something, anything.

Things seemed easy, straightforward. Wesley's mind was racing. Several ideas knocked around his head at the same time, and he knew exactly what to do about them. It was like he'd been allowed to see his own life from a different angle, a little more removed than usual.

"This shit's awesome, menó. Makes you feel, uh . . ." Wesley paced up and down the kitchen. "Fuck it, I'm smoking a cig. We can just spray some air freshener later." Washington decided to join him.

Wesley wanted to tell his brother about all the things that

felt different to him and how. In his mind, body, outlook. But he couldn't find the words, let alone arrange the sentences. Everything felt so quick and intense, like it could all explode any second. Wesley got the urge to go outside, see folks, drink a cold one. Only then did he remember the UPP and everything else that lay ahead of them.

Just thinking about it made him nervous. The confidence he'd felt only a second ago vanished and gave way to anxiety. Wesley dashed to the living room window and gazed out at the streets. There was no one around. Nine p.m. It seemed impossible. The quiet.

Needing to keep busy, he went to his bedroom, determined to clean up. He started in the closet, grabbed all his crumpled-up clothes, and tossed them on the bed. Then he folded them one by one. Washington walked in while he was doing this and stood there staring at his brother.

"This shit's a godsend when you're tanked on booze. Perks you right the fuck up." Even with Wesley as his partner in crime, Washington still felt guilty as hell about doing lines at home. He wanted to talk, to hash things out until he was confident he'd made the right decision.

Wesley sorted his pants, shorts, and T-shirts into piles. As he did, his mind was already on the next thing: soaking his sneakers.

"Just can't get hooked."

"For sure."

"How many times you done coke?"

"Four, counting this one."

Wesley went back to the task at hand. It was amazing to not feel lazy. Or tired. He could get a jump on a bunch of things he'd been wanting to do forever. Errands that snow-balled in his mind until they became a priority. It wasn't long before he forgot everything that was about to happen on the hill.

"But I'm chill, bro, for real. I don't crave it or nothing like that. Only reason I brought it up today is that I'd've had to throw it out. Which would've sucked big-time."

Wesley wasn't listening. He wanted music. He had this song stuck in his head but couldn't remember what it was called. He went to his computer. Before he had a chance to go on YouTube, Facebook swallowed him whole. He scrolled down his timeline. Everyone he knew was talking about the same thing: the thousands of officers selected for Operation Choque de Paz, Nem da Rocinha's prison sentence, and whether or not there would be a shootout. Also, would the power stay on all night long or would they cut it during the invasion?

It was too much information to take in at once. Suddenly, every thought he had seemed small and meaningless, nothing in the grand scheme of all that could happen. Wesley forgot about the clothes he had to put away, the sneakers he'd wanted to soak, and just scrolled mindlessly. Down and down until he came across a post by an old friend of his from school. A montage of Rocinha at night, all lit up. Behind the houses, against the skyline, was a silhouette of Christ the Redeemer. The caption read: Lord keep us.

PART II

RIO—November 13, 2011

It sounded like the chopper was inside the apartment. The whole building practically shook from the noise. Biel woke up but refused to peep out the window until he was sure the bird was far the hell away. When he did look outside, Travessa Kátia was dead, quieter than he'd ever seen it. Usually, at that time of day, the green market was already set up on Boiadeiro, and people could be seen walking around with their groceries and their Sunday morning hopes and worries. Soon after, the bars would raise their shutters, and the early-bird customers would file in. A bit later, around nine, service would begin at the Neo-Pentecostal church in the building next door and at the Our Lady of Aparecida chapel down the street. But as Biel peered out the window that morning, he saw nothing, not a single sign of life.

At least if he'd had some weed, he could've fallen back asleep. No dice. Biel got up to take a leak, then peeked into the bedroom. He wanted to check if anyone else had been woken by the helicopter. The bedroom was still dark. He stared over at Douglas and Murilo, but neither of them moved.

He went back to the living room to mess around on his laptop, curious to see what people were saying about the operation on Facebook. But the internet was down. He tried refreshing the page and restarting both the router and his computer. Nothing. He should try the TV. Every channel was probably running the same story: *Military police invades Rocinha, Latin America's largest favela*. But to Biel's surprise, all he got was the same blue screen. He looked up at the kitchen wall clock. It was five to eight.

There was no point lying down and closing his eyes when his brain was moving so fast. He couldn't remember hearing any gunfire the night before. The silence they'd fallen asleep to had been broken only by the earsplitting drone of the helicopters. The fact that there'd been no hostilities was proof that the police operation was a success. But that was only half the story. It was the stuff that happened while nothing was happening that kept Biel up that morning.

Outside, the shops were still closed. Slowly but surely, the occasional pedestrian started walking down Travessa Kátia. They moved cautiously, with tentative steps. You could see from their faces that they were working men and women, the kind with formal jobs on the blacktop. Biel wished he had somewhere to go outside the house. At least that way he'd be headed toward a destination, not walking down the stairs like he was then, aimless, with no clue where he was going.

The second he set foot on Via Ápia, an authorized NET vendor approached him with a limited-time offer for cable TV. Biel didn't want to stand around listening to the guy's spiel, so he apologized and kept walking. He'd barely gotten rid of him when another authorized vendor, this one for Oi, tried to sell him on a once-in-a-lifetime plan for TV, internet, and phone. That's when Biel realized that gatonet, the favela's pirated cable and internet system, wasn't coming back anytime soon.

There were almost no residents among the cops, reporters, and authorized vendors crowding the entrance to the favela. He made his way uphill. At the corner of Estrada da Gávea and Via Ápia, he lit a cigarette. A BearCat trundled up the street ahead of him. Though Biel wanted to check out the situation higher up, in the heart of Rocinha, away from the cameras and authorized vendors, he quickly pushed that thought out of his head. He'd be a lot safer down on Largo das Flores.

On the floricultural sidewalk, near the mototaxi rank, there was a swarm of law enforcement vehicles: military-police cruisers, riot-police Blazers, BearCats, the whole nine yards. There was even a police bus with a massive BOPE flag stretched across it. The minute Biel saw the image of the knife in the skull, it hit him: when folks in Rocinha started obsessing over the UPP occupation, they'd mostly focused on the day of the invasion. No one had ever talked about what might come after.

There was no question. He had to move out of Rocinha, and fast. Preferably someplace on the blacktop, where there was no risk of pacification. Sometimes, just for the hell of it, Biel would scroll through rentals online. Flamengo, Glória, Catete. Second-division South Zone. Murilo and Douglas thought he was tripping; for that price, you could rent a mansion in any favela in the city. That attitude annoyed the hell out of Biel. He was convinced people were lying when they said they were proud to live on the hill. As far as he was concerned, they only said that so they wouldn't have to admit they couldn't afford to live anywhere better. Instead they went on about how there was more freedom in favelas, how growing up on the blacktop must be a drag, that rich kids played marbles on carpeted floors and flew kites in front of fans, how you couldn't have a decent churrasco in a condo without worrying the noise would get you in trouble with the building manager. It was funny how their memories worked. In these moments, it was like they forgot about the water shortages, open sewers, cops kicking down doors, garbage collection being subject to the whims of COMLURB. He wanted to see where they'd shove their pride if they ever got the chance to move into a condo with a twenty-four-hour doorman, gas-powered showers, elevators, trash sorting, and the security of knowing the police would only show up at your door to protect you.

Biel walked a little longer. Not even the Universal Church of the Kingdom of God had the courage to open its doors. Any other Sunday, the place would've been crawling with brothers and sisters passing out newspapers and taking down names to add to their book of prayers. Instead, there were cops pacing back and forth. Biel had seen enough. It was time to head home.

He only noticed O China was closed when he was back on Travessa Kátia. This shouldn't have come as a surprise, given that it was the same for every other establishment in the area. But for some reason, the sight of that shuttered pastelaria meant so much more. In the time he'd lived there, Biel had never seen O China close its doors. Once, he'd come home from a New Year's party in Copacabana to find the place open. Carnavals, bailes, World Cup games, nothing stopped the owners from slinging pastéis, juice, and soft drinks. Biel pictured O China and his wife sitting at home wondering when they'd get to serve customers again. Had the chopper woken them as well where they lived?

As Biel walked up Travessa Kátia, he couldn't shake the image of the shuttered pastelaria. It seemed to be screaming something all of them would be forced to open their eyes to eventually: the Rocinha they knew was gone.

It all happened fast. The second he thought of turning around, the muzzle was in his face. The cop with the rifle started shouting at him to explain what he was doing there.

"I live here," he managed to say after the initial scare.

"Then get the fuck in!"

Biel obeyed. Inside, Murilo and Douglas stood in a corner of the living room, their heads down. Next to them, a pair of riot-police officers held their rifles across their chests.

"What were you trying to get rid of out there?" the officer asked, gun still pointed at Biel.

"I went out for some bread."

Another cop, who wasn't directly involved in the conversation, took issue with Biel's reply. He started speaking, inches from his face.

"Bread? Where, asshole? Everything's fucking closed."

Coroa walked downstairs, stood near the door, and peered in.

"What is this, a goddamn party?" The guy with the rifle turned to Coroa, weapon raised.

"I own this building, officer," Coroa said. He didn't look down, nor did he seem scared of the gun. The cop lowered it.

The pig told Coroa that their informant had tipped them to pushers living in that building, and that those three individuals fit the description. Then he moved on to the usual threats. He said the three of them had better hand over the product stat; if they were forced to conduct a search only to turn something up, things would get ugly. Cops loved fishing.

"These boys are all workers . . ." Coroa explained to the cops.

But there was no stopping them. The police turned the house upside down anyway. They even checked the ashtray for roaches and looked through Douglas's tattoo equipment. Good thing they didn't ask to see a receipt.

Biel tried to get Douglas and Murilo's attention, to communicate with them somehow, but they kept their heads down. One of the pigs was watching them. As if they'd try something against three armed police officers.

The hate Biel felt was so intense that he finally understood why players fired at those assholes and tossed grenades under BearCats. Nobody should have to take that shit—some guy stepping into your home, rummaging through your stuff, treating you like a criminal even though he'd never seen you a day in his life. Who was the mole? How many people lived in Rocinha anyway? 70,000, 100,000? How did they even figure out that kind of number, when there were five, six people living under one roof, when every month saw more folks coming down from the North, the Northeast? Out of all the thousands of people who lived in Rocinha, how many were actually in the business? It couldn't be more than 1%. Cops reaped what they fucking sowed.

At some point, the pigs got tired of looking. They found no contraband, which pissed them off even more. But they had eyes on them now, they said. Things around there were about to change. They'd better not catch them mixed up in anything shady, because they knew what the tender trio looked like now.

The cops left to knock on other doors. Coroa looked over at Murilo, Douglas, and Biel. All three gave him a thank-you signal at the same time. Coroa nodded, then left.

RIO—November 18, 2011

He got there in the nick of time, threw on his uniform, and kept a low profile, sorting silverware and folding napkins. Washington thought he could go unnoticed, blend in with the other staff. No dice. Half an hour before the restaurant opened, the manager came up to him.

"Don't forget to iron your uniform, Washington. Your clothes look like they came straight out of a lion's mouth." The man smiled to lighten things up.

Washington hated ironing his uniform in that heat. Zero breeze in the dressing room, and when the iron went on, the place became an oven, hot and stuffy.

He had no choice. If he wanted to move up in that restaurant, be a server one day, he couldn't dream of slacking off. After three months grinding there, Washington was clued in to the rules of the game; the only folks who worked the dining room were from Ceará and Paraíba, the lightest skinned— Galicians, as they called themselves. Meanwhile, the darker you were, the farther they kept you from the patrons: in the kitchen, on cleanup duty, et cetera. Once he clocked what things were like there, he realized he couldn't afford to kid around.

With any other job, Washington might've appreciated not having to look patrons in the eye. The issue was that at this restaurant, with commissions, tips, and all that, the money stayed in the dining hall. It was the smooth operators, the people who knew how to sell the menu, who came out on top at month's end.

Back in the dressing room, Washington carefully ironed his clothes, top to bottom, leaving not a single wrinkle. He was practically dripping with sweat. Washington tried to focus on the silver lining: before he knew it, it'd be four o'clock, then he'd swing by the boca, cop a joint. Gleyce would come over to smoke up with him, the two of them home alone. It almost gave him hope.

When Washington joined the other staff, the manager didn't pass up the opportunity. He gave his employee a once-over, then nodded with satisfaction.

"Excellent. That's the standard."

Washington agreed.

"Tell me something. You got a handle on the food yet?"

"Sure do. I'm a quick study."

"I'm going to need you as a runner. Augusto just called to say he can't make it."

It was the break he'd been waiting for. All he had to do was show his worth in that position, and he'd be promoted in no time. That's how things rolled there: runners were always first in line to become waiters because they were used to handing out dishes around the dining room, and they knew the menu back to front. He needed to seize his chance; Augusto was up next.

"Charge double time today, all right? Damn Augusto, he's always leaving me hanging when I need him."

It was his third time doing doubles that month, always to cover for a no-show. Every weekend, somebody went off the deep end and cut work. Washington had started welcoming the doubles; he was planning to use them to move up. When the time came, he'd have the backing he needed at the restaurant.

"I'm here to work," he said, even while he knew all his plans for that evening were a wash.

The manager smiled big, from ear to ear, patted him on the back, and bounced. Washington smiled back, tense with rage, but also, somehow, truly grateful.

It was eleven at night by the time he left the restaurant, bushed. He pulled out his cell and saw that all Gleyce had texted him back was *ok*, which left him wondering if she was pissed or couldn't be bothered to type anything else. His coworkers invited him to get a drink with them, Friday nights out were constitutional, but Washington decided to go home instead. He had an early start again tomorrow.

He had it all laid out in his head: he'd swing by the boca in Valão, cop some green, head home, spark up, pass out. No internet. He didn't want to know about shit. After work, he was too tired to even think.

He rolled through the part of Larguinho where the boca

was set up but couldn't pick out the dealer right away. He stared at the kids hanging in the area to see if one of them crossed eyes with him, gave him some sign. Nothing, fuck-all. He saw three dudes sitting on the stoop of a bar, looking like they were waiting on something. Washington sat beside them.

"Yo, anything happening round here today?"

One of the guys told him that a shorty had booked it outta there, but his friend said he'd be back in no time. Washington thanked him, relieved not to have to make another trip up to Pedrinha. It made him mad as hell to climb all those steps only to find out there was nothing going on.

The organization still hadn't gotten their act together since the UPP had posted up. The bocas were constantly changing location, and most of the time all they had was coke. Worst of all, the weed was different. The second the police occupied the hill, pushers swapped bengala for some dry-ass, old ditch weed. That was one thing he couldn't wrap his head around. Players would go down whether the weed they sold was good or bad. *So why not do the residents a solid?* Washington wondered whenever he ground the new schwag.

Another thing that was really different was that getting hold of drugs had become a huge ordeal. You had to be on your toes all the time, on the lookout for cops. A group like the one loitering on that stoop was sure to get stopped. Assholes came down merciless, and if no one else was around, they really let it rip. Worst of all, nobody in Rocinha was used to the new normal yet. There'd never been any cops on the hill before.

The whole time he sat there, Washington stayed alert,

eyes on the alleys up top, on the alleys down low, on every entryway. If he saw a gun, a vest, or a uniform, he'd bounce. He was so busy looking out for police, he didn't even see shorty roll up. The kid was around nine years old.

"What y'all want?" the little man asked.

Washington respected the line and let the other guys order first. They threw together some cash and ordered a bunch of coke. When it was his turn, Washington pulled out a twenty from his wallet and asked for two dime bags of weed.

"We're all out. It's just hash today. Want some? It's nickel bags." Shorty talked fast, eyes running up and down each alley.

"Gimme four," Washington replied, handing over the money. "Is it any good?"

Before the kid could reply, he got smacked upside the head. No one had any idea what was going on: the aggressor was a woman, another resident, short but apparently as strong as a construction foreman. She whacked the kid, then came down on him, trying to get him in a chokehold. He stumbled but managed to get away from her and hotfoot it to Rua 2. The woman cut eyes at Washington and the other guys before setting off after him.

"Damn, that bitch is no joke. Straight-up ninja, samurai, or some shit. You see that? She came outta nowhere!" said one of the cokeheads.

"She's slicker than BOPE, sneaking up like that, without nobody seeing her."

"The woman gave that kid a reality check. Shorty must be seeing stars now." The guys laughed about what they'd just witnessed.

"Who was she?" Washington asked before lighting a cigarette.

"Hell knows. His ma, maybe?"

After laughing some more, the cokeheads started bugging out. They'd already paid. Who were they meant to chase up if the little man didn't come back? Lieutenants and soldiers were like ghosts, there was no sign of them, ever. The bocas were putting a different kid out front every day. The paranoia came down hard. One of them wondered if it was all just an act, a trick the woman and kid had pulled to pocket the dough. Washington listened and kept his opinions to himself. But that stuff really wigged him out. He thought about how Dona Marli was always telling her sons that if either of them got mixed up in crime, she wasn't visiting anyone in prison or begging reporters to put her on TV when they were killed in a shootout. It was every mother's worst fear.

Close to an hour ticked by with no sign of shorty. Hanging around there sucked so hard Washington seriously considered packing it in, forgetting the twenty reais, and calling it a day. Except, every time he was about to get up, something kept him there, waiting.

The cokeheads wouldn't stop bitching, sure they'd been stiffed. Washington decided to put some distance between them; they were attracting the wrong kind of attention. He stood up. The cokeheads cut eyes at him. It was like throwing in the sponge was as good as admitting the little man wouldn't be back. He felt sorry for them and pissed at the same time. He should just call it a day and go back home.

That's when shorty turned up on Larguinho. Washington was on his feet facing the stoop when the kid planted himself in front of the two guys. He stuffed his hand in his shorts pockets and pulled out the drugs, handing the coke to the cokeheads and the hash to Washington.

"That woman your mom, little man?" Washington had to know.

"This shit's bunk," he said before vanishing back up an alley. The cokeheads had already pushed off too. Washington checked the two blocks of hash, slipped them into his shoes, and made for Boiadeiro.

He managed to hail a mototaxi before crossing paths with the cops outside the pharmacy. He got on the bitch seat and felt relieved.

"Cachopa, please."

"She can't handle that hill, man." The driver pointed at his Honda CG125, clearly in iffy condition.

Washington eyeballed the street around him, the cops nearby. It was after midnight.

"Then drop me at Casa da Paz."

The motorbike chugged forward. Even with a helmet on, with no wind on his face, Washington was happy as hell to be cruising around the hill, watching folks on the streets. Shame it was over so soon. He'd just started enjoying the ride when the driver stopped. Washington paid for the run, crossed the street, and peered up the stairs. Seventy-eight steps later, he'd be home.

RIO—December 3, 2011

It was funny, really. All it took was a couple of bumps for Wesley to notice the world was crawling with folks living double lives. At work, in the street, everywhere you'd never think to look. Older people, parents, even Evangelical pastors. After the initial surprise, Wesley doubted nothing and vouched for no one. Anybody could be a closeted cokehead: the baker, the girl next door, the cleanest-living dude in the building.

That night out, it was his co-worker Lucas Butterfingers who put down the blow. Dude was mellow, kept to himself. You'd never think he fucked with illicits. When he pulled out that baggie of yellow, rocky powder, Wesley got a little anxious: it was nothing like the snow in Rocinha or Chácara do Céu, which was the only kind he'd ever tried. Lucas explained he'd copped the powder in Vila do João, that he went there all the time and their coke was bomb. Butterfingers skillfully cut lines while flapping his gums. He seemed like a whole

other person. Wesley couldn't get that out of his mind—how
you thought you knew somebody just because you were on a
first-name basis, because you lived in the same neighborhood,
because you worked together . . .

After doing coke a few times, Wesley could finally pin-
point its effects on his body. It was funny, how the high
seemed to start before he even touched the stuff. The second
he clocked the capsule, he felt jittery, his hands shook, his
breathing became irregular. Just seeing the powder made him
want to take a dump. Lucas finished cutting lines.

The way that coke hit—with a rusty bitterness, pupils
instantly saucering, making everything around him seem
small—Wesley could tell it was different, A-grade. You only
really know something's bad once you try the good shit, he
thought to himself as he glanced up from his card and faced
his reflection in the bathroom mirror. Trouble was, soon as
you got a taste of premium, there was no going back to junk.
Wesley tripped. If he thought about it, it was stupid to com-
pare the drugs sold in North Zone favelas with the ones sold
in Rocinha. A joke, really. In the bengalinha era, you could
still get a decent high off half-decent weed, but those days
were long gone. It wasn't easy for anybody anymore. If things
were less-than-chill before, now that the UPP had occupied
the hill, they were totally fucked. Everything was worse quality and way more expensive. Wesley looked at his reflection
and did a final coke-ring check.

There was no question, the second he had some time off,
he would go on a mission farther afield. Wesley had always
been the crew's missionary, and he usually managed to cop

weed for himself from the commission he got copping it for others. He'd hit Maguinho, Jacaré, B2, Primavera—all they had to do was say where the fire was for him to haul ass there. But once the UPP invaded the hill, he stopped showing face. Crossing the city with contraband had never been a cakewalk, and he always got nervous en route. But Wesley had a new fear to contend with: getting busted at his front door. That's what really got him. Back in the day, whenever he made it back to Rocinha after a mission, he felt safe—enough to break out the product right then and there and light a metaphorical candle in celebration. But these days he had to stay on his toes no matter where he was, whether the blacktop or the hill. He knew tons of guys who'd been stopped by the UPP. Motherfuckers were merciless when they got you on possession, and Wesley knew plenty who'd been set as examples.

Trouble was, it was worth the risk. In part because Wesley had the money. Meaning that if he made it back to his home base with the gear, he was set for weeks. Besides weed, he could also cop some eight-balls of coke and pay Butterfingers back for his generosity. That perk-up had saved him. Wesley had been wiped from working several parties in a row.

Every year ended the same: it was like rich folks conspired to get laid at the same time, popping out kids in November or December. Seriously insane. He'd pulled doubles every weekend. The first party ran from ten in the morning to two in the afternoon while the second kicked off at four and wrapped up by eight.

That Saturday, Wesley was stuck manning the trampoline for both shifts. The morning was a cinch. Most of the guests were babies, nowhere near old enough to tumble around. Whenever any kids did come through, it was with their nannies. But the afternoon shift was a birthday bash for a seven-year-old, and every kid there had the devil in them. The second the nannies looked away, the little assholes started duking it out.

What sucked is that their fights lacked grit. They mostly just grabbed each other and pulled, sometimes sinking teeth or yanking hair—none of that slugging everyone loved to crowd around. The second a fight broke out, Wesley played dumb and headed to the bathroom. He made the most of his time away to catch up with co-workers, see if Talia was around, do some constitutional slacking off.

For all the bullshit Wesley had to put up with on the trampoline, he was pretty happy not to be on the entertainment team anymore. At first, when they went back to assigning him parties as a server, he was kind of pissed—he'd been making bank on entertainment. But it didn't take him long to realize he was better off this way. Take the current party, for example. Seven-, eight-year-old rich kids treated entertainers like garbage. They thought that shit was for toddlers, so when a grown man with a whole-ass beard started doing baby voice, they showed no mercy. Picture being in a situation like that, biting your cheeks, having to take it in silence.

Wesley was on his way back to the trampoline when Talia showed up. Around other people, she talked to him like she did anyone else, but he couldn't stop thinking about how it was with just the two of them. All that pretending made him thirsty as hell, and Wesley wasn't particularly good at playing it cool. He was always looking for some excuse to be near her.

When Talia walked into the kitchen, Wesley decided to have another glass of water.

"Hey, what you up to later?" he asked in a low voice. Talia smiled.

"Dunno . . . Might just head home. Been a tough week."

"A beer won't make any difference. C'mon, I'll walk you to the bus after." Wesley's favorite thing about coke highs was the confidence.

"Gotta go. These kids are acting all crazy today."

By the time Wesley got back, there was no one left on the trampoline. It was super mellow. By the sounds of it, all the kids had left to play in the field area. Without anything to distract him in that headspace, Wesley studied the party, especially the guests: their designer clothes, always-straight hair, the easy way they had of ordering around anybody in uniform. He started getting riled up. His mom worked for people like them. His aunts and uncles and grandparents worked for people like them. They cleaned and rewired their houses, looked after their kids. Now Wesley was doing the same thing, fulfilling the same destiny. Serving. Obeying. Wesley had worked several parties over the last few weeks and managed to pocket a good chunk of money. Enough to pay his monthly fees at the driving school, chip in at home, and save a little to spend on himself. He used to be okay with that, but now, as he looked around at those people, all he felt was rage, because he knew that the money he broke his back to make didn't mean shit to them. They could wipe their asses with it, and it still wouldn't put a dent in their lives. Worst of all, they knew this. Which is why they could look down their noses at people and order them around with soft voices, never breaking a sweat. They knew it, took advantage of it, and every day, including holidays and holy days, they made a point of passing this knowledge on to their offspring.

"I was thinking . . . Maybe one beer would be okay." Talia's voice pulled Wesley out of that hole.

He looked around him, then at Talia, and felt like he'd just been beamed down.

"Another time, maybe. Head's killing me."

She left without a word. Wesley remembered his friends saying how, sometimes, when you're high on coke, this huge depression will hit you, a sudden gloom, and that doing more lines could either snap you out of it or make things a hell of a lot worse. His eyes welled up. At least he'd finished the theory portion of driver's ed. All he had to do now were the practical and written tests. It'd be no time before he was renting a moto and cruising all over the hill. This thought gave Wesley some hope. If everything went according to plan, he'd never have to work outside Rocinha or deal with those bougie assholes again. But, until then, his aspirations were being funded by the money he made at the party venue. Meaning, he had a few more months of gritting his teeth and bearing it.

The kids came back in a stampede, high and wired. Wesley stood in front of the trampoline, clenching his jaw. They started shoving each other, fighting over who got to go first.

"I'm the one in charge in this joint. Now get in line or scram." For a second, Wesley forgot he needed that job. It didn't even occur to him to check if there was anybody within earshot who could make him pay later for what he'd said. The kids were scared straight and immediately formed a line.

He spent another hour watching them tumble around the

trampoline. The party ended. Wesley was dying to get home. He was almost at the bus stop when he spotted Lucas Butterfingers, who was also walking solo, away from the rest of the crew.

"Yo, VJ, wanna hit a baile?" Wesley had 120 reais in his pocket, plenty enough for a good time.

"The party doesn't start till two. What you wanna do in the meantime?" Wesley asked, even though he already knew the answer.

"Pregame, duh," Lucas replied while doing a karate chop, a gesture known to every cokehead in the city.

Wesley knew he had work the next day. And that he should be trying to save money. He also knew that if he got back to Rocinha later, chances were high he'd get stopped. For all these reasons, it didn't make sense for him to go to the baile. But he was all in. Today would only be back tomorrow.

RIO—December 17, 2011

There was no excuse: the sofa had come in that door before, now it had to go out. Murilo and Douglas hung on to that thought while trying every angle. No luck. Rubber's truck was parked on Via Ápia, right on their corner, and it wouldn't be long before he got on their case to hurry up. As if that wasn't enough, Biel was acting like one of those flanelinha guys who helps you park, then watches your car: he stood there telling them to turn the couch clockwise, then counterclockwise, without ever getting his hands dirty.

"You sure this thing doesn't come apart?" Douglas's forehead was dripping.

They set the sofa down without a word, relieved to be free of its weight. Murilo felt around the couch for a groove, anything. It was their third time doing that.

"Fuck yeah, check this out," Murilo said, flashing a joint. The thing was bent, banged up, dusty. But a joint no less. It was coming up on ten in the morning, and smoke had yet to pass their lips.

"The hell. I lost that fatty days ago," Biel said, taking the joint from Murilo. "I looked every fucking where for this shit. It's laced with hash."

"Only you, Biel," Murilo said, then stepped back to the sofa. "Let's fire this baby up."

"No way. Coroa's gonna bitch about it." Instead of perching on the sofa arm like before, he lay all the way down, beat.

"Fuck Coroa. We're moving, ain't we? This should be the happiest day of that sad motherfucker's life. How much do you wanna bet he sets off a bunch of bottle rockets the second we're out of here? Coroa's probably so fucking happy we're leaving, he'd smoke this thing with us."

"Fuck it, let's burn this shit." Douglas was dying to smoke anything. In the end, Murilo agreed as well.

Biel didn't think twice before looking around the apartment for a lighter. But that mess of boxes made the simplest tasks impossible. The other two joined the hunting party. They unzipped backpacks, patted down short pockets, peeked under furniture. The sofa sat there waiting.

"Yo, what's the holdup? I got another move later, damnit," Rubber yelled from the street in his high-pitched voice, which made any complaint sound comical. Murilo went to the window to say they were just sorting out a couple of final details.

"Let's save the joint for the new place, pô. We don't know if the boca's running up there or not." Douglas took his position next to the sofa.

"You're up, Biel." Murilo sat against the wall and felt the heat pressing down on him.

Biel hefted up the other end of the sofa, and they started again. The problem was they just kept trying the same positions as before, as if you could exhaust a piece of furniture into submission.

"Wait, wait, wait, I got an idea!" Murilo leaped up. "Turn it over and lay it down, that side first. No, that one." Their communication wasn't flowing, so Murilo showed them what to do.

And what do you know? The sofa started inching through the door. It inched and inched and inched until the other arm jammed.

Murilo was so furious that he threw up his hands and socked the door with his foot. They'd never have thought it, but that's exactly what it needed: the sofa squeezed a little farther through the door. Another three well-aimed kicks, and the problem was solved. All that was left was for them to haul the thing down three floors and come back for the rest of their boxes.

Now that the truck was packed full, it was time to get going. Coroa even poked his head out the window to make sure it wasn't a dream. Murilo sat in front while the other two rode in the truck bed to make sure nothing fell out. Douglas held his tattoo equipment in his lap, protecting it from any sudden bumps.

"Y'all duck if you see any cops, okay?" Rubber yelled back at them from the driver's seat. "It's not allowed anymore. Taking folks in the back like that."

"What's not allowed?" Murilo asked just for the sake of it.

He'd been zoned out, thinking about the apartment they'd left behind and what the future held for them. Even though they were staying in Rocinha, it was still a pretty big move.

Every part of the hill had its own vibe, and most of their friends lived near the bottom, on the side streets connecting Via Ápia, Largo do Boiadeiro, and Valão. They didn't know anyone in the upper part who could tell them how things worked around there.

"Cops, man. They fined my buddy the other day. Listen, I been doing this for twenty-five years and never had any trouble. Ever. What's the point of changing things up on us now?" Murilo shook his head. "You hear about that store in Valão that got robbed?"

"Yeah."

As they neared Curva do S, Murilo started thinking about the hill up to Cachopa, that steep incline folks called Ladeira da Cachopa. It had driven plenty to tears: motorcycles, cars, trucks.

"What I wanna know is what the cops were doing when they robbed the place. Ticketing folks? Towing some poor family man's work bike? You tell me."

Murilo pictured the three of them having to get out of the truck and push it uphill, furniture and all, beneath the noonday sun.

"Not saying I approve of drug dealers, bocas, or none of that stuff. I don't approve or disapprove, see? Makes no difference to me. They do their thing, I do mine, and none of us sticks our noses in the other's business. That's just how it is. But let me tell you something. All this nonsense about stores getting robbed in Rocinha? It never happened back in my day. So, what I wanna know is, what are cops good for? Ticketing working folks, making people's lives hell? Is that it?"

They reached the ladeira. From inside the truck, it looked

even steeper, near impossible. Rubber started maneuvering the vehicle, bracing it for the slope.

"What now, Rubber?"

"What you mean what now?"

"You think we'll make it?"

Rubber said nothing, switched gears, and smoothly accelerated. The truck started and stopped a couple of times, wheels spinning out. Murilo peered up the hill, which seemed miles away. Rubber tapped the pedal, messed around with the gears, and finally got the truck to gain traction and climb up, slow and steady.

"Listen, kid, I been at this for twenty-five years now, twenty-five. You think what you got back there is heavy? Please. I've hauled some stuff in my life, lemme tell you. A mountain of stuff. Up and down, left and right, all over this beautiful hill. Rocinha is a whole world. Boy, have I traveled, have I got stories to tell."

They'd only been inside the new place once, the day they went to see it and sign the paperwork. In retrospect, it hadn't seemed so far uphill. But all it took was them picking up the fridge to realize it wasn't so close either. To make matters worse, they were sure the alleys had shrunk since last time. The power lines hung lower, and utility poles seemed to crop up out of nowhere. Plus, foot traffic was so heavy that a bottleneck of people formed behind them. One thing was for sure, though: you only really get to know a place once you've been through the ringer in it. By the time they were done moving, they felt like they'd met the entire neighborhood.

It was dark when Murilo unloaded the last box. His body was wrecked. Everything ached: back, arms, legs. And they still had to put things away. But not before cooling their heels for a second and catching their breaths. The three of them sat on the floor, each in a corner, at once defeated and triumphant. They were happy with their new home. Sure, there was only one bedroom, but the living room was big and the kitchen was decent. Not to mention, it was basically the same size as their old place, except for half the price. Now, they just had to get a sense of the new neighborhood, figure out who they could trust, who was a deadbeat, scope out the best grocery store, the bar with the coldest beer.

"How about that joint we found earlier?" Douglas asked at exactly the right time.

"Fuck, we forgot to get a lighter."

"Yo, Biel, how did you light your cig on Larguinho?"

"Asked some dude I saw smoking. He had matches."

"Let's go out and buy one. We're gonna need it, anyway. Plus, I bet it'll be easier than trying to find one in here," Murilo said while pointing at the mess of boxes.

"Will you go? I can give you some money," Biel said from the floor.

"Nah, let's do rock-paper-scissors."

"Hold up, neguim. There's somebody out there smoking. Lemme go light my cig on his. I'll bring back the cherry." Douglas was peering through the half-open front door.

He pried himself off the floor and headed outside. Besides the smoker, there was also a woman hanging her laundry. Douglas said hello, ready to win over the neighbors. The woman smiled at him, then went back inside.

"Sup, man. Can I get a light?"

"I got you," Washington immediately replied.

RIO—December 30, 2011

Forty-five C in the shade. Decembers were killer. It always felt like the hill would either melt or explode. That was another reason Wesley wanted to smoke a bit of grass on Larguinho on the way back from the beach. It was way too muggy indoors. At least out there, he could knock back a beer, maybe even luck out and catch a breeze. It was his first day off after a busy period at work, and he was in the mood for a good time.

Around then, the streets were usually crawling with folks headed up and down the hill, either looking to make or spend money. There was meat grilling on terraces, music blasting. The place was popping. Before UPP invaded the hill, Larguinho was the heart of the party in Cachopa. A must-go for anybody looking to burn one, or share and hear stories about the talk of the neighborhood. But it was under heavy scrutiny these days, and folks were hanging out there less and less. Nobody wanted to get bagged for no reason.

"What's the scoop, y'all?" Wesley cracked open a can, then sat down beside Twiggy and Early Bird on the stoop.

"Throw in two reais, and Early Bird will go on a weed mission. Then we can burn one on the terrace."

"I got some grass right here, neguim. Copped some Colombia. My buddy's got a playboy connect. Hooked me up real nice." Wesley pulled out a pack of cigarettes from his pocket, took one for himself, then passed it around.

"Say less, cuz. Let's burn that shit right now. Papers?"

"Whoa there, menó. You in a hurry or something? Let's have a beer first."

"You don't wanna hang out here too long with contraband, neguim. You know this place is hot." Early Bird figured he should give Wesley a heads-up.

"Pfft, menó. Whatever. Just one beer. Can you go get it, Twig?" Wesley handed him some money. "A 600ml and three glasses."

Twiggy was almost at Bar do Bá when he turned around and asked:

"Brahma or Antarctica?"

"You know I only fuck with Brahma." Wesley pointed at the can he was holding.

"The sun's crazy hot today. Just one beer, okay?" Early Bird was trying to act cool, but you could tell his eyes were extra peeled, scanning the streets around him for cops. Twiggy came back with the beer.

"My bad, neguim. The only cold ones were Itaipava."

"When it's this goddamn hot, anything goes." Wesley downed the rest of his beer before pouring himself a glass.

"Damn, neguim, some crazy shit happened at home the other day. The shower cut out in reverse."

"What the hell you talking about, Twig?"

"It's what I said, pô. The shower cut out in reverse. Only spits out hot water now. You think it's funny? I'm telling you, we've had no cold water for days. I swear, it's three in the morning, you turn on the shower, and the water's scalding. Sun's burning up the water tank. Burning it up something fierce."

"At least y'all got running water. Three days straight, I've had to wash in the faucet on Vila Verde!"

A half dozen beers later, they'd more or less stopped stressing over five-o. By that point in the day, the cops on duty were probably trying to make some quick cash; dudes always got extra intense around Christmas and New Year's. And money was a lot easier to come by if you set up a checkpoint on Estrada da Gávea and pulled over some sorry sucker on a minor violation, or else raided a boca and negotiated a bribe. Anything beat chasing down junkies and potheads on the street. It was settled, there'd be no cops on Larguinho that night. They were sure of it. So they could knock back some more beers, another ten if they wanted. Things were chill.

More folks started coming through. Biel was out on a spin when he spotted Wesley and decided to stick around. They'd only been neighbors a couple of weeks, but it was like they'd known each other their whole lives. Pot brings people together like that. The day they moved in, once Washington and Douglas introduced themselves, they'd all smoked up. The three of them told Washington and Wesley all about Coroa and having to move. After that, Wesley started introducing them to his friends, and the crew was formed. Even though the end of the year was always crazy busy, they still managed to have a good time in the building. Gaming on the PS2 and smoking weed laid the groundwork for their friendship. A few beers later, Murilo joined the crew on Larguinho. "Ah, menó. Y'all got no clue what things were like before, do you? Damn, back in the day—you tell them, Early Bird—it was popping down here. There'd be spliffs going round, outta nowhere some dude would bust out a TV and another buddy would throw down his PlayStation, then pfft, forget about it. We'd fire up Bomba Patch right here on the street, kick back and chill. And music on the block every Wednesday! Beer coming out of your ears, live bands, tons of dimes. Good times we won't ever get back, pô. Cachopão was lit, no denying it. It was Rocinha's very own VIP area," Wesley told his neighbors while the others nodded along.

Even though they were buzzed, no one forgot about Colombia. The dank shit, the fire, the killer green. When Wesley said Biel was the one with the playboy hookup, everybody wanted to know how much it was going for, what he had. Nobody could hack the schwag they called weed in Rocinha anymore. Biel figured he could make good money selling grass in the area, but then started freaking out about getting caught running a covert boca. Once they were done speculating about the weed, they went up to the terrace together. Down below, everything glowed.

"You had to be there, menó. It was scary as shit. So the cops roll up, right? They're shoving their guns in our faces, saying hands on the wall and whatever. We're shook. Keep our heads low. Say yes officer, no officer, we're all workers here, officer. You know the drill. I think it was me, Curly, Lesk, and Dôdo. Anyway, since we don't have any contraband on us, we're thinking they'll let us go in no time. Fat fucking chance. Assholes jerked us around, they jerked us around real good. Dudes wanted to know where the boca is. You tell me. These fools think snitches grow on trees or something. Whatever. We're all like: Officer, all we know is that we don't know, you know? For what, neguim? That's when they really let it rip. They tell us that if we don't fess up, they're gonna take us downtown, that there's a kilo of product in the cherry-top with our name on it. I'm freaking the hell out, you know what they like. But then, fuck, the funniest thing happened. The pigs want to know all our names so they can pull up our priors or whatever. Cool. So, I tell them mine, and the whole gang turns to me like *what?* Then Curly gives them his: Luciano. Then Lesk, whose real name is Alex. And Dôdo, who's Jaílson or Jeimerson or something. It was fucking hysterical. Been friends all our lives and none of us knew our real names." Twiggy laughed and coughed at the same time.

"C'mon, neguim. You cough, you pass."

"Dude thinks it's a microphone or something."

Dona Marli passed them on the street below. She walked at her usual clip across Larguinho on her way back home. Wesley almost called out to her but then thought better of it. His mom didn't like her sons smoking weed out in the streets.

"Yo, Early Bird, your pops still got that hardboard?" Wesley asked.

Biel and Murilo could never have guessed what that question meant, but the guys from the hill knew exactly what Wesley was scheming.

"Aw, nice. You looking to set up some table tennis?" Twiggy got excited.

"Pô, man. Pretty sure my pops would wig out, you know? He's always telling me to stay away from Larguinho."

"C'mon, Early Bird. You tell Joel I'm the one asking." Wesley picked up his glass of beer, but it was empty. "You tell him. You know your pops loves me."

"I still got some rackets," Twiggy said, jumping to his feet.

They set out on their respective missions. Early Bird went to fetch the hardboard and Twiggy the rackets while Wesley and the others went looking for Curly and his sawhorses. It took them about half an hour to get everything ready. Another buddy threw in a two by two for them to use as a net.

Since everybody had pitched in, chaos struck when it was time to play. Nobody wanted to be left out. But nothing you couldn't solve with a quick game of rock-paper-scissors or odds and evens.

In the end, Wesley and Early Bird won the right to start. Funnily enough, it was only when they were standing in front of the table that they realized they'd forgotten the ball.

"Fuck, I can't believe it!"

"Try Venâncio's, they'll have some!"

But Venâncio's was closed, and nobody else in the area sold balls. The gang considered resorting to deodorant but then ditched the idea. Roll-on balls were heavy and slowed the game down.

"Fuck it. I'm gonna figure this shit out."

Wesley took Biel with him. He'd been itching to do a line since the first beer but hadn't wanted to show his cards. None

of the guys from Cachopa knew he'd been enjoying the occasional bump.

They went to Valão, did a few lines, then went looking for
a ball. Back at the makeshift table, they were floored by the
size of the crowd waiting for the match to begin. It was like
the feeding of the 5,000. The five guys they'd left waiting had
multiplied into twenty. It was in that electrifying, packed-
stadium climate that Wesley and Early Bird kicked off the
evening's first table tennis match.

———

As usual those days, Washington was dying to get home,
shower, take it easy. Work was a steady grind that late December, and he barely had time to spend the money he made.
He was thinking this while riding double on the moto when
he saw the whole crew gathered on Larguinho. The first thing
that popped into his mind was that something tragic had
happened: somebody dead or killed. Not for nothing, either.
A couple days earlier, he'd peeped some BOPE officers wandering the hill with shovels. There wasn't a doubt in the mind
of anybody who saw them: get busted by one of those dudes,
and you don't even become a statistic.

"Just the man we were waiting for!"

Washington's arrival livened up the circle. Everybody
there knew he could do some serious damage with the racket.

Washington paid the driver and headed toward the crew.
He wasn't sure what to do next. The natural thing would've
been to kick back with them there; smoke, drink, play. On the
other hand, his desire to head home was strong. Ever since

he'd started hustling at work, he'd been going out less and less. All he ever wanted to do on his time off was lay low, burn a fatty at home, or hit the streets with Gleyce or his co-workers. Right then, as he saw Larguinho popping like it used to pre-UPP, Washington realized he was losing touch with his old friends.

"Who's last in line?" He'd made a decision.

"Always he who asks, fool!"

Washington waved to everyone, then stood next to Wesley. He grabbed a glass of beer, lit a cigarette, and kept an eye on the match. He wouldn't be up for a while. In a game of winner-stays-on, the more players there are, the longer it takes for everyone to have a go, and the larger the audience. He felt a rush of adrenaline; he'd always had a competitive streak.

"Yo, menó, wanna hit this up on the terrace?" Wesley flashed him a joint.

They went to the terrace. Wesley sparked up while Biel rolled another. They were burning through the weed, and Washington worried he was going to lose control. He'd been smoking a lot less on account of work. It used to be five, six, ten joints a day; now, with several shifts a week, and one Sunday a month, he tapped out at two, three Js max. As a result, he got stoned on way less.

"When I saw you standing there, bro, I was sure you'd make a beeline for the house. All you do these days is work."

"It's rough. I think I've left this kid stuff behind me."

Truth is, Washington wasn't the least bit happy about having almost no downtime. He got the feeling work was gradually taking over his life; even when he wasn't on shift, all he could think about was resting up for the next day. At the same time, no way was he letting go of that job. Besides the benefits, having a signed work card gave him security. Whenever the cops stopped him, Washington busted out his papers and felt them ease up.

"That's when you're not with that chick. What's her name again?"

"Gleyce."

"Right. You tapping that?"

"Cut this dude off, he's starting to run his mouth." Washington got up joint in hand and stood watching the street below him. "Where Douglas at?"

"Home. He's got a tattoo lined up this week, so he's working on the design," Biel said from the other end of the terrace.

Wesley went up to Washington, feeling sorry about what he'd said earlier. Sometimes he got pissed at his brother for acting like he was the only one with responsibilities, now that he had a full-time job. The way Washington talked, you'd think Wesley spent all day in the streets or on the beach, when the truth is he'd been stuck in the party venue all month listening to every Lottie Dottie Chicken album under the sun. Nonfucking-stop. He hadn't even made it to driver's ed yet, which he'd been looking forward to after hours and hours of theory classes, all on account of the parties he had to work. But Wesley didn't want to go into it. The year was ending, he was healthy, he had money in his pocket, the best thing for him to do was just let it go. Wesley lit a cigarette next to his brother, and the two stood there watching the match on Larguinho. Wesley filled him in on the table tennis mission. How they'd only found the ball toward the end, after going down to Boiadeiro, and how crazy it was seeing Larguinho crowded with people again.

"Remember when we used to play on tile?" Washington asked.

"No shit."

"Bro, I'll never forget the sound the ball made when it hit the tile. TAC, TAC, TAC. There was days I heard that shit so often it snuck into my dreams. Swear to God, I'd be sleeping and outta nowhere I'd hear TAC, TAC, TAC. In my goddamn head!"

"I was thinking about that time we went all the way up the hill to Sítio dos Macacos. Man, that was something else. On a hot day like this, the whole crew setting off so we could splash around in waterfalls and shit. No better life than that. Playing hide-and-seek in the jungle! Remember?"

"What about that time we stole fruit and cookies and stuff from the old macumba woman?"

"We were fucking starved. It was our early days smoking weed. Man, we used to get some serious munchies."

The game down below was louder now, the crowd shouting after each serve and razzing the players. It was time to head down. When they got there, they could tell by the smell that the crew had decided they didn't need to leave Larguinho anymore to toke up. The other thing that was different was the speaker blasting a Racionais MC song about the end of the year. Then most of the crew started singing along:

Pobre é o diabo, eu odeio ostentação
Pode rir, ri, mas não desacredita não . . .

Washington joined in on the chorus. Buzzing from the beer and weed, his body felt light, and he was happy to be kicking back in the streets.

RIO—January 8, 2012

Douglas jolted awake and nearly fell out of bed. After several hours of twisting, turning, and roasting in that heat, he had no idea when he'd actually drifted off. Biel was sound asleep in the still-dark bedroom. What time was it, anyway? Murilo was getting ready to go to work when he saw Douglas shuffle into the living room.

"What's up?"

"Can't sleep," Douglas said before throwing himself on the sofa.

His body ached from exhaustion, but he had no idea it was *that* early. He grabbed a roach from the ashtray and lit up in the hopes it would help him doze back off.

"I wouldn't get outta bed till noon if I could," Murilo said with the indignation of someone who has no choice.

Douglas didn't have the energy to talk, so he pulled on that joint until his fingers burned, then lay back down on the sofa. He closed his eyes and listened to Murilo moving around the apartment, head pounding nonstop. His heart was beating so fast it seemed to consume all the oxygen in the room.

"Real talk, neguim. When're you gonna let me tattoo you?"

Murilo was constantly avoiding that subject. He'd come up with some random excuse about the Army or else say he was still mulling over the design. This time, he opted for the silent treatment. He continued putting on his sneakers.

"I know how it is. You don't think I'm up for the challenge. Just say it, bro. Be straight with me."

Murilo got up, shrugged on his backpack, and lit a cigarette.

"Nah, man. I gotta bounce. It's almost six. They really come at you if you're late."

Douglas was left alone with his neuroses. Never in his wildest dreams had he thought the news that he dabbled in ink would get around Cachopa so fast. Of course, his friendship with Washington and Wesley had helped. The best thing anybody could do when they moved someplace new was get in with the locals. Still, the number of people willing to put their skin in the hands of a newbie was unreal. Douglas was up to his neck in guinea pigs.

He'd been getting so much interest from people that, even without a lot of experience, he'd had to start charging thirty reais just to stay in the black. Each session required new needles and grips, not to mention paper towels, plastic wrap, and surgical gloves. As expected, the mention of money scared off the majority of volunteers. Even so, Douglas was starting off the new year fully booked. He had four pieces scheduled for January, one for each Sunday of the month.

But the first Sunday snuck up on him, and what used to

be a source of joy now made his body shudder and his heart race. Everything he'd been working toward was finally beginning to happen. The only issue was that acquiring a new skill usually went hand in hand with making mistakes.

"Sup, DG. Wanna hit the beach?" Biel walked into the living room, face creased with sleep. It was almost eleven in the morning.

Douglas studied Biel's shoulder piece. After the touch-up, you couldn't even tell some of the letters had been janky.

"Curly's coming over later for a sesh."

Douglas decided to get up. He'd been glued to that sofa for hours. He went to the bedroom, grabbed his folder and pencil case, turned back, and then spread it all out on the table.

"Damn. This dude's seriously getting a Maltese cross?" Biel was looking at the drawings Douglas had made on A4 sheets of paper. Considering Biel himself pulled for Vasco da Gama, his shock came as a surprise.

"Yup. Some folks have started getting all intense over Copa do Brasil." Douglas arranged the sheets side by side. The red crosses looked practically identical.

"Least it's easy, right? A couple of basic lines, and bam."

Douglas wanted to explain to Biel that when it came to tattoos there was no such thing as a basic line. For starters, you couldn't use a ruler. Plus, every body that hit your table was different. Some were hard, others soft, some a little crooked. Not to mention that even the most basic line lasted forever. But Douglas didn't want to get into it; talking about his fears and anxiety only fed his insecurities.

"Yeah, it'll be cool. Fast, at least."

After Biel left, Douglas scavenged around the apartment

for something to eat before Curly got there. That weird pit in his stomach had killed his appetite. He went for the fastest option: a bowl of chicken-flavored instant noodles and hard-boiled eggs that he inhaled so quickly he barely tasted them.

Curly was at his front door in no time. He walked in talking a mile a minute, grinding weed, the uzh. Douglas was kind of weirded out by Curly's excitement. He couldn't help wondering how he'd act as he walked out of there later.

Curly went to the table to look over the designs. He liked each one better than the last. Douglas shrugged off the praise and started arranging his workstation. He covered the area in plastic wrap, then set down two grips and two needles—one liner, one shader, all disposable, sealed, to be opened in front of the client. Then he turned to the ink and picked out two: matte black and red. He stood the cups side by side. Lastly, he made some room for a pack of paper towels and a spray bottle filled with soapy water. Curly watched in silence as he finished rolling his joint.

"You shave your leg?"

Curly nodded.

It was the first time Douglas could remember getting annoyed by the scent of weed stinking up the house. He'd been dead set on not smoking until the job was done. Curly took a couple of drags and passed the joint. The thing was a cannon, rolled with a single blue Smoking paper. Douglas took it from him, not because he wanted any but because he was scared to admit that on the inside, he was shaking like a leaf.

"Yo, neguim, I was thinking. You sure you want a Maltese cross? I looked into it, and, like, did you know the Portuguese had this same cross on their ships? That's right, the same motherfuckers that rocked up here and started murdering Indians, enslaving folks, you name it, then packed up one day and bounced, leaving us to clean up their mess. So, what I'm saying is: getting one of these crosses is basically the same as some kid who came up in the favela getting a skull with a knife. See what I mean?"

Curly burst out laughing.

"Whatever, neguim. Flamengo was full of rich white kids until they realized they wanted in on some favela action. Why don't you look *that* up, bro? Look up what team was the first one to let Black guys play ball. Catch up, man. Cruz de Malta is the Giant of the Hill. Respect our history."

Douglas couldn't think of anything else to say to get Curly to change his mind, so he sat at the table and transferred his drawing onto carbon paper. He pulled on a pair of surgical gloves, placed the Maltese cross on Curly's calf, and adjusted the tattoo gun.

"Now all I gotta do is trace it."

Douglas decided to start with the red ink. First he'd sketch the outside, then he'd fill it in. Only after he was done with that would he outline the whole thing in black. It was hard to believe that living your dream could be so damn terrifying.

Two gunshots went off right near the building. Douglas switched off the machine, immersing the apartment in silence. They waited for the counterfire. Things didn't seem to be evolving, so after a while Douglas went back to work.

"That was a handgun," Curly said with full confidence.

"What was the vibe out there?"

"Things were chill at the boca earlier," Curly said with a pained look on his face.

Douglas clocked his expression and wondered if maybe he was applying too much pressure. Judging that sweet spot was the hardest part of the process.

"Did you know anybody in Roça before moving here?" Curly asked.

"Did I know anybody? *I'm from here*, born and raised. It's the other two who aren't. Biel's from Cruzada, and the other guy, Murilo, he's been here since he was a kid but was born in the West Zone. His mom moved back that way recently. Me, I was born in Valão, pô. But I've lived all over the hill: Raiz, Rua 2, Via Ápia . . . Always renting, you know how it is." When Douglas spoke, he switched off the machine and saw the relief on Curly's face.

"Word. I moved here when I was a kid too, from Nova Iguaçu, up north. But I think of myself as being from Roça. I don't remember anything else."

"Life here's good, neguim. Rocinha is everything."

An hour later, they took a break. All that was left to do was the black outline. The fact that Curly's calf was swollen and red made it difficult for Douglas to tell how the finished piece would look. Curly rolled a joint while they rested, one as fat as the first. Douglas stared at the tattoo taking shape on Curly's calf and forced himself to believe everything was going to be fine.

"Real talk? This shit hurts like hell. Anybody that says different is lying. But I'd much rather be here than home. It's fucking rough over there. Did I mention my sister's pregnant? Like about to pop. Anyway, she's staying with us for a bit so we can help out, that kinda thing. Fuck man, lemme tell you. She asks for literally everything. If she's thirsty, it's *Luciano*.

If she's hungry, it's *Luciano.* I mean, fuck. Sometimes she calls me over just to change the channel because her finger's swollen or some shit. It's been a week of that crap. But whatever, it's family, you gotta step up. But check this out: the other day, we're walking home after an ultrasound when she looks down and says: Oh! Money. Then she bends over and picks up a twenty-real note. I was flipping out, neguim, like, what? So I said to her: How come you didn't call me over to get that money for you, huh?"

Douglas laughed halfheartedly. The truth is he hadn't really been listening. His eyes were fixed on the design on Curly's calf. He pictured putting the finishing touches on the piece, black ink tearing Curly's skin. He thought beyond that too, to the effect his design would have around there as everyone admired the clean, straight lines.

"You like your piece so far?"

Curly glanced at his leg.

"I trust you, neguim."

RIO—February 13, 2012

Biel always lost his mind over those built-in wardrobes. Good wood, indestructible. Nothing like the plywood stuff they sold at Casas Bahia, the kind that fell to pieces after one move. As he took in the room, he was so distracted he didn't even realize Marcelinho had already hit the slopes and was holding out the plate and straw.

"So that's what's up. My connect flew that shit in, and I picked it up myself. Be honest, is this grass chronic or what?" Marcelinho asked.

It was his third time telling that story, coke-jawed. At least this time he opened the suitcase and showed Biel the stash. There were probably eight kilos of shake. So loud it stank up the room.

"And you didn't freak out or nothing? I mean, damn, getting busted for that shit is no joke."

The more smoke Biel blew up Marcelinho's ass, the higher

his chances of getting a nice discount. He had his re-ups pegged: he knew just how much they got off on telling people about the dangers of the job.

"Fuck yeah, there were mad cops, airport security. The place was hot. But you gotta put your ass on the line if you want to come out on top."

Someone knocked on the door.

"What?" Marcelinho asked, irritated.

"It's Ivone. Your mother asked me to bring you some food. She's worried because you skipped lunch."

They hid the evidence as best they could before opening the door. A white-haired woman in a housekeeping uniform walked in with a tray. It was stacked with cake, sliced bread, cheese, and a jug of orange juice. Biel got annoyed that he was high on coke. If they'd smoked pot instead, he'd have gone to town on that spread.

"That's business for you, homes. No risk, no reward. Amirite?" Marcelinho served himself some orange juice.

Before Ivone left, Biel noticed that there was something about the way she wore her hair that reminded him of his mother.

"So how much? For friends."

Biel knew he could move caviar like that on the blacktop for as much as thirty reais a gram. Folks would be lining up to hand over their money. If he closed with Marcelinho for thirteen, max fifteen reais a g, he could make a pretty penny.

"Buddy rate's twenty."

Marcelinho probably had a ton of people coming after his weed. In February, every playboy in the city suddenly wanted to be a dealer. All so they'd have some stories to tell around Carnaval, so they could stunt in front of the girls. It wasn't going to be easy to talk him down.

"Yeah, cool. That's legit, for real. Especially after all the trouble you went through to get the stuff. Gotta have hair on your chest to do what you did."

For someone as coked out as Marcelinho, Biel's little speech was an ego-massage. Marcelinho decided to tell the story a fourth time, play by play. He talked about cutting a deal with this matuto up in Bahia, a big-shot, high-ranking airman. About the trip there and back, the ride in the taxi, the clothes. He hyped himself up the whole time, going on about how badass he was.

"That's why these other guys can't get ahead, bro. They don't have your vision, your drive. Even when they got the money to put down, they settle for the same old contacts."

"That's what I'm always saying. They don't make moves. They push one key here, one key there, convinced they're making a killing. I fought for this stuff, homes. I stuck my neck out. Now it's time to rake it in. For real, if I told you how much I paid per g, you wouldn't believe me."

"How much? My lips are sealed." They'd finally made it to the interesting part. If Biel knew how much Marcelinho had ponied up, it'd be easier to negotiate the price.

"Six reais a gram. Cha-ching!" Marcelinho railed four lines, one after another.

"If I buy bulk, would you give me a good deal?" Biel asked after taking a bump.

"Nah, homes, this is OG manga rosa. Chronic. You could sell this shit on the blacktop for forty a pop." He illustrated the point by grabbing a nug and showing Biel the resin. "I mean, damn, get a whiff of this."

"C'mon, Marcelim, you know what it's like. There's too many dudes pushing drugs these days. If I try and charge more than the going rate, I'm gonna strike out, you know that."

Now that Biel had a sense of how much the product had cost Marcelinho, twenty reais sounded like extortion. They were both aware that Marcelinho could and would charge less. And that's the thing that really messed with Biel, having to go through the motions and butter the dude up, nice and slow.

"All right, listen, since you're a real one: take half a key, and I'll give it to you for fifteen."

Biel knew that was the final offer. Take it or leave it. He also knew he could double his money with that dank. The problem was he didn't have the cash. Ever since the UPP took over the hill, he'd had to keep a low profile, avoid bringing too much product home. It was peak season, and he was strapped.

"Fifteen's dope, for real. But I was only looking to cop two hundred."

"Now you're trying to play me, homes. You know there's mad dudes out there ready to pay the asking price, right?" Marcelinho closed the suitcase.

"I'm tapped out, Marcelim. A lot of shit went down at the end of last year, so I've been having to lay low. Listen, I got three hundred on me right now. If it's all right with you, I'll leave this money here, take half a key. I can get you back in a week tops."

Biel had a crazy idea right then: What if he sold that stuff to the players themselves? Almost none of the boca's top dogs smoked their own weed. Most of them got their stuff off the hill, sometimes even from the competition. If he could unload this Colombia on them, he'd make up the shortfall in no time.

Marcelinho opened the suitcase again. Sometimes the dude acted like he was in a movie or something. He pulled out his precision scale from under the bed and started weighing nuggets.

"In that case, I'll have to give it to you for seventeen."

He got down to work. When the scale showed 100g, he'd slide the bud into a ziplock bag. Biel stared at the weed. All he could think about was how he was going to get to Rocinha with that much gear on him. If he was caught, there was no talking his way out. It was straight to Bangu.

"Thanks, Marcelim. You're ride or die."

Biel put the weed in his backpack. The stuff was pungent. He hadn't even left the apartment, and he was already shaking. But hand to God: he was going to make it to Rocinha in one piece, set his boca plan in motion, sell the rest on the blacktop, and go back to living the high life.

"Lemme show you something before you bounce."

Marcelinho stepped up to the wardrobe and opened the door. Biel almost felt angry at the sight of his clothes—all designer, all original. They were arranged by color. He couldn't stop picturing the housekeeper in there, organizing it. Marcelinho reached for a shoebox all the way at the top. Nike. Then, smiling like a little kid as he opened it: a silver, 9mm Glock. The thing practically gleamed.

RIO—March 3, 2012

It all started with a picture of Murilo's sister on campus. In her Facebook post, Monique described how important that moment was: she was the first in her family to get into a public university. Then she talked about her grandparents, about her mother busting her ass to bring up the kids, about how hard it was to study while holding down a job. When he first read the post, Murilo had actually been touched, but then, as he scrolled down to comment on it—just one person among many—he got kind of annoyed. Was it really so hard to shoot him a text, ring him up? In the end, he didn't like the post or send her a message. He did nothing.

Now, as he walked along Valão toward Rua 2, Murilo tried to remember which of the alleys was the one to her house. He'd only visited his sister once since she'd moved. That time, they'd met on Via Ápia, and he'd followed her without paying any attention to the route.

How could they have grown so far apart when they were

both from the same place? The question had been nagging at Murilo since he found out Monique got into college. He thought of them back when they were kids and still lived on Travessa Roma, how Monique was always standing up for him with the other boys on their street.

"Y'all must think you have two dicks to be beating on my brother like that!" she used to yell, to Murilo's despair; he knew they'd razz him for it later.

There were other issues when Monique became a teenager. Everybody started calling him "in-law." If that had been the extent of it, he'd have managed okay. But the guys liked detailing what they did with her. How she'd take it on all fours and go down on them, that sort of thing. In cases like those, there was no escaping it: five minutes of throwing hands was fair game in any favela.

But in spite of all this, they'd still hung out a lot at home. They used to cover for each other, help with the cooking, laugh their asses off at the same movies and cartoons. Suddenly, Murilo was staring at a boteco at the end of an alley. He got the feeling he'd seen his sister stop there for a soda the last time he visited. But he wasn't sure, so he kept walking, glancing around for clues.

His friendship with Douglas, the tension at home after their mom moved out, and the fact that Monique had left on bad terms to live with a friend all pointed to them growing apart at around that time. But if he really thought about it, he was sure it had started earlier, around when he'd enlisted in the Army. His sister had always been against it. Whereas the rest of the family believed it'd be a good opportunity—he could earn some money, learn to be a man, maybe even make a career out of it—Monique was always pressuring him to finish school. He was just one year shy of graduating. She used to go on and on about how he'd always been good at sports like surfing and soccer, and he could try for a degree in sports science, then work at a school, the gym, get a job where he wasn't a doormat for some sergeant, where he didn't have to handle weapons.

"What're you looking for, motherfucker?" When Murilo saw that rifle in his face, he was the most scared he'd ever been. He was so lost in his memories that he didn't see the three guys in black. "Looking for the boca, are you? You can tell your buddies their time is up, asshole."

"No, officer. I'm just looking for my sister's house," Murilo said after recovering from the shock.

"Do we look like clowns to you, dickhead?" The cop picked Murilo up by the shirt and threw him on the ground. "How the fuck don't you know where your own sister lives?"

"You got drugs? Better show us now, or it'll be worse for you later," the other pig yelled from farther behind.

Murilo had the feeling they were out for blood. Cops weren't usually this fired up so early in the afternoon. Had they bumped someone off already? Were they headed to an operation?

"I don't do drugs, sir. I'm in the Army. A soldier at Duque de Caxias Fort."

He immediately regretted not having papers on him. Everybody knew how important it was those days to carry an ID, work card, or student card, anything that could help in a situation like that. But it takes time to get used to a new status quo. Especially if you've grown up walking around that hill without a worry, only carrying your ID when you go down to the blacktop.

"So where's your papers?"

"C'mon, this guy's clearly a goose."

"Zero, one, zero, zero, two, zero, zero, zero, one, dash, eight."

"The fuck is that?"

"I don't have my ID on me, but that's my registration number."

The pigs glanced at each other, and Murilo had the sinking feeling he was watching other people decide his fate.

"Listen, soldier. This is what you're gonna do: Beat it," one of them finally said. "And I mean beat it. If we catch you here again, it's not gonna be pretty."

Murilo didn't know where to go, so he just went in the opposite direction and wound up right at the alley he'd been looking for. He bought a loosie at the boteco and started walking up, head dizzy and heart filled with hate. His body shook so much, he had trouble getting up the stairs. Ever since the cops had invaded Rocinha, he'd been stopped by the military police, the riot police, and now BOPE. But what really made him mad, so mad he couldn't see straight, was knowing he was one of the lucky ones. If those guys had caught him in an empty alley in the dead of night, things could've gone a lot worse.

It wasn't long before he was outside the building he'd been looking for. He recognized it from the tag on the wall: REST IN POWER MN BAFO. All he had to do was walk inside, the door wasn't even latched. But first he lit a cigarette to help him cool off. Fat chance. He only got madder and madder. His heart beat louder, his breath faltered over the smoke. Murilo couldn't remember why he was there. Or maybe he'd never known. Anyway, he should probably head home again, smoke up, wait for the day to end. He dropped the cigarette butt on the floor and started walking back. It was all downhill from there. He was almost out of the alley when his phone rang.

"Hey, Dona Vanderleia. How's it going?"

His mom said she'd been thinking about him, which is why she'd called. Murilo hadn't visited since Christmas.

"I'll come see you next time I'm off duty. I miss you too, Mom. But it's been hard, nonstop work."

She thanked God for that because idle hands are the devil's tools. Then she told him about her job, their pregnant dog, and Monique getting into college. Apparently, she'd been on the waitlist. They called her up at the last minute.

"I saw on Facebook. I've been wanting to link up with her, get a drink or something. You gotta celebrate that kind of thing." Murilo felt his breath slowly return to normal, his heartbeat become more regular. "Why psychology, though?"

Dona Vanderleia burst out laughing. Then she said Monique had picked psychology because there wasn't a single sane person in the family. Then she burst out laughing again, and Murilo laughed with her.

"I've been wanting to talk to you about something, Mom . . . I'm thinking of leaving the Army later this year."

The vibe immediately changed. Dona Vanderleia asked Murilo if he'd found another job or if he was planning on living on a dime. Murilo was about to tell her he'd find something to tide him over while he figured out his next step when he was interrupted by a slap across the face that flung his cell phone away from him.

"That was my ma, damnit!" Murilo yelled before realizing it was the same cops as before.

"Thought I told you to get the fuck outta here."

Murilo was frozen still. He didn't know what to do, in part because one wrong word or move could cost him everything. Other residents looked at him as they walked past, but none stopped. No one wanted trouble. Murilo was on his own.

"I'm just heading home. I didn't want to bother you all, so I went this way instead."

One of the cops pointed a gun at him, to keep him on his toes.

"Only junkies run from cops. Or didn't you hear?"

"Mr. Ganja over here thinks we're a bunch of idiots."

The pig pistol-whipped Murilo, who dropped to the ground. Warm liquid instantly trickled from his head. He staggered to his feet, wiped the blood from his forehead and turned to face the cops around him, picturing all the painful ways he could kill them.

RIO—March 23, 2012

By the look of her underwear—a red, lacy number—Wesley got the sense Talia had walked out of the house looking for trouble. Sure, they'd fucked a couple times before—at his place in Cachopa, when his mom and brother were out—but that round motel bed, the dozens of mirrors reflecting their bodies, the knowledge nobody would disturb them . . . It made the whole thing feel like their first time.

Now, he pressed his body into Talia's and ran his hands down her back, dick pushing against his briefs. While he kissed her neck and shoulders, he stealthily tried to undo her bra, but it was a tricky piece with double hooks. Wesley was nervous.

Not wanting to kill the mood, he turned Talia around and kissed the back of her head, then moved down her back, making her shiver all over. He managed to undo the stupid hook. Talia turned back around, breasts out. Wesley kept kissing her, this time all over her body. She was moaning louder now, so he slipped his hand in her underwear. His fingertips felt wet. Time to get the party started.

A few hours earlier, Wesley had been kind of confused when Talia had sat next to him at the bar. All their co-workers were there. Ever since getting back together with her ex, she'd avoided talking to Wesley, especially in front of other people. He still remembered her icing him out, so he tried to play it cool, like he didn't care that she was there. But he couldn't keep up the act. She started coming on heavy. There was nothing he could do: the flesh is weak. Their first kiss that evening happened right at the table while their friends and co-workers cheered.

Wesley usually came faster than he liked in the first round. But he held his own that night. The two of them made moves around the bed. They did it side by side, from behind, cowgirl, missionary. When he finally came, they were both exhausted. Wesley wondered if the line he'd snorted in the bar bathroom had improved his performance. He'd always heard coke could make guys go soft, but on him it had the opposite effect. Being high made him more alert; it put him in full control of the situation. Which is why, when Talia fell asleep, he ran to the bathroom for another hit. He wanted to be ready for round two.

Now that Wesley was wired again, he started feeling pressed down by all those mirrors. It was a crazy experience, seeing yourself buck-naked from a load of different angles. Talia was deep asleep, letting out the occasional light snore. He went to the window to smoke a cigarette. It was coming up on two in the morning, and there was hardly anyone out in that neck of Barrinha.

A patrol car pulled over outside the motel. Just seeing the siren flash made his heart pound harder. Wesley felt a pang in his chest. He'd done his fair share of clowning at friends who got all paranoid after doing lines. He saw the cops get out of the car. Instead of heading toward the motel, they made for a canopy and raided a homeless encampment. One of the unhoused guys tried to resist and got whacked on the head. A woman immediately shielded the kid sleeping beside them with her body. Wesley went to the bathroom and did two more lines.

He lay back down in bed. Talia was sleeping more fitfully now, twisting and turning. Freaked out by his reflection in the mirrors, Wesley decided to switch off all the lights. Now the only thing he could see was the police siren. A few minutes later, Talia woke up.

"Wesley?"

He responded with a hug. The two of them lay like that for a while.

"Honest, I don't remember the last time I had such a good lay," Talia said, breaking the silence.

Naturally, Wesley felt proud. But his head was someplace else, and he didn't realize she was suggesting they go again. He only got the message when Talia put her hand on his dick. Since he didn't get hard as fast as expected, Wesley flipped Talia over and went down on her.

He was skillful with his tongue, increasing and decreasing the speed of his movements as he felt Talia squirm. Her moaning grew louder. Wesley liked the sensation of pleasuring another person, of her thighs locked around his head.

"Fuck me."

That was Wesley's cue to work harder. He gripped Talia's thighs and felt her shudder until she came. Trouble was, she wanted to return the favor with a blow job. After a few minutes of unsuccessful licking and sucking, Talia quietly went back to her pillow.

"I don't know what's going on. This has never happened to me before." It may not have seemed it, but it was true.

Talia curled into Wesley's lap.

"It happens. We were drinking and stuff. You'll be back in action in no time."

Wesley kissed her and pulled her hips closer.

"Don't worry about it, babe. There's no reason to get nervous. We're just having a good time."

Talia got up and went to the bathroom. Wesley buried his head in the pillow. He pictured Talia telling a friend, the gossip spreading around work like wildfire. Only when he heard the door close did he remember he'd left the coke on the sink. The toilet flushed.

"Now I know why you can't get it up!" she shouted, storming back into the room.

"You flushed it?"

"Motherfucking junkie asshole!"

"C'mon, Talia. Don't make a scene. Calm down, pô."

"I'll calm down . . ." Talia started getting dressed. "I'll calm right the fuck down." She clumsily put on her sandals.

"Chill, baby. Let's talk about it."

She glared at Wesley.

"You have any idea how many times I seen my mom beaten black and blue on account of this shit? My stepdad snorted coke too, just like you, then he'd lay hands on her. I was ten years old." She started crying from the nerves.

"I'm not your stepdad, Talia."

She fixed him with a stern look.

"He was the one that beat her, not the coke," he said.

"Go fuck yourself!" She slammed the door on the way out.

Wesley got back in bed, exhausted. The radio clock showed the time was 3:05 a.m. What he needed right then was a joint to lower his adrenaline, give him some perspective, but he'd left his weed at home. At one point, he got up and grabbed his clothes so he could leave, but then he thought better of it. He may as well spend the night there, seeing as it was paid for and all. It wasn't safe to head back to Rocinha at that hour; he could easily run into a cop. Wesley glanced at his stuff on the nightstand. At least he had four smokes left in the pack.

RIO—April 3, 2012

They were so busy talking they didn't even notice the water boiling hard on the stove. Gleyce ran over, but it was too late. Washington's habit of throwing the coffee grounds right in with the water rarely panned out. The water overflowed, spilling all over the stovetop.

"But, like, do you think he's gonna die?" she said, picking up the thread of their conversation after switching off the burner.

"I mean, c'mon, Gleyce, dude took a bullet to the head. Only a miracle, Jesus Christ or whatever, can save him."

Washington brought over a wet dishcloth to clean the stovetop while Gleyce grabbed the milk pan and strained the coffee. She knew her way around his place, where everything was kept; she felt at home there. Even though people seemed to think there was something going on between them—they spent a lot of time one-on-one—Gleyce was sure Washington saw their relationship the same way she did and felt secure in their friendship.

"Shit's gonna hit the fan, and I don't wanna be around when it happens."

"For real. It was bad before. Now they're gonna be out for blood."

Like most of Rocinha's residents, Gleyce and Washington were discussing the previous day's operation. It wasn't unusual for bullets to be flying—there'd been shootouts every day for the past two weeks or so, but that operation had been different. It was the first time a police officer was seriously injured since UPP had occupied the hill.

"And a riot-cop motherfucker to boot . . ." Washington finished wringing out the dishcloth over the sink.

"All we can do is wait for a miracle."

They took their coffee back to the sofa where a joint awaited them. It was weird rooting for a cop to pull through, but that's what a lot of people were hoping for that morning; everybody knew that the worst operations were the ones that followed the death of a police officer.

"I mean, c'mon, though. Dudes are firing shots every day. Did they really think one of their own wouldn't fall? So far, this bullshit has killed like ten players and three residents. If it's war they want, then they've got it: you never know who's gonna go down next." Washington lit the joint.

"Holy shit, this stuff stinks. It's straight-up ammonia."

Another thing people talked a lot about was the quality of the weed. Every pothead on the hill was griping about it: the flavor, the smell, the price. But without the courage or the money to hit up another favela, they went on buying it all the same.

"Yeah, Dona Marli's about to change her mind about letting us smoke in here. She says it was false advertising, that Wesley and me started with the good stuff and then moved on to this reggie shit."

There was no lack of theories about the weed crisis. Many believed that the grass being sold in Rocinha's bocas had been buried in the jungle for a while to guarantee there'd be enough product to go around during the UPP occupation. Others believed the police was the new supplier, which meant zero quality control. But no one was sure of anything. Whenever anyone asked at the boca, they always got a different answer.

"What about your ma, how's she holding up?" Washington passed the joint.

"She's pissed. About the ENEM thing and me not wanting to take any of the classes. Mama's real mad . . ."

"I don't get why you didn't go either."

"I wasn't interested in any of the classes, library sciences or whatever, geography, pharmacy. Bunch of stuff I never wanted for myself."

"I mean, a diploma's a diploma, right? At least it gets you a special cell in prison."

All that talk about university blew Washington's mind. Before meeting Gleyce, he'd thought of college as this impossible thing that existed only in movies. But now he more or less understood how the entrance exam worked. He'd even read up on some prep courses on the hill and the blacktop. Sometimes, though he couldn't bring himself to admit it to anyone, Washington thought that if he managed to get his high school diploma, through EJA or whatever, he might just have a shot at college too. It would make his mom happy as hell. "I mean it, man. I gotta stand my ground. Think about it: How many people do you know that got to choose their profession, what they were gonna do for a living? Pô, man, I live with my mom, we own our house, I got an all right job that gives me time to do other stuff . . . I don't wanna rush it, that's all. But I can't seem to get my ma to see that."

Washington often felt that Gleyce took too long to make her mind up, and he worried she'd pay for it down the line. At the same time, he admired her courage and confidence when it came to making decisions. Washington himself had been working a job that sucked up practically every ounce of his energy—taking on poorly remunerated doubles and extra hours—for six months now. And even though he'd shot up the ranks from dishwasher to commis, his promotion to waiter still felt far away. But he'd convinced himself that even when things were at their worst, they were okay.

Someone knocked on the door. Gleyce and Washington looked at each other at the same time, wondering who it could be. All that talk of operations made it near impossible to imagine it was anyone but the pigs.

"Yo, I can smell that marola. Y'all holding out on me?!" The voice on the other side was Douglas. Washington got up to open the door.

"Sup, man. Don't just knock like that without saying anything."

Douglas walked in and was surprised to see his buddy wasn't alone. Gleyce jumped off the sofa.

"Douglas, this is Gleyce."

"Pleasure," he said, going in for the two kisses. "Washington's always talking about you."

The three of them went back to the couch. Washington passed Douglas the roach, and they sat in the silence that follows an unexpected arrival. Douglas kept his eyes glued to the ground, watching a few ants hard at work.

"You off today?" Washington was uncomfortable.

"I'm off for fucking ever, my man. I ditched that dumb job."

"For real? What're you gonna do?"

"I'll figure something out, neguim. Do a gig here, another there, carry shit, help out with a move, whatever. But, for real, I can't work there anymore. I need time, you know? To do my own stuff, practice my designs . . ."

Douglas had wanted to quit his job for months. After Biel started slinging that playboy weed in the boca and raking it in, the decision was made. Douglas knew that if he came into hard times, Biel would have his back.

"What do you wanna do?" Gleyce repositioned herself on the sofa, interested.

"I'm gonna be a tattoo artist." He always felt proud saying that.

"He's done some cool pieces already. Tell her, DG."

"Just gotta do yours now."

Curious to know more, Gleyce blurted out a ton of questions. She asked him where he'd learned to draw, when he'd decided to be a tattoo artist, if it made him nervous.

"But listen, be honest. You tattoo artists are kinda sadistic . . . right? Stabbing clients with needles, watching all that blood pour out . . ."

The question took Douglas by surprise, and his mind immediately went to two experiences: inking Biel and Curly. What had he felt when he'd seen their skin tear?

"Okay, so here's the deal: the thing I like most about tattooing people is that your art gets to travel all over the place, you know? Like, tags, graffiti . . . that shit doesn't move from the wall. And there's always the risk that somebody will come along and knock the wall down, or paint over it or whatever. Same for an oil painting. But tattoos, they last forever. They follow people wherever they go." He'd never given it any thought, but he knew it was true. "That's the thing that scares me the most about it too."

The news that Douglas had left his job had Washington putting pressure on himself as well. How much longer was he going to stick around the restaurant without a promotion? Three more months, he decided. Without gratuity, his salary didn't amount to much. Now that he was helping his mom with rent and groceries, by the time the second half of the month came around, he was broke, busting ass just to buy cigarettes.

"What about you?" Douglas asked after a while of them sitting in silence.

"Film," Gleyce said after waiting a beat. "There's loads of great stories on the hill . . . I could make some kickass movies."

The conversation went on in that vein; sometimes picking up steam, others stalling, made awkward by the lack of intimacy between them. Washington was trying to play midfield, to be the link connecting his two friends. But at the same time, it rubbed him the wrong way when they hit it off too much.

The sound of gunfire shot through their conversation. Startled, they all fell quiet and fixed their eyes in the middle distance, waiting for the next round, which never came. Little by little, the street noise returned to normal.

"Y'all hear about that cop over on Miguel Couto?" Douglas asked after the silence.

"For sure. That's all anybody's talking about. Me and Gleyce were actually talking about it right before you got here. About how weird it is to be rooting for a cop to pull through."

"Y'all didn't hear? Dude kicked the bucket!"

"You're fucking kidding me!" Washington didn't want to believe it.

"I'm telling you. It was in the papers. That shit was all anybody in the street was talking about as I walked up here."

Hearing that, Gleyce took out her phone and shot her mom a text.

"Another J?" Washington said, like he could read his friends' minds.

RIO—April 23, 2012

He arrived at Barreira do Vasco in uniform, 7.62 across his chest, shoulder to shoulder with the other soldiers in his battalion. It was Murilo's first time entering a favela as neither guest nor client. The second they got there, they were greeted by a series of bottle rockets, a sign that the boca was closed until further notice.

The convoy stopped outside the police station, and the soldiers filed onto the square. Mothers shouted at their children to run home. A soccer match ground to a halt. People loitering on the benches made scarce. By Murilo's count, judging by how long ago they'd left Leme, it was probably around noon.

One of the first things Murilo learned in military training was that rifles weigh four kilos. But they always felt a lot heavier. Sometimes, he still had trouble walking while carrying one. The muzzle would bump against his knee while the strap slipped off his shoulder. He tried to blend in with the other soldiers as they advanced in pairs down the street. Then, something really weird happened: even though Murilo had never set foot in that favela, he felt as if he'd experienced that moment before, to the point that he wasn't even startled when one of the soldiers tripped and fell. The way the squad laughed and the sergeant scolded the guy—he recognized all of it.

The soldiers stopped outside a house. The sergeant stepped forward and knocked on the door. Some of the neighbors peered at them through their windows. No one answered. The sergeant knocked again, harder this time. The sound of his fist on the wood door was strangely familiar. Murilo felt like he was watching a movie he'd seen before. Only he couldn't remember how it ended.

"I'm cooking, damnit!"

"Police. Open up!"

The door opened. A woman came out carrying a little girl who couldn't have been much older than one.

"Is this the address of Robson dos Santos Pereira?"

"Yes, officer, sir. That's my grandson." The woman looked old enough to be the sergeant's mother.

"The Brazilian Army has issued an arrest warrant for Robson. Your grandson's been AWOL for two months."

The child started crying. The more the woman tried to quiet her, the harder she bawled. A vein popped in her forehead. Murilo averted his eyes, praying for that scene to end as soon as humanly possible.

"Robson isn't home, officer." The woman did her best to talk over the tears while also trying to get the girl to rest her little head on her shoulder, but she just kept throwing herself back. "Believe me, we all want to know where he is too. This baby girl is his daughter."

The sergeant didn't believe her, though, and asked to look around the house. He walked in before she had a chance to object. The woman trailed him, crying baby in arms. Murilo had never liked that sergeant; he was a health nut, a wannabe athlete who over-gelled his hair. But the way he treated that woman had filled him with true hatred. He couldn't take it anymore. He needed a new job.

The soldiers stayed outside. At the ready. Though no one spoke, it was clear they were on edge. Flaunting their rifles in the middle of the favela with no superior in sight. What if the players started firing at them right then and there? Soon, they began entering the house, one by one. Murilo went last. When he stepped inside, he saw the toddler sitting quietly on the sofa while her grandmother cried.

"It's been two months! Two months since he's been home!"

The soldiers each focused their attention on a different aspect of the room, all so they wouldn't have to watch the woman cry. Murilo studied the furniture, which was perfectly tidy and clean. He thought about his grandma's place in Bangu, her backyard, the almond tree that kept the house cool with its shade, about showering under the garden hose.

"He's in the West Zone. Favela do Rola, somewhere like that." Once the sergeant was satisfied that the deserter was not to be found in the apartment, he started trying to wrap up the mission. But the woman kept pleading, "You've gotta find him. Please. We don't know if he's dead or alive!" The little girl stared vacantly at a blank TV screen.

The apartment was very small. The kitchen spilled into

the living room. There was a bathroom in the back and a single bedroom. From where Murilo stood, he could see a pair of old legs. Motionless legs that seemed indifferent to the confusion caused by the ten armed men squeezed into their home.

In the corner of that room was an altar with an image of Our Lady of Aparecida. Next to her, Francis of Assisi held Baby Jesus in his arms. Murilo was impressed by how little dust there was in there, everything in its rightful place. How did a woman with a sick husband and a small grandchild manage to keep everything so tidy while Murilo and his friends, who were young and able, lived surrounded by filth?

"I was sure the barracks would whip that boy into shape," the woman said as the sergeant gestured at the soldiers to make their exit. "Are you gonna find him?"

Out in the street, everything was back to normal. After sitting tight for a while, the residents of the favela had realized that the soldiers weren't there for a showdown. Murilo wondered where Robson was hiding. Had he gotten mixed up in crack? Died on the blacktop with no ID on him? Or had he simply run away from the barracks, leaving his grandma to cry crocodile tears?

The soldiers walked back to the truck in silence. The sergeant headed up the front. A group of kids paused their kickabout to let them pass. A bit farther on, Murilo heard some guys speculating over the prices of each of their rifles.

"Sixty grand! Sixty grand for sure if it's new."

They were about to turn a corner in the alley when they came across a young man without a shirt on. The guy got scared and booked it out of there, leaving behind one of his flip-flops. The sergeant signaled to the group to chase him.

The soldiers swiftly obeyed, but judging by how smoothly he navigated those alleys, the kid must've been born and raised there.

Murilo ran alongside the rest of the squad, sort of confused about what exactly was going on. Were they supposed to shoot him? Arrest him? Why had he run off like that? Murilo pictured himself pulling the trigger. His heart raced, and he trembled from head to toe. The guy they were chasing was so young, maybe even younger than most of the soldiers in that battalion.

The kid cannily vanished into the alleys, which pissed the sergeant off even more. He decided to split the squad up into groups in order to corral the target. Murilo went with the soldiers closest to him. He could see the tension on their faces. Was it that they were scared to shoot? Or that they were raring to pull the trigger?

The soldiers hugged the wall, weapons trained forward. Now and then, an oblivious resident would walk past them, get spooked, and shield their heads with their hands, as if doing so could protect them from a bullet. But since none of these residents were their target, the soldiers immediately waved them away.

Murilo's legs shook and his blood pressure dropped. He was sure he'd keel over at any moment. The rifle weighed heavier on him. What if the guy showed up right in front of him? The sergeant kept trying to gesture orders at them, but none of the privates paid any attention. They were all busy aiming their weapons.

As if the stress of having to shoot another human wasn't enough, Murilo also had to contend with the possibility of being shot at. He tried to catch his breath and thought about how he was under the protection not only of his squad but of the entire Brazilian Armed Forces. Surely nobody was crazy enough to shoot a soldier for no reason. There'd be tanks, helicopters, BearCats. They'd turn the favela upside down. Murilo held fast to this thought, but the truth is it wasn't enough. What use was revenge if he got shot in the head? There'd be no tomorrow.

That's when Murilo's vision started tunneling and his legs buckled. He caught himself on the wall and tried to communicate with the other soldiers, but his voice faltered. The rifle was dragging his body to the ground. Those alleys were a maze. *Which way should he turn?* he asked himself as he heard the bottle rockets: *Pah. Pah pah pah. Pah. Pah.*

RIO—May 5, 2012

"Bring down another, fam!"

It was close to four years since Washington had celebrated his birthday. Truth is, he always went kind of cold on that day and kept to himself. What was there to celebrate when time passed, things stayed the same, and every year brought more of the same fucked-up bullshit? Growing up seemed to come with nothing but problems; all the dreams you had as a kid became more and more impossible while reality seemed increasingly limited, until eventually life just felt like a chore. But Washington didn't want to think about that right now. What he wanted was to celebrate; twenty-three years, signed worked card, nice chunk of money in his pocket.

Washington told folks to come through at four so they'd get there at six, right at a bar on Via Ápia. He couldn't help himself in the end and went down early with Wesley and

Douglas to get the party started. Except Wesley wasn't in the same headspace. Ever since he'd left his job, scared of getting pegged as a limp dick, he hadn't been able to find anything else, not anywhere. He'd done some of the standard one-off gigs in Cachopa—carrying construction material and crates of beer—but competition was fierce, and there were plenty of days when he couldn't even pocket one miserable cent. Wesley had always made his own money, paid his own way, leaned on no one but himself. Now, if he wanted to smoke a joint or a cigarette, he had to ask someone to spot him. Which is why he spent most of his time at home, so that he wouldn't turn into one of those freeloaders he'd always hated.

On top of all that, there was the fucking driving test. After paying for the whole course, taking the dumb theory classes, and getting his ass all the way out to fucking Flamengo for driving lessons just to learn to ride a motorcycle, something he'd done since he was knee-high on way harder streets than the flat, trafficless road where he'd been assessed, Wesley couldn't stop reliving that test in his head, the moment he'd put his foot down and been automatically failed. He wanted to see those instructors ride around Rocinha without putting their feet down.

Wesley wasn't in a party mood, and he only went to the bar to support his brother, who wasn't to blame for his problems. After a few beers, Biel arrived, lifting Wesley's spirits. He rocked up buzzing, saying he had some quality coke on him, the good stuff, rich-folk drugs, so they could have a good time. Washington hadn't really planned on doing any lines; some of his friends would be coming through any minute, and he hoped to give each of them his attention. But not wanting to disrespect Biel's gift, he did a quick bump, his first and last of the day.

"Fuck . . . y'all snorting that shit while I'm sitting here dying to toke up!" Douglas had never tried cocaine, and he didn't want to either. Truth is, it made him trip to think of all the money people sank on a single night of karate; spend the same on weed, and you'd have a full stash.

"Don't kid. The cops down here are out for blood." Of course, Washington also wanted to burn one, but he knew that smoking grass near Via Ápia or even Valão was rough; the place was crawling with cops raring to fight.

"You think I don't know? Dudes can't even lay eyes on me anymore: those fucks have threatened to take me in ten, fifteen times since they occupied this hill." Douglas spat poison on the ground.

"They're always stopping me too. Last time was fucking rough, though. I was down in Venâncio to cop a loosie, right, minding my own—it was like nine, nine something at night—when I bumped right into the riot police. I tried acting like I hadn't seen shit, but motherfuckers called me over for a chat. Cool, I got nothing to hide, so I went up to them. These dudes ask me: This your fucking flip-flop? I look down and see a Kenner on the ground. I go: With all due respect, officer, but I'm *wearing* my flip-flops. And I point down to my Havaianas. Asshole gets real mad and says: Fucking answer me. Is this your flip-flop or not? And I go: Officer, my flip-flops are the ones on my feet. Why? Then the motherfucking pig slaps me across the face with the motherfucking flip-flop. The hate I feel, I swear. You ever been bitch-slapped with a Kenner?"

Wesley had told that story loads of times, but being high,

he decided to tell it again. He got angrier the more he thought about it; he'd even played it out in his dreams. The red and black Kenner, the thwack of the flip-flop against his face.

"I been pretty lucky with this shit. Cops haven't stopped me once!" Biel told his friends.

More and more people started showing up. First Murilo got there, kind of quiet. Folks had been worried about him for a couple of weeks now. A few minutes later, it was Chico, Rubinho, the restaurant crew. The table filled up, beer flowed, and they ordered some chips, it was an atmosphere of excess. By the time Gleyce made an appearance, looking fine and made-up, Washington was already tanked.

"Here, let me introduce you. This is Joyce, and this is Aline, that friend I told you about," Gleyce said after giving Washington a birthday hug.

The whole table was turned up now that the skirts were there. Up until then, it'd been nothing but pants. Gleyce slipped into a seat next to Douglas and settled in; her friends did the same. Washington, meanwhile, played musical chairs so that he could talk to everyone.

"So, how old are you now?" Aline asked when Washington sat near them.

"Twenty-three," he said slowly, still getting used to his new age. "What about you?"

"Same age as yesterday. It's your birthday, not mine." The way Washington laughed was too loud and too drunk, especially for Aline, who'd just gotten there. "Twenty. I turned twenty at the end of last year."

"Cool."

The two didn't say much after that. Instead, they weighed

in on topics circulating around the table. Basically, about Ambev not having any competition. Brahma, Skol, Antarctica were all theirs. Which is why sometimes, the good beer was Antarctica, and other times it was Brahma; they kept switching it up like that to give customers the illusion of choice.

"But Skol's always nasty!" Everybody agreed. "Itaipava theirs too?"

"Please, that stuff doesn't even qualify as beer."

Then they went back to the start of the conversation, everyone talking over each other, louder and louder by the minute.

"You know what sucks about getting old?" he said to Aline, picking up the thread of their previous conversation. "That, like, you gotta try real hard to make it seem like everything isn't going to shit. See what I'm saying? It's not the beer talking, I swear. I'm being serious. Been on my mind for days. Like, I keep thinking about when I was a kid. Back then I figured that, by my age, as a grown man and shit, everything would be cool, I'd be swimming in dough, traveling the whole-ass world. The U.S., Japan, you name it. But now I stop and look around me, and you know what I realize? I never even been out of Rio de Janeiro. See what I'm saying?! Then, like, I get all worked up wondering what that kid, meaning me, would think if he saw my life today."

Washington stopped talking only to realize he was a lot drunker than he thought. Aline, who was looking at him very seriously, took her half-empty glass of beer and knocked it back in one gulp. She'd been drinking fast since she got there, maybe to get herself on the same level as the people who'd arrived earlier.

"I only been out of Rio once." To Washington's surprise, she stayed on topic. "Went to Vitória, in Espírito Santo. My mom's family's from up there."

"Was it cool?"

"Honest? I thought the city was kinda ugly. Like really plain, zero character. But I was only there three days, that's not a whole lotta time to get to know a place. We went up for my uncle's wedding."

"Word."

"The wedding was pretty awesome, actually. I met a bunch of cousins my age—big family and all. But, anyway, the funny thing about it is that it was my first time drinking in front of my mom. I was, what, fifteen, sixteen years old. I'd gotten lit a bunch of times before while cutting class or at bailes, but never in front of her. So, anyway, we're kicking it at the wedding party when this waiter stops at our table and I say something about how I'd like a beer instead of Coke. I was just kidding around, really. My aunts were there, other folks too. I just wanted to tease my mom a little, but then, man, I almost couldn't believe it, I hear her say to the waiter: She can have beer, she's not a kid anymore. And I was like, Excuse me, what? I was so excited. Drank the beer, went up to the bar, ordered cocktails, caipirinhas, got wasted with my cousins. But like, juiced up. I'd never seen so much free alcohol in my life, not sure how I didn't puke. Anyway, so the party's winding down now. I'm on the dance floor, tapped out, when my mom calls me over. I'm thinking: That's it, I'm screwed, I drank too much, she's gonna ream me out in front of everyone. Man, you're not gonna believe what happened. We're off to the side when she pulls out this bottle and says: Go stash it in your purse! I know it's big enough. And I was like, huh? I had no idea what to do. But then I went and did what she said, scared shitless that somebody had seen me. And you know what the best part is? My mom doesn't even like whiskey! The bottle's still sitting on the living-room shelf, like a trophy or something. Every time I see it I think about that night. I was thinking about it today, actually . . ."

Washington and Aline started laughing, oblivious to the rest of the table, where the discussion had turned to how much more expensive cigarettes were now.

"You fly there?"

"Nah, we bussed. Took all day."

"Damn."

"It was cool, though. There's some beautiful places on the road. So much open space. Forest, mountains, cows. Big world out there."

For a moment, Washington tried to imagine the open spaces: mountains without houses, people, or power lines. He considered saving up money to go on vacation someplace like Minas Gerais, Vitória. Anywhere, really. He wanted to experience the journey there.

"Looks like Joyce is into your brother," Aline said. He looked over at them. Girl did look thirsty.

"You got eyes on anyone?"

"Depends."

"On what?" Washington leaned forward in his chair, bringing his face closer to Aline's.

"On whether the guy I got eyes on isn't into somebody else." She looked over at Gleyce Kelly without a hint of subtlety.

Washington had glanced at the end of the table at various points in their conversation and seen Gleyce and Douglas inching closer together, using any excuse to touch. The weirdest thing was that, right then, Washington didn't feel jealous, only worried about what his friends would think: that Douglas was cockblocking, or that Washington had wasted all that time marinating meat for somebody else to grill. He considered explaining everything to Aline, but just the thought of saying it aloud made him realize how dumb it all sounded. He excused himself and went outside for a smoke.

Wesley followed him and pulled a cigarette out of his pack. Not that smoking indoors wasn't allowed. Sometimes, Washington just liked stepping out for a smoke. Watching people, getting some fresh air.

"I think I'm going on a mission with Biel."

"What do you mean, a mission?" Washington acted like he was confused.

"A mission, pô. Biel's tapped out. Your work buddies are in the mood for snow."

"What are you now, a gopher?" The question came out louder than Washington had intended.

"C'mon, bro. What's the big deal?"

"Dude, Wesley, everybody's having a good time. Why do that shit now?"

"Cause I want to." He made to leave only to hear his brother say:

"Remember what you said to me? *Just can't get hooked . . .*"

"And am I?"

"Man, your broke ass can't afford shit, and now you wanna do rails . . . If that's not being hooked, I don't know what is." They were talking louder and louder, and Washington worried his friends would hear them.

"Go fuck yourself. I'm not asking for your permission."

Wesley went back into the bar to get Biel, and the two headed toward the boca. With any luck, they'd find what they wanted in Valão. But if there were cops in the area, they'd have to go up to Terreirão or Pedrinha. Either way, at that hour, the chances of them getting picked up were high. The night-shift MPs were vicious.

Washington stayed outside even after finishing his cigarette. He was thinking about the day UPP invaded the hill, about the two of them doing lines at home, the adrenaline rush of knowing everything was about to change, the feeling there was nothing they could do to stop it.

"You okay?" Gleyce stepped out of the bar to check on him.

"All good." He lit another cigarette, mostly to justify him still being out there. When he took the first drag, he felt a pang in his chest.

Gunfire rang out in the distance. Then there were a few scattered shots in a range of different calibers. It went on for nearly a minute without interruption. The noise was intense but faraway enough that people on Via Ápia were unfazed. After the initial shock, it was business as usual.

"Enjoy the gunfire? I ordered it specially for you. From Nemzão himself! It's your birthday, I had to tell the world," Gleyce said once the shooting stopped. She was talking funny, visibly affected by the booze.

Washington took a good look at Gleyce. She was prettier

than ever. More than her features, curves, clothes, there was this energy about her, something unique that made him want to always have her close. It was hard to explain . . .

"What the hell?!" Gleyce wriggled away from the stolen kiss.

Washington immediately tried to come up with an excuse—he was lit, he didn't want to complicate things, there was nothing to complicate, really, and he wasn't even sure why he'd done that—but, right then, Dona Marli showed up. She walked up excitedly holding a chocolate cake, one of those bakery cakes that practically glow in the display case. Gleyce gave her a quick hug and went back to her spot at the table.

Dona Marli's sudden arrival may have spared Washington from an awkward conversation, but it also brought back another point of distress. There was no avoiding her inevitable question.

"Where's your brother?"

"Oof, Mom. He's smashed. You know what beer's like. He just went to get some baile cigarettes. At Juarima's, I think." That was the best he could come up with right then.

It didn't take Dona Marli long to settle in and start joking around with everyone, laughing like she hadn't in ages. Soon enough, she was steering the conversation, bringing up embarrassing stories about her sons, making everyone at the table crack up.

"Happy birthday, son. You've earned it," she whispered to Washington, after polishing off another beer, surrounded by high-volume chatter.

"Thanks, Ma."

He couldn't stop thinking about Wesley. Was he coming back? If he didn't, what would Washington tell his mom? It wasn't long before his questions were answered. With one eye on the street, Washington was the first to see Biel walking back with his brother.

After copping the powder in Terreirão and snorting the first couple of lines, Wesley had started getting anxious. He shouldn't be fighting with his brother, not on his birthday; he needed to go back and apologize. But he never imagined he'd walk right into his mom, sitting there with their friends.

"Took you long enough!" Dona Marli said when she saw her son.

"Sup, bro, you find those smokes?" Washington quickly asked, so that he and Wesley could get their stories straight. Wesley nodded, eyes bugging out of his face.

All of a sudden, he was terrified that he might have coke on his nose. What if Dona Marli figured out what was going on, in front of everybody? Instead of sitting back down at the table, Wesley started heading toward the bathroom.

"Wesley!" It was his mom. He stopped in his tracks. "Come sing your brother 'Happy Birthday.'"

Dona Marli took the plastic lid off the cake, placed two candles in the middle, and lit them. The crew leaned into the buzz and sang at the top of their lungs:

Parabéns pra você
Nessa data querida
Muitas felicidades
Muitos anos de vida.

RIO—May 27, 2012

The news caught Biel off guard. Everything had been fine until then. It was Saturday, sunny. He was about to hit the beach, bring in some money. Why did he have to go online? Now, as he kicked the ball around with his blacktop friends in a game of altinha, he couldn't really focus. His body moved on autopilot while his mind was someplace else.

Biel couldn't get Marlon out of his head. They'd been next-door neighbors in Cruzada São Sebastião, childhood friends. He remembered the two of them tiptoeing across the pipe over the Jardim do Alah canal, taking jiu-jitsu classes together at Santos Anjos school, riding a piece of cardboard down sand dunes formed by the never-ending canal maintenance. Memories of a life Biel thought he'd left behind came flooding back after he heard the news.

"Water break?" They stopped playing and walked back to their beach chairs. It didn't take them long to find a matte leão vendor.

"Yo, hang on a sec." Biel drained his cup. "Top us up."
The vendor filled his cup again and left.

They watched a footvolley game happening at a net nearby.
The two sides were neck and neck, and the crowd cheered
louder with every point scored.

"There's a lot of money in the game today. Like twenty
thou on each match."

"Whatever, that's nothing. Last week, when that dude
Alecsandro was here, the pool was a hundred G." The crowd
was mostly made up of former athletes turned businessmen
or of businessmen who wished they were athletes.

Biel hadn't been to the beach in ages. Once he'd started
selling his green to the players in Cachopa, his Rocinha clien-
tele had skyrocketed. The news was walkie-talkied around.
Hour after hour, at boca after boca, people got a noseful of
that fresh grass, or at least of the Colombia Biel was slinging.
It must've driven users up the wall, catching a whiff of that
marola at the boca while they were sold schwag that stank of
ammonia. But whatever, we've all got problems, and the fact
of the matter was that Biel's new arrangement put him in a
comfortable position; he could afford to spend less time on
the blacktop. Now that he was back at his old post, he found
those guys' conversations increasingly bizarre.

His mind drifted to Marlon again. The guy had been a
beast at soccer. At almost every sport, really. He was a good
fighter. At one point he'd dabbled in surf. And when he
worked as a ball boy, he owned the tennis court, even got
himself hired as a practice hitter at the Jockey Club. "He'll
probably never walk again." Biel reread the message on his
cell phone.

"I think the guy that lost a hundred stacks was Fernando. And dude *still* bought everybody a round."

"I mean, he's a millionaire. It's pennies to him. As soon as he got back from the States, he bought, like, five or six apartments."

It'd been years since Biel had spoken to any of the old gang. How did Marlon's sister find him on Facebook, anyway? And to drop a bomb like that? She'd DM'ed Biel her brother's room number, claiming he needed to see some friendly faces because he was getting depressed stuck in that bed.

"He's a slick motherfucker too. I heard he's been skimming millions, moving it out of the country. They won't even let him into the States anymore. But here? Here he gets to live like a motherfucking king."

"Skimming from who?" Biel asked sort of without thinking.

"Who knows. All I know for sure is that he's rich, like filthy fucking rich."

Biel glanced over at him. He was lounging back, watching the game. How much had he put down on that match? Either way, he seemed to be shouting less out of worry than because he was having fun. It was all good times over there.

The playboys sparked up, and for the first time since he'd known them, the way they did it kind of grated on Biel. They never looked around to check for cops, not before or during. They just fired their lighters and let the marola of weed mix with the smell of salt air.

"We hitting 00 tonight?"

"Is that a rhetorical question?"

"Mariana's gonna be there with her friends."

"Mariana Weber?"

"No, Bianco."

"Ah, that Mariana. She's a babe."

"What about the Michael Douglas?"

"Well, we've gotta buy it."

"Vini's running a sale. It's one fifty a gram after five."

"Not bad."

"Good shit too. I tried some last week."

"So that's what's up."

"That's what's up."

Biel said nothing, even though he knew they expected him to chip in for the MDMA. The second he pictured the packed club, the flashing lights, the same old music and same old Marianas, Biel knew he wasn't going with them. He'd been hanging with that crowd for three years. What had really changed in that time? What about his plans? What were the chances he'd ever earn enough to rent a nice apartment, move up in the world? Especially considering all the money he had to make just to pretend he didn't need it. From that day on, their relationship would be strictly professional. He could easily live off what he earned distributing on the hill, even though he risked getting busted on his way home; the UPP was becoming more and more unhinged, coming down hard on residents.

The guys started getting ready to leave. Biel stayed put. As he watched them picking up their shirts and wallets, smacking their flip-flops together, it was like he wasn't there—the things they did and said just washed over him.

"Yo, Biel. We're getting food. You deaf or something?"

"I'm cool, thanks. Gonna visit a friend at the hospital."

They left, and Biel sat around the beach on his own. As he peered out at the ocean, he was almost offended by how blue it was. Morro Dois Irmãos, the sun, that slice of the city they called Rio de Janeiro—it all felt like an affront.

He thought about the friends he'd made in Cachopa in the last few months. All the stories. The guys were hilarious, the girls fine as hell. Despite the occupation and its effect on the hill, he was digging life in Rocinha. Back when they'd lived in Via Ápia, he basically only went home to sleep, pouring all his energy into his social life on the blacktop. Now, up in Cachopa, he actually took part in the neighborhood; he felt more welcome there than he had anywhere else in his life.

Biel was still zoned out when he heard a voice. He didn't have to look up to know it was the kid he'd tripped a few months back, helping the lynch mob catch up to him. After that day, Biel had seen him on the beach selling bananada and paçoca. These days, it was crackling. Every time Biel heard that voice, he was reminded of what he'd done.

"Yo, kid. Over here!" The boy came closer. "How much for one bag?"

"One real."

Biel handed him a coin and in return got a bag of crackling with a packet of ketchup taped to it, as usual.

"So, listen, I know you probably don't remember me or anything, but—"

The boy looked at Biel for the first time, and his face clouded over.

"Fuck if I don't remember. You call me here just so you can screw me over again?" the kid shouted.

"No, man, I . . . That day, I dunno, man. I'm not one of them, menó, hand to God. I'm just like you!"

"Whatever. You're nothing like me. Eat shit, asshole!"

RIO—June 6, 2012

Favela fuckup. Wesley did another line on the track and thought about the kind of person he'd become. Obviously, everybody would believe him when he said he'd been busted by the cops; he'd run missions plenty of times and never jerked anybody around. The problem wasn't so much whether or not folks believed him as it was that *he* would always know. Just as he knew that money was scarce, Rocinha weed was garbage, and his friends were all counting on that grass to get them through the week.

Which is why Wesley couldn't really wrap his head around what happened when he stopped outside the boca on Fazenda, the most hyped spot in Jacaré that week. All Wesley had to do was cop some joints for his buddies back home. After that, he'd still have another thirty reais left over for himself, all on commission alone. But in the end, every last penny turned to dust.

Wesley wanted to forget all about what he'd done, so he

scanned his surroundings for something, anything, to distract him. There were a ton of people all around the tracks and the station. Some smoking out of cups, others showering under a leaky pipe, a handful of uniformed schoolkids huffing loló.

But one scene in particular caught Wesley's attention: a couple arguing over a cigarette. The woman was screaming at her partner about how since *she* had gotten them that Derby, *she* should be the one to smoke it first. The guy held her off with one arm while shielding the cigarette with his free hand. The woman cussed him out at the top of her lungs: cuck, limp dick, rent boy, crackhead. Things were mostly fine though, and no one but Wesley seemed to be paying them any attention. Folks only started spectating when she grabbed a rock from the ground and threatened to smash the man's head in.

The second the guy saw he had an audience, he flipped his lid. He shouted loud enough for everyone to hear that she'd best not miss or else he'd beat her to a pulp, right then and there. That was the cue for the crowd to start yelling too, encouraging her to throw the rock at him already. The guy lit the cigarette like he wanted everybody to see he didn't give a damn what they thought. The woman got even more pissed, and the crowd egged her on. He was going to smoke the whole thing unless she threw the rock soon, they warned her.

The woman started swinging the rock back and forth. She was so focused she even stopped shouting—she knew she only had one chance. The guy kept smoking the cigarette with his left hand while covering his head with his right. She threatened to throw the stone a couple of times, then wussed out. The cigarette was half-done. It was only when the crowd and her partner stopped believing she would do it that she finally hurled the rock.

It soared through the air in what seemed like slow-motion. The guy tried to duck but in the end had to raise his arm to guard his head. He instantly started bleeding. Everything screeched to a stop: the crowd fell quiet, bracing for his reaction. The man grabbed a piece of wood and ran after the woman, who'd already booked it to the other end of the station. He chased her, faster and faster, foaming at the mouth. But before he could catch up to her, some guys from the boca told him to drop it, they didn't want any trouble on those tracks. Pissed, the man pointed at the cut on his arm and said he had a right to defend himself.

"Hey, want an umbrella?" Wesley was so absorbed in the scene that he jumped.

"It's a pretty good one," the man went on, opening the umbrella to show Wesley that it worked. "Give it to you for two reais."

Wesley looked at him for the first time. He was tall and wore jeans that seemed like they hadn't been taken off in weeks.

"It's not even raining, dude."

"That's why it's so cheap. Otherwise, I'd be using it myself or selling it for five times the price."

The man closed the umbrella and started leaving. Right then, Wesley was reminded of what it was like to talk to another person. As he watched the man draw away, he was hit again by the agony of being alone. He called out:

"Hey, you like blow?"

The man grabbed a brick and sat down beside him. He didn't say a word. Wesley pulled a capsule out of his pocket, tipped some onto his ID, and started cutting lines with his RioCard.

"Name's Marco, but folks here call me Teach. Cause I used to teach drums."

After they each did a line, Wesley started rambling. He said he'd just been laid off after being at a job for three years, with a signed work card and everything, which is why he had some severance pay to throw around. He'd gone on that drug mission to stock up for the week and only done a couple of rails to check the quality of the gear. Wesley wasn't sure why he was lying through his teeth. He was the one spotting the guy, so he owed no explanations. Plus, Teach wasn't exactly asking questions. He just listened and nodded along.

"It's not like I'm that into cocaine either. It's just for special occasions. Like, it's my birthday next week." The lies flew out of Wesley's mouth with such conviction that he started buying into his own cock-and-bull.

"You've got to be careful with coke. It's tricky business. I started snorting when I was, hmm, fifteen, sixteen max. I'm forty-eight now. Damn, the stories I could tell you. Like you wouldn't believe. After a while, I realized that the trouble with cocaine is that it's fake, really two-faced. At the start, my brother, it's the best thing in the whole goddamn world. You take a bump and feel like you're floating on air, so high on energy you could party all night long. I swear, I remember to this day the first few times I snorted powder. You get this feeling, right? A whole-body rush. And your heart's like boom, boom, boom. Right then, at the start, it's like you almost can't believe stuff like this exists—it's so perfect. But soon enough, the drug shows you another side of itself, and next thing you know it's taking you places you never wanted to be, places it's real hard to get back from . . . That's it, done and dusted. The coke goes from the parties to your home and turns everything upside down. Families are tough. You got kids? I have two—"

"I'm always telling my friends, there's a time and place for it. Bailes, birthday parties. Start using on a weekday, and it won't be long before you go off the deep end. Next thing you know, you're just another one of those fools that's all beaten down . . . I was watching them just now, and I thought: Everybody starts somewhere, you know? Nobody's born a zombie." When he was done speaking, Wesley wondered if what he'd said might offend Teach, but there was no taking it back now.

"No, man. That's not what I'm saying, not at all." Teach pointed at the junkies around them, at the trash strewn all over. "This here, cracôlandia? This shit's got nothing to do with drugs. I mean, just think about it. There's drugs everywhere. In the South Zone, in any city in the world. I told you I was a musician, right? Was. Am. I'm taking a break now . . . Anyway, listen, brother, I've played in some fancy places. Hotels, cruise ships, the whole nine yards. The amount of drugs those folks put in their bodies—it's out of this world. Trays of cocaine, waiters passing out straws. Brother, I've seen it with my own eyes. Loads of times. People cutting loose, noses bleeding. Shooting up in any vein they can find—feet, arms, neck. Ain't nothing I've not seen. Rich folks, man. You tell me, where's the cracolândia in Leblon, in Jardim Botânico?

This here's got nothing to do with drugs. It's poverty makes a place like this. Misery. The despair of wanting to survive but knowing you've gotta work like a goddamn dog just to put money in other people's pockets. Riding crowded buses, all that horseshit. Not to mention the folks who've lost loved ones to stray bullets. There's so much crap going round, it's something new every day."

Wesley lit a cigarette and offered one to Teach. The guy was getting his ideas in a knot. Besides, if Teach knew as much as he said he did, how come he'd ended up like that? Torn clothes, missing teeth. Wesley wanted to ask. Truth told, though, he was scared of the answer.

"You're right, Teach. Best stick to weed. Straight up."

"Weed's good, yeah." Teach took a long pull on his cigarette, like he was remembering all the killer grass he'd smoked in his life. "Helps you relax. Nice assist for that afternoon nap, or a night out with your girl . . . Weed's good, real good. But that's another whole-ass problem, isn't it? Folks burn one and don't even realize the shit they're getting mixed up in. You ever stop to think why cops go after stoners like they do?" He paused, maybe waiting for Wesley to say something, which he didn't. "Orders from up top. Senators, suits . . . Those dudes see weed as a problem because it makes us not want to do anything. Am I lying? And if all of us down here aren't doing anything, brother . . . If all of us down here aren't mopping floors or guarding banks or making food, then all the guys up there are screwed. Because then the whole world stops running. Those dudes can't do shit on their own except order other folks around. That's why they need us working for them 24/7. That's why they'd rather see Black men behind bars than

Black men smoking weed. That way, at least they get to make an example of them."

Three gunshots rang out not far from where they were. Wesley was startled, like he'd just woken up from a nightmare. He sat up straight, on high alert. Everybody in the city knew what operations in Jacarezinho were like. Even people who'd never set foot on that hill knew from reading about it in the papers, watching it on the news. Despite Jacarezinho's reputation, the gunfire wasn't enough to scare the folks on the tracks, who calmly went about their business.

"You hear that? They wanna bring UPP up in here too."

"Yeah," Wesley replied, unnerved.

He wanted to get up and catch the train home but thought he'd peeped some police officers near the other end of the station. He couldn't tell what was real and what was a figment of his paranoia; he knew that he was keyed up, that he was carrying contraband, that he was smack in the middle of Rio's very own Gaza Strip. He also knew that plenty of folks in his position had never lived to tell the tale. They heard another volley of gunfire from a machine gun.

"They're gonna pacify us! Pacify *us!*" Teach hollered louder and louder, as if competing with the bullets and fireworks all around them. He hollered against the clamor of war and laughed with his mouth wide open, baring even more of his missing teeth.

RIO—June 13, 2012

After tidying, sweeping, mopping, washing a week's worth of dirty dishes, and kicking Biel out of the apartment, Douglas stared at the clock and worried he was being stood up. He paced around the spotless living room, unsure what to do with himself. Two hours and a couple of text exchanges later, Gleyce finally arrived.

"Don't mind the mess," Douglas said, though he couldn't hold back a smile. The truth was he wanted Gleyce to know all he'd done to make her feel welcome.

Gleyce didn't buy it and sat on the sofa to roll a joint. She knew he'd cleaned the place for her and that the fact that no one else was home was more than just a coincidence. Douglas sat on the other end of the sofa and waited for her to finish.

"How about that movie?" she asked out of the blue.

"Huh?"

"Thought you'd invited me over to watch a movie . . ." Gleyce couldn't help laughing. What was this, a rom-com?

She'd known exactly what she wanted when she'd walked out of her house. The cleanliness of the apartment also made Douglas's intentions crystal clear. And yet there they were, going through the motions.

"Oh, right, yeah, we got some good options," he said, pointing at a stack sitting on top of the DVD player. "*Die Hard, The Fast and the Furious.* Or that really crazy one with the dude from *Titanic* . . ." Douglas was a lot more nervous than he'd bargained on. He had a knot in his stomach and his body suddenly went hot, even though it was cool outside. This was the moment he'd been waiting for. Now he just had to seal the deal.

"That PS2 over there work?" Gleyce asked. She gestured at the PlayStation, then lit the joint.

"You play?"

"Just fighting games."

Douglas started up Mortal Kombat, though he wasn't particularly excited about it. By the first match, he realized he was going to have to wise up. Gleyce started kicking ass with Kitana. And she wasn't even pressing a bunch of random buttons at the same time like most people did in fighting games. No, Gleyce actually knew the special moves, the combos.

"When I was a kid, I used to like playing with Sonya Blade, except then I found out she was a cop and went off that shit."

Douglas was too busy trying to stay alive to register anything she said. And he still had his ass handed to him in two rounds, on top of getting a fatality.

"Gonna stop going easy on you now."

Gleyce was used to hearing people say that the first time they played against her. Douglas chose Sub-Zero. He knew he could put him to work if need be, but it didn't matter, she crushed him anyway.

"You should put on another game if you wanna win." While waiting for the game to load, Gleyce pulled on the roach, nearly burning her fingers. "My aunt's got a bar over in Paula Brito. I grew up playing this shit on the arcade in there."

Douglas wanted to keep going. He tried every character at least once, as if winning were just a matter of choosing the right player. At least duking it out in the game eased some of the tension between them. They chatted a bunch while playing. Gleyce said she'd changed her mind about film. Now she was interested in journalism. The way favelas were portrayed in the news made her angrier by the day. She spoke about the importance of having people on the inside telling their own stories, of residents weighing in on what was happening. Douglas didn't know where she got these ideas from, but he agreed with all of them. He more than just agreed, he was in awe. It was obvious Gleyce loved that hill as much as he did, except she took things a step further. She wanted to make change, to do her part to improve the situation. The more they talked, the more Douglas understood why Washington was so fascinated by her.

Thinking about his friend was dangerous territory. While he'd waited for Gleyce, cleaned the apartment, and texted her, in the back of his mind he couldn't stop wondering if he might be stabbing Washington in the back. He knew he wasn't doing anything wrong, not in practice, anyway. Especially considering what had happened at the bar. Gleyce was annoyed at

Washington. But that was beside the point. What mattered to him was their friendship.

Washington was a good guy. It'd taken him no time at all to win Douglas's trust and consideration. Trouble was, from the minute Gleyce Kelly walked into Douglas's life, he hadn't been able to get her out of his head. To make matters worse, it looked to him like she felt the same way. Douglas started running back all the times they'd hung out since the day they met. About the interest she'd shown in him, even when they were with a larger group of people. The smiles, the looks. The gratuitous touching. On his hand, his leg . . .

"C'mon. Just pick one already."

He'd been scrolling through the characters without actually paying attention to what was onscreen. He snapped out of it and picked Liu Kang, one of the game's main guys, modeled on Bruce Lee.

"I used to slay with him on the Super Nintendo."

The fight started out slower this time with Gleyce backing off a bit. Douglas couldn't tell if she was going easy on him or if he really did play better with Liu Kang. Either way, he won the first round.

"Can I have some water?" She paused the match.

"Go right ahead."

As he sat alone on the sofa, Douglas wondered if he'd gotten the wrong end of the stick. Maybe she was only interested in hanging out and smoking weed as friends, just like with Washington.

"You had a Super Nintendo?"

Gleyce walked back to the sofa, unmoved by everything going on in Douglas's head.

"Nah, this is the first console I ever had. I bartered for it with some dude at work."

They started round two. Gleyce was kicking ass again with a mix of special moves and combos. The match ended in no time. Douglas put the controller down. They turned to face each other on the sofa, bodies inching closer.

"When you mentioned the Super Nintendo just now, it made me think of something. I never had a video game console growing up, but I still played all the time, like 24/7. And the reason I did is that my best friend when I was a kid had one. So, like, when you said Super Nintendo, it took me right back to the day he got it. It was Christmas, and it was drizzling, kinda like it is today. I went over to his place a bit after midnight. I didn't go there for a specific reason or nothing, just to pass the time. Cause we were super tight, and his mom liked me. So, anyway, when I got there, they'd just started opening their Christmas presents. My buddy was the oldest of three. I swear, Gleyce, I remember it like it was yesterday. There were these huge boxes all wrapped in colorful paper. And as I'm thinking and talking about it now, I can legit see the looks on our faces the moment we peeped that black box covered in Nintendo cartoons. Mario, Donkey Kong, you know the ones. We were like, Whooooooa! And the funniest thing is that, now that I mention it, in my memories, the box is, like, practically glowing and shit, like it's this sacred object. I mean, this must've been, what, '98, '99? Man, I was so fucking happy. Cause, see, I was this dude's best friend, right, which meant I'd get to play my ass off. When I saw that Super Nintendo, I kinda felt like it was my present too, you know? I mean, I basically lived at his place. I was there every goddamn day. We'd watch *The Fresh Prince of Bel-Air*, *My Wife and Kids*, and like a ton of cartoons—*X-Men*, *Static Shock*, whatever. Anyway, what I mean is, I knew I was gonna be playing Nintendo all the time from then on and that no one could accuse me of only looking out for number one, you know. Cause that's something that used to happen back then. Dudes would try to weasel their way into friendships with kids that had video games at home. We called them *abeiros*. Not me, though, I was already best friends with the guy with the Super Nintendo, and man, did we play the hell out of it . . . Those were the days."

"Y'all still friends?"

"You know, we'll say hello and shit when we see each other around, but it's not the same . . . We drifted apart back in our teens. Cause his mom, his whole family, became religious. Like, mad, mad religious. Evangelical Christians. The other day, I saw on Facebook that he got married. And I wouldn't be surprised if he was still a virgin when he walked down that aisle. Church is fucking weird."

"So, you're not religious?" Gleyce left the controller on the sofa and leaned forward. Her body language made it perfectly clear: there was no turning back.

"Nah, but I do believe in God," he replied. That was the cue for the two of them to move forward at the same time, toward their first kiss.

RIO—June 16, 2012

It was pitch black by the time they made it to the forest. The last street and lamppost were behind them, and they couldn't see a thing, the whole world shrouded in dark. Sounds became crisper—the rustle of the wind against the leaves, the animals. It was all so strange and last minute that it felt a bit like a dream. After a week of trying to set a date to hike the mountain, the plan had come together suddenly, on a late Saturday night, while they were all kicking back and smoking grass.

Armed with the flashlights on their phones, half a dozen hot dog rolls, three bottles of water, and enough weed to tide them over, they set off on the trail to Pedra da Gávea, the tallest mountain in the city. Shame there was no time for them to try and get better weed someplace else; ever since Biel had ditched Ipanema beach and lost nearly all his contacts, they'd had to go back to smoking Rocinha mids. Better than nothing, though.

It was almost one in the morning by the time they were actually on the trail. Murilo's guess—he was the only one who knew the way—was that they'd reach the summit by dawn. Right in time to see the sun slip out of the ocean.

By the first steep incline, Biel was already asking himself why he'd been so gung-ho on hiking that day. Maybe he didn't think anyone would have the guts to get up off the couch that late at night to tackle a mountain. Also struggling uphill, Wesley thought of what a boost it would be to have some blow right then. The only reason he didn't mention it was that Washington never passed up a chance to tell his brother he was on the verge of losing control.

"Whoa there, soldier. None of us here as fit as you!" Douglas yelled from the end of the line.

"Y'all got no one to blame but yourselves for dragging ass." Murilo did not slow down. "Worst case scenario, there's always these." He pointed his cell-phone flashlight at a yellow arrow on the tree marking the trail.

Out of the five of them, Washington was the most stoked. With all the time he'd been putting in at the restaurant, he rarely did anything on weekends and slept through most of his Mondays off. All that hard work had earned him the pride of his mother, as well as the respect of his neighbors and the old heads in the street; people had even started setting him up as a role model for kids in the neighborhood who didn't seem to care about anything. Still, as much as Washington liked the way he was treated and having a guaranteed salary, the truth was he felt his body getting more and more tired while he lost the will to do anything at all.

"What the fuck, menó. We passed this before!" Wesley was pointing at a tree.

"Quit tripping. I know my way around. I've done this trail twice already."

"Nah, menó. I'm telling you. I seen this tree already."

"Let's burn one while y'all hash this shit out." Biel pulled out a pack of cigarettes, which held a couple of pre-rolled joints.

"Word. Pass the water while you're at it." Douglas sat on a rock and tried to catch his breath.

"I know cause of this branch right here. Can't be two that look exactly the same."

"Damn. No way we're getting there before dawn if we keep going in circles."

"Going in circles? You believe this guy? There's more than a thousand fucking trees up in here. Dude's just trying to slow us down. You're all a bunch of chumps," Murilo protested while also sitting down. "Washington worked all day, he's on shift tomorrow morning too, I'm getting up early on Monday, and your weak asses are acting like you're not gonna sleep in all afternoon!"

"Washington's out of his mind, though. Remember all the times we invited him to kick it and he was like, Nah, I got work the next day? Look at him now, tagging along on a five-hour midnight hike." The minute Douglas said how long the hike was, he regretted leaving the house all over again, especially as he knew there was no way but down once they reached the top.

"Fuck, man, even I don't believe I'm hiking up this shit

with you all right now. But that's how it is, you gotta go wild sometimes, or all you're good for is working and paying the bills." Washington also took a seat. His legs felt heavy after running around all day at the restaurant.

"Damn straight, cuz. Specially today. Soon as the weather cleared, you had to come. You deserve a good time." Douglas was trying to keep the conversation going in part so they could rest as long as possible but also because he'd been trying to feel things out with Washington for days, to make sure they were still okay. There were a bunch of times when he'd wanted to tell Washington what had gone down with Gleyce the previous week, but he always gave up before he even got started.

"When y'all were trying to figure out whether to go or not, talking about hiking trails and all these different places, I kept tripping, like, fuck, I'm a carioca, right? Rio de Janeiro born and raised. But the truth is, I never been to the Christ, to Vista Chinesa, Pão de Açúcar, nowhere. Hell, I never even been to Dois Irmãos." Washington had always wanted to hike Pedra da Gávea, but something inevitably got in the way.

"I told you this a million times: Rio's only a *cidade maravilhosa* for other people. There's no marvelous city for us. Gringos come here, dudes from Minas Gerais or from the south. They have a great time, hit up cool parties, stay in ritzy hotels in the South Zone, hike trails, see all the beaches . . . Cariocas, meanwhile, can get fucked."

"Not cariocas, Biel. Favelados. Rich folk on the blacktop get to enjoy it just fine—it's us from the favelas that don't." Wesley got pissed every time Biel said *carioca* like everybody from Rio was the same. Maybe he was still under the influ-

ence of his Ipanema friends. "You know Makita, my buddy
from Vidigal? Kid was born there, raised there, whole family's
from that area. You think he wanted to leave the hill? What
was he supposed to do, though? The city's crawling with gringos, rent's getting steeper by the day, the market's cashing in
and twisting the knife. Dude had to pack up and bounce. And
let me tell you, they got lucky and all, locking down a place
in Roça. Loads of fools wound up in bumfuck Santa Cruz,
Sepetiba."

"No doubt. It's the same bullshit as the World Cup and the
Olympics." Douglas seemed to have perked up. "I get crazy
just thinking about it. Cause I remember, man, I remember.
Being a kid, watching that shit on TV, Brazil getting picked
to host the World Cup, everybody celebrating. My buddies,
family, my cousins, all of us happy as hell, thinking we'd
get to watch our team in Maracanã and whatever. But things
shaped up different, didn't they? We're busting ass to pay rent
and buy the essentials. Where we gonna get the money for a
ticket? Word is the cheap seats are going for six, seven hundred reais. And that's just for the group rounds."

"Makes you mad, doesn't it? Like, I don't even wanna pull
for Brazil, no joke."

"C'mon, Wesley. It's Brazil. You can't not pull for Brazil."
Murilo stubbed out the joint and got up to start hiking again.

"Let's dig into some bread, smoke a cig, get us nice and
ready for the rest of the trek."

"Don't play, Biel. We're not even halfway there . . ."

"For real, though, Brazil's gotta watch out for France. Get
them back for the ass-whooping we took on their home turf.
If we beat France, then it's smooth sailing." Washington was

thinking about the time he and his buddies cried in front of the TV during the 1998 final.

"It's Germany we gotta watch out for. There's some beasts on that team." Douglas had liked playing Germany in video games since he was a kid.

"Whatever. Let them try and come at us—France, Germany, you name it. Brazil's gonna crush this World Cup. My man Neymar's on fire!" Murilo knew that if he wasn't careful, they'd start rolling another joint, so he stopped talking and started walking. "See you up top."

The crew was back on the trail, but this time, buzzed, they were having a blast. They talked about the animals, wondered if there were any jaguars, snakes, or monkeys. Murilo said he had a buddy who claimed he saw a sloth one time. Douglas and Washington hung back, though without losing sight of the rest of the crew. It seemed like the slope would never end.

"You talk to Gleyce lately?" Douglas blurted out, not knowing what he would say next.

"We talk all the time, man."

Douglas sensed a hard edge in Washington's voice. What if Gleyce had already said something to him? Washington might get even more upset, think his friend was two-faced.

"She came over last week." An uphill trail was definitely not the best place to be having that conversation, but Douglas didn't want that stuff on his mind anymore. Washington kept walking like normal.

"She told me the same day, cuz. It's cool."

"I swear I was gonna tell you, man, but, you know, we ain't seen much of each other this week. And after everything that went down on your birthday . . ." Douglas couldn't stop explaining himself.

Being stoned, Washington even had the urge to laugh at his buddy's confessions and justifications. But then he realized Douglas was legit stressing about the whole thing, so he decided to put an end to the rumors once and for all. He said things between him and Gleyce had been worked out. That he'd talked to her the next day, tail between his legs, and apologized for his behavior on his birthday. That he'd said it was good in the end because it helped him understand the truth about their relationship. They were friends. Family. That he couldn't fall into the trap of other people's expectations. That one of the things Gleyce had taught him was that there could be real friendship between men and women. Then Washington said that Gleyce was crazy about Douglas, and he'd better not screw things up.

Now that they'd hashed everything out, Washington and Douglas walked faster to catch up with the rest of the crew. Murilo, Biel, and Wesley were barely talking, and they joined them in their silence. The noises of the jungle grew more intense and also more familiar.

Even though they were exhausted, the trail seemed to get easier the more progress they made. Their eyes adjusted to the gloom, and their legs moved on their own, picking the best route between rocks and surface roots. Their breath adapted to the rhythm of their gait. They went on like this for a while, without speaking. But they never stopped communicating. Together, they walked faster or slower, chose specific paths and strategies with gestures and whistles as if they'd hiked that trail countless times.

"How about that joint?!" Washington burst out when he spotted a rock with a perfect view of the ocean. It was the question on everyone's minds.

As soon as they settled down to smoke, after more than two hours of trudging uphill without a break, they felt the tired weight of the hike. They decided to eat a bit of bread and drink some water.

"Let's stick to the pre-rolled joints. Or else we'll run out of time." Murilo was focused on reaching the summit before sunrise, aware that once the heat turned up, they wouldn't want to hang around long.

"We're almost there, right? My legs are like dead weight, man."

"Almost!" Murilo pointed to the summit, as if to corroborate what he'd just said. "The way back's easier. Just gotta stay on our toes so we don't get lost. The first time I hiked up this thing was rough. I was a kid, like fourteen or something. Hadn't even started smoking weed yet, so you get an idea. I was with some guys from my street. The way up was a cinch. We were young, you know, surfers, all excited. We spent a long while hanging out on that rock. But on the walk back down, no clue what went wrong, but somehow me and a buddy got separated from the rest of the group. It was crazy, neither of us knew our way around this place. So we kept walking and walking. Through thick jungle and shit. We started wigging out, like, fuck, how're we gonna get out of here? But we just kept going downhill, cause, like, we'd have to end up somewhere eventually, right? And we did. We wound up in this gated community or something. Tons of crazy-ass mansions, you had to see it. A whole other world. Anyway, we still didn't

know our way out, right? There were loads of different streets
and stuff. Truth is, we had no fucking idea where we were,
Barra, or São Conrado, or whatever. And we'd been lost for,
like, hours. I mean, just getting there had taken us for fucking ever. We were dead on our feet. Starving. Just wanting to
get home. Anyway, so we see this old man headed our way.
Shit, I was so happy I could've cried. I rock right up to him to
ask for directions. I swear, I'll never forget the look on the old
guy's face. Second he sees us, dude goes white as a sheet and
books it outta there stat. Laugh all you want. Motherfucker
ran like lightning. We couldn't figure why. I mean, we were
chill and all, done nothing wrong. So we keep walking and
walking, trying to find the fucking exit. A couple minutes go
by, and this security car zooms up to us, screeches to a stop.
The guards climb outta the car and put their guns right in our
faces, even check my nose for coke. And there I am, desperate
to get home. After holding us for a while and asking us a ton
of questions, they drive us to the gate, and we make scarce."

Just over an hour after their last stop, they finally made it
to Carrasqueira. The sky was beginning to change color; an
orange tint creeped up and took over the dark blue of night.
The time was 5:20 a.m.

"Are you shitting me?"

"How the hell are we supposed to get up that thing, Murilo? Are you crazy or something?"

"Just don't look down."

Murilo led the way, scaling the rock. His friends followed,
each at their own pace and with their own concerns. Biel was
focused on keeping out of his mind all the stories he'd heard
of people who'd fallen on that section of the trail. Wesley was

coolheaded, skillful, and it wasn't long before he caught up to Murilo. Washington wasn't scared either, but, for a moment, without meaning to, he wondered what would happen if he didn't show up at work, if, for example, he plummeted off the side of that rock. Meanwhile, Douglas took longer than anyone to make up his mind, whether to go right or left, which leg to use first. Naturally, he was last. When he realized how far behind them he was, he got a bit nervous. Still, he wanted to take things one step at a time. He knew he couldn't afford to get it wrong.

At one point, he stopped to rest and couldn't help looking down. From where he was, all the way up there, it was impossible not to think about death. Not in a scary, paralyzing way but as this strange phenomenon that was hidden among all the other life stuff people had to deal with but that could crop up at any moment. One false step, one gunshot, one car, and people died. In other words, this thing everybody knew about burst into their lives as a huge revelation. He looked up again and kept climbing.

The rest of the crew waited for Douglas before tackling the last leg of the Carrasqueira, and they all reached the summit of Pedra da Gávea at the same time. The sun had just slipped out of the ocean, and the dark blue of the sky gave way to a lighter, bluer blue than any of them could ever have imagined.

"Check that out!" Then they all shouted every curse word they knew, electrified by the feeling that Rio de Janeiro was finally at their feet.

PART III

RIO—July 29, 2012

Even though it was the middle of winter, there was plenty of sun to go round. The heat felt different there, Murilo thought to himself as he and his sister stepped off the bus. The journey from Rocinha to Campo Grande had taken about two hours, and there wasn't even traffic on Avenida Brasil. At least Monique had been with him, and they'd had plenty of time to chat on the way.

"Are you gonna tell her right off the bat?" she asked as they stood outside the front door.

"It's her birthday. I'll tell her some other time."

Dona Vanderleia opened the door, already tipsy. She hugged her children while awkwardly clutching a mug of beer, then complained about how they never visited. She spoke loudly, competing with Arlindo Cruz's "Ainda é tempo pra ser feliz," which played at full blast.

"Almost everyone's here."

In the backyard were uncles, aunts, and cousins Murilo

hadn't seen in forever. His mother's family was scattered all over the city—some in the Center, others in the West Zone, a few in South Zone favelas, and a handful in the North Zone. Getting everybody together in one place was always a big ordeal.

"How old are you again, Ma?"

"Fifty!"

Murilo and his sister sat at the table, away from the guests and the loudspeakers. Roni brought them a can of beer and two glasses.

"Gotta wet that whistle on a scorcher like this one!"

Murilo hated when their stepdad acted all chummy. It rang false.

Everybody toasted to Dona Vanderleia's health. Murilo saw some of Roni's friends in the crowd. There was no helping it, not in a neighborhood like that one. The men were all potbellied, decked in rings and chains. They stank of militia. Murilo counted at least three at the party.

After the toast, Murilo and Monique headed back to their spot. Dona Vanderleia had already vanished into the backyard, where she cheerfully twirled and sambaed, beer in hand. Murilo liked to see his mother happy, but the celebratory atmosphere just hollowed out a pit in his stomach.

"I'm gonna demolish this churrasco." Murilo pulled out a cigarette and saw that there were only two more knocking around in the pack. "I haven't had any meat in forever. Shit's been rough at home. It's instant noodles every day," he told Monique, trying to make her laugh. But he couldn't help thinking about the time their rent had been past due and he, Douglas, and Biel had had to hawk their phones and other valuables at the street market, where the vendors kept offering them pennies, convinced they were cokeheads who'd accept a measly twenty reais for their devices.

"You still into the chicken-flavored one? These days, I'm liking tomato better."

"That's the last thing on my mind right now."

He got up and went to the table with the food. There was rice, farofa, potato salad, and tomato, green pepper, and onion salsa—all of it practically shining. The clean tablecloth, spotless silverware, and glass serving platters nearly made Murilo miss the days when he lived with his mom. Before long, he was remembering how it felt to have clean, nice-smelling clothes in his closet.

"I swear! He meant it."

"Only in Rio, man . . ." Murilo's two uncles were laughing together at a table strategically located next to the beer cooler and the grill.

Murilo quietly served himself food, avoiding eye contact so that he wouldn't be pulled into conversation. Not that he had any beef with his uncles; the two of them were pretty chill, funny even. The trouble was that when it came to catching up with family after months of not seeing each other, they always wanted to know how things were at home, at work, in life in general. Straightforward questions that Murilo had no clue how to answer.

"Wait until you hear this." The two men approached Murilo.

"So, I was just telling your uncle about the other week, when I was in my cab, driving around. You know I can't stand traffic so, if I can help it, I try and go out at night. Anyway, I'm cruising around São Cristovão, and everything's cool, quiet, when I pick up this passenger. The guy gets in, says 'good evening,' yada yada, and to please take him to Copa. I was happy to. I'd been wanting to get to the South Zone anyway. I'd taken that route so I could get closer to Leopoldina. So we start talking and stuff, nice guy, laid-back, the conversation's flowing, then for some reason we hit on the subject of insurance. He says to me, Listen, brother, I'm always telling car owners, even if your ride's a clunker, even if it's old, none of that matters, you better get it insured. And I say to him, You know, some cars just aren't worth the trouble. And he goes: I'm telling you. It's my job, so I know what I'm talking about. I'm thinking he's an insurance broker or something when he says: I jack cars for a living. Minimum five a day."

"Fuck! You're messing with me, right?" Murilo left his plate on the table, grabbed a plastic cup, and filled it with beer.

"Hand to God. Then he says to me, Here's another bit of free advice: Don't resist, cause when we're jacking cars, we're pumped up on adrenaline, and we might get it into our heads that the driver's armed, and that's it, the sucker goes and dies for no reason. That's why I always tell everyone: Get insurance and be cool. And if you don't, then deal with it. All I know is no car's worth dying over. So, anyway, there I was thinking I'm next, right? Swear to God, Murilo, my asshole was so tight you couldn't fit a needle in it. But I can't help myself, so I say: But, I mean, if you think about it, you risk your life jacking cars. What's the difference between you and the driver? I regretted those words the second they left my mouth. I mean, what if he thought I was threatening him?

But he says: Sure, but that's my job, isn't it? There's risks and there's rewards, just like any other profession. Plus, I'm not risking my life for *one* car, right? What can I say? It comes with the territory. Now, if somebody tries to steal from me one day, they can take it, I'll get over it. That's why I'm always going on about insurance . . ."

"So, did he try and jack your car or what?" Murilo laughed in earnest.

"No!" His uncle paused to refill his glass. "The guy gets off at Copa, pays me, says goodbye, and goes on his merry way. Guess he must've met his daily quota!"

Murilo hung out with his uncles a while longer, laughing at all the stories they told. But when his turn came to talk, he got up and went back to his table, claiming he'd left his sister waiting long enough. But first, he grabbed two more beers from the cooler. The heat and his desire to be anywhere else were making him drink faster than normal.

"It's for the best . . ." Back at his table, he found his sister chatting with Angelita, his mother's best friend.

"I'd get the hell out too, if I could. But I own my place . . ." Angelita was probably a decade older than Dona Vanderleia. "What about you? Still in Rocinha?" she asked, turning the conversation over to Murilo.

"Nah, I'm living it up in Ipanema now." Murilo was trying to be funny but instead sounded sarcastic.

"How come you haven't invited me over then? I'm in desperate need of some beach time." Angelita got up and pointed at her arms. "See? I'm going yellow!"

Murilo thought back to when Angelita and his mom used to work together, to all the nights she spent with them in

Rocinha. She and Dona Vanderleia would stay up chatting and kidding around. Sometimes, they even ordered pizza. Angelita seemed to have a transformative effect on his mother. In her company, Dona Vanderleia became funnier and lighter, arguing less and laughing more. Maybe that's why Angelita had no trouble at all winning Murilo and Monique over and becoming, in a way, part of the family.

"That's all. Just wanted to tell you how proud I am. I swear, I cried my eyes out when your mom told me the news. I just knew you could do it. I always knew." They hugged again, then Angelita went back to her spot at the table.

"Funny how much she's aged since Mom's last birthday." Monique couldn't figure out what to do with the dregs of warm beer in her glass. In the end, she downed the whole thing. "But she hasn't changed one bit," Monique said, making a face and reaching out her glass for her brother to fill up.

"So, where you getting the hell out of? I feel like I missed something," Murilo asked, though he already knew the answer. He filled his sister's glass, then his own.

"Rocinha. I'm looking into university housing. And if that fails, an apartment share in the area."

"Right . . ."

Murilo knew that, even though they both lived in Rocinha, they never saw each other and spent less and less time together. Which is why it wouldn't have made sense—and was also kind of ridiculous—for him to say he felt abandoned. Yet that's exactly what he wanted to say. He lit his second-to-last cigarette.

"Things aren't okay where I live anymore. There's shoot-outs every day. Every single day. With all those bullets flying, one day they might just hit someone," Monique said.

"They've already hit a few someones."

"You haven't heard the half of it," Monique continued. "Twice now I've been caught in the crossfire while walking home. And I swear, you just can't know what the hell to do in that situation. Do you keep walking? Do you turn back? And while you're trying to make up your mind, the bullets are getting closer and closer." Murilo genuinely believed his sister was torn up about it. At the same time, he couldn't help feeling she was blowing things out of proportion, that spending time with college kids and rich folk from the blacktop had messed with her head.

"Honestly, Mu, nobody should get used to that kind of thing, it's not normal," she continued, probably annoyed by the skepticism in Murilo's eyes. "And it's not just the gunfire either. It's everything. I mean, shit, I didn't have water all last week. A whole week! I had to get it in buckets. I'd come home after work and still have to stand in fucking line just so I could wash." Monique drained her glass again. She tried to pour them another round, but only a dribble came out of the can.

"It's not about getting used to things, sis. What we need is money. Cause money equals opportunity, right? We only live where we can afford to."

Monique didn't like where the conversation was going, partly because she hadn't asked for anybody's opinion. Murilo seemed drunk, and he had a hostile gleam in his eye. She didn't want them to fight, so she got up to get more beer. Out of nowhere, Murilo grabbed her hand.

"I know you can do it."

The day whizzed by, and the party wound up being a lot quieter and more laid-back than Murilo had imagined. The family cracked the usual jokes, making it easier for him to say what was expected of him. Thanks to the ice-cold beer, everything was funnier and more refreshing; proof of this was the raucous laughter later that evening, when all the guests came together to sing "Happy Birthday."

Murilo was busy housing a third slice of cake. Drunker than he'd have liked, he didn't have the energy to make the trip back home. But staying over in Campo Grande wasn't an option, either. He didn't have any weed with him; besides, he was on his last cigarette. Murilo was debating whether or not to light it when Roni came over with a friend.

"This is my stepson, the one I was telling you about." The two shook hands. Murilo spotted his sister across the backyard, saying goodbye to family. "I was waiting for you to stop by at our table. Hoped you'd join us for a drink."

Murilo hated when his stepdad pretended they were friends. Ever since Roni and his mom had gotten together, it'd been pretty much impossible to get any help from her. When she did lend Murilo and his sister a hand, on the DL, she'd ask them to keep it to themselves because she didn't want to upset her husband.

"Next time." Murilo gulped down the last bit of cake and got up like he was in a hurry to throw away that plate.

"Souza was in the military as well. That's why I wanted to introduce you. He started as a lieutenant, then passed the police entrance exam."

"So you're a cop?"

"Reformed," Souza said, and all Murilo could hear was *militia, militia, militia.*

"What's important is that I was talking to him about getting you a place on a prep course. With a scholarship, maybe."

Murilo lit his last cigarette. As he tried to enjoy the smoke, the reformed police officer leaned in a little too close.

"You've got a good physique, kid. If you quit smoking and lay off the drink a while, you might just have a future . . ." Souza said while sizing up Murilo.

"I resigned from the Army a month ago," he blurted out. If he'd had the wherewithal to think before speaking, he'd have smiled and nodded, then excused himself to throw his plate in the garbage, kiss his mother goodbye, wave at the few remaining guests, and go home.

"Your mom didn't mention it."

Dona Vanderleia was walking past them with a bagful of empty beer cans when she heard Roni say her name. She stopped.

"What didn't I mention?"

"I resigned from the Army, Ma. A while ago. Things aren't easy at home. We're all broke. It's a mess. But I had to get outta there," Murilo said, voice slurred by booze.

"It's okay, son. We can talk about it later."

"I wanted to tell you sooner, but I had to figure some things out first. Like, I went to EJA to see about my high-school diploma. I need to get all the paperwork together, go back to my old school, and talk to the principal. Then, it's just a matter of getting down to work ASAP so I can finally gradu-ate. That's the plan anyway."

Dona Vanderleia could see that her son needed her, so she walked him to a table in the corner, where they sat across from each other.

"Why didn't you say something, Murilo? I could've helped. Just the other day, a friend told me about this job opening at a market in Copacabana . . . I'm still your mother, you know, even if we don't live under the same roof."

"I tried like hell, Ma, I really did. Excuse the French, but it's a fucking bitch. I tried, but I couldn't do it—I couldn't stay there another minute. And you know what the worst part is? I wasted two years there. Two years, and I got no savings, no skills. Unless I wanna sell drugs in the boca, join the police force, be in the militia . . . Cause, like, I don't really know how to do anything. Except carry shit. I'm strong, that's for sure. But I see people around the hill, their bodies are all fucked up from hauling construction material, furniture. It sucks, but that's the only work available these days. I promise, though, I promise I'll find *my* thing, Ma. I'll find my thing and do it right. I know I got time still. That I'm young. Whole life ahead of me and whatever. Things are gonna change, Ma. Trust me." Tears had started rolling down Murilo's cheeks.

"I know, son, I know. What's got you so worked up, though? I mean, it was just a job . . . You quit, it's behind you, now you've just got to find something else, like you said."

"But that's the problem, Dona Vanderleia. It was more than just a job. Or is it just a job when a guy shoves a gun, a loaded seven-six-two rifle, in a fifteen-year-old's face? And what if I told you that that guy was me, and that I was *this* close to pulling that trigger? No . . . It's more than just a job."

"Jesus Christ, Murilo. What do you mean? Where did that happen?" Dona Vanderleia, who'd also been drinking all day, immediately sobered up.

"It happened the week before I resigned. And the worst part, Ma, the worst part of all is I didn't do it because someone told me to. I did it because I *wanted* to. It was some other soldier that stopped the kid. I was just with him. I didn't have to act. But I did. I did because I was pissed, because the kid had annoyed the hell out of me, because he was clowning right in our faces. I remember we were hot as hell in our uniforms, our boots. But, the truth is, the honest truth is I did it because I could. Because I felt I could. I was the one with a loaded weapon, meaning, like, I was the one in fucking charge. So I pointed it at him. Right at his face. But you know me, Ma, I'm not that person. I'm not . . . and I don't want to be. I'll show you. I promise."

Murilo was sobbing by the time he finished his story. Dona Vanderleia got up, pulled him into a hug, and gave him her shoulder to cry on. A few curious guests approached them. She signaled with her hands that everything was okay, her son was just a bit drunk. Then she took Murilo inside, helped him into the shower, and stroked his head until he fell asleep.

RIO—August 9, 2012

It was intense, the rush of adrenaline Douglas felt when he lifted the transfer paper and saw his stencil of Pedra da Gávea on another person's skin. That was the most complicated piece he'd done in his short career as a tattoo artist, and it had come at the perfect time. After working on a string of names, phrases, and butterflies, Douglas realized he needed a challenge if he wanted to up his game. Of course, things at home—everybody broke and unemployed—helped him find the courage to skip a few steps. Douglas honestly believed his Pedra da Gávea design could be the fuel that pushed him to do better and better work.

"This piece is gonna be dope as hell," Washington said, studying the lines on his shoulder and remembering the moment they'd reached the summit of that mountain, the freedom he'd felt seeing the city from way up high.

"There'll be shading too, and I'll freestyle some stuff around the sun . . ."

"Take a pic for me. I want a before-and-after shot." He handed Douglas his cell. Ever since he'd bought himself a smartphone—in twelve installments, no interest—Washington had become obsessed with documenting everything. Sometimes, he even took pictures of his lunch. His friends were floored when they heard how much the thing cost him, but then he told them it was more than just a phone: it was the world at his fingertips. It didn't just text and call, it did everything.

Douglas took a photo and then turned to his workstation. He gave it a satisfied once-over. The equipment was clean and neatly arranged, ready to kick off a new session. Douglas was prepared to put everything he had into that design, not only because he wanted to improve his portfolio but because he thought Washington deserved some killer ink. Though they hadn't known each other long, Douglas felt he'd found a true friend. Just last month, Washington had lent him money to pay back rent. Now, there he was, entrusting Douglas with a kickass tattoo, which was the same as putting his faith in him.

Not even Gleyce had managed to come between them. Truth told, ever since Douglas and Gleyce had started seeing each other, it was like he and Washington had gotten closer. All three of them often went out together. Sometimes, they invited one of Gleyce's friends so that Washington wouldn't have to feel like a third wheel. A few days ago, they'd decided to travel to Minas Gerais together to visit one of Douglas's cousins, just as soon as they had some money to spare.

Douglas wavered over what grip to use before finally settling on the liner. He'd start with the foundation of the design, a sort of sketch, before moving on to the shading, which was the hardest part. These days, Douglas felt a lot more at ease with the machine, with the way it vibrated when it kicked on. He carefully began his line work on Washington, whose skin tore and spilled blood.

"This is actually pretty chill. Doesn't even hurt that bad," Washington said.

It was still early though, and he would probably change his mind a few minutes, or hours, into the process. Except hearing this made Douglas wonder if he was applying enough pressure. He still hadn't figured out the perfect depth. Some clients complained of too much pain while others barely felt a thing. Weirdly, though, he'd had tattoos fade in both groups, meaning there wasn't a clear pattern.

"People say shoulders are pretty easy."

Douglas realized there was no avoiding it. If he wanted to be able to judge the pressure, he'd have to tattoo himself. Just the thought of it made him shudder. He'd never liked needles.

"What about you? When are you getting inked?"

"I was legit just thinking about that, neguim." Douglas paused to wiped blood from Washington's shoulder. "I'm gonna do something on myself. Probably on the thigh, cause I can get good purchase that way."

Douglas finished wiping Washington's shoulder and was jolted by the sight of a janky line. He took a deep breath to calm his nerves. Thankfully, he could fix it with shading.

"What's it gonna be?" Washington lit a joint. His shoulder was starting to burn.

"Dunno, something simple, like a pot leaf or whatever."

"The fuck, neguim. Are you insane?" Washington choked

on the smoke. "The way cops are acting now, if they catch you with a pot leaf tattoo, you're a dead man. Didn't you hear what happened to Bristles? So, dude was on his way home from school . . ."

Douglas lit a cigarette he'd bummed from Washington, then peered down at the messy line again. Could Washington see it in the mirror? Sometimes, clients didn't notice. Like when this guy got his family name tattooed on his back: he'd left the parlor feeling stoked about it only to show up again the next day, convinced it was fucked up, all because somebody told him so.

"It's gnarly out there. The pigs are full of hate. Now that the players have started shooting back, they're running scared . . ."

After nearly a year of the UPP, the dynamic between the cops and the drug traffickers had changed. Though at first the players kept on slinging drugs on the DL, these days it was like they were raring to take back every inch of the hill. This naturally scared the shit out of the police. At the end of the day, though, it was the residents who got the raw deal. Washington had noticed that cops were a lot more aggressive when they stopped people. Luckily, his signed work card made it easier to get around.

"Yeah. The World Cup'll be here before we know it. I wanna see what happens if there's still constant shootouts by the time it comes around. They're gonna be screwed."

Douglas switched on the machine and got back to work. He tried to reconnect with his earlier calm, but all he could think about now was the janky line. Maybe he should just fess up to Washington. At least then they could shoulder the anxiety together, and Douglas could get back to work feeling just that bit lighter. He opened his mouth to say something a couple of times but kept chickening out. He decided to finish up the more detailed work with the liner needle and then move on to shading. After giving it some thought, he concluded that having a client lose faith in him would make him feel even worse than that line.

"The thing I'm really freaking out about is Wesley," Washington said, not noticing how Douglas was sweating bullets.

He'd already told Douglas his brother had been missing since the weekend. But he couldn't stop thinking about it, partly because he'd been so sure Wesley would resurface on Sunday night, Monday morning at the latest. But time ticked on, and as they closed in on Tuesday, he started running through worst-case scenarios.

"I even made up some shit about him being at a girl's house, so Dona Marli wouldn't stress. But it's rough, man . . ."

Douglas switched off the machine again, this time to swap out the grips and needles. He wanted to start shading so he could fix the messy line ASAP.

"The thing that really gets me is that I know he's going off the deep end . . . Wesley's been kicking with some sketchy fucking people. They're trouble, man."

Once he was done messing with the machine, Douglas turned his attention back to the design. The pause had cooled Washington's blood, and the light burning sensation had turned into a sharp, unrelenting pain.

"Plus, I can't stop thinking about how, like, I was the one that introduced him to that shit, you know? I get really torn up about it."

Douglas stayed focused while Washington talked, determined to fix the line to the best of his abilities. It was harder for him to see what he was doing with the round shader because there was more blood, but he was bent on not screwing up again. When Douglas needed razor-sharp focus, he craved silence. But clients always wanted to talk. His solution was to half-listen. He just nodded along and got on with it. Barely anyone noticed that he wasn't really there, maybe because most of them didn't actually care whether or not anyone was listening—they just wanted to flap their gums. But in this case, Douglas knew that Washington desperately needed to work through some things. He grudgingly switched off the machine.

"Honest? If I was you, I'd sit him down and talk to him, man, cause a talk's a talk, right, especially with family. But enough of this bullshit of blaming yourself, or whatever, because that's beside the fucking point. I mean, for real, this shit your brother's going through is normal. To be expected. Everybody has a wild phase. Even me. I didn't snort coke or anything, but I went heavy on the booze. Like, basically every day. I'd get home shit-faced, wilding. I'm not kidding. I'd be fucking trashed. So, my mom: she warned me once, she warned me twice, three times, and then, when she got sick of me, she kicked me out. And it was for real the best thing that could've happened. It was exactly what I needed to get a grip, you know? You think my old lady spent any time thinking, *well, he did see me drink a lot,* and *well, I used to let him have a glass of wine every Christmas, and sneak sips of my beer?* Fuck no. And she was right, bro. If I hadn't started drinking at home, then I'd've done it someplace else. It's all fucking there, man, right at our fingertips: booze, coke, cigs, all of it, any drug you could dream of. The choice we have isn't to do drugs but *not* do them, get it? It's doing drugs that's normal. So, what I'm saying is your brother's just going through a phase. There's time's we're in the deep end, and we don't even realize. I mean, I drank around the clock. Weekdays. I used to cut class and sit in the square bingeing. And I drank some disgusting shit too. Vodka. Cheap whiskey. Soda mixed with Cachaça 51 . . . Back then, I used to think that was it, that that's what I wanted . . . Now I realize it was just a period in my life, one that started when my grandad died. So, anyway, the best thing you can do is talk to your brother, man, see what's going on with him. Cause a lot of the time we think the reason dudes get hooked is that they're weak and shit, but there's a story behind everything. There's always a story . . ."

Washington listened in silence. He thought about Wesley but also about a lot of things that had happened that past year. The police occupation had changed the lives of every resident in Rocinha, and even though people were always talking about these changes, telling stories, getting outraged, they seemed incapable of expressing how it made them feel, deep down, to be stuck in the middle of all that.

Douglas went back to the tattoo, grateful for the silence. For a while, he and Washington only said the bare minimum. The design began to take shape. The line that had annoyed the hell out of Douglas melted into the shading. He freestyled new ideas. He was so deep in the zone that he managed to stop thinking about the before and the after. Not even the final result really mattered, only the mountain, the clouds, the sun, and the steady buzz of that machine. Until, suddenly, his flow was interrupted by a knock on the door.

"Hey, fam! What's good?" Wesley appeared out of nowhere. His clothes were dirty, and by the look on his face, he hadn't slept in days. He also seemed skinnier. "Damn, DG. That piece is shaping up real nice."

He said a couple more things about the tattoo before explaining he'd just stopped by to shower and change before heading home. Dona Marli would lose her shit if she caught him looking like that. Washington was so relieved to see him that he gave himself permission to feel angry. At the same time, he had so much stuff to get off his chest, that he decided the best thing to do was stay quiet. Meanwhile, Douglas tried to ignore the interruption, hoping to get back in the groove.

Wesley grabbed a towel and hit the shower. Douglas went back to tattooing Washington, who felt his friend was being a bit heavy-handed; his shoulder was beginning to throb. He tried not to obsess over his brother and instead focused on the design on his shoulder. Even though he'd picked the tattoo very carefully, it was weird to think he'd carry it with him for the rest of his life, just like the scar on his knee, his first kiss, the first time he'd been stopped and frisked, the 2002 World Cup final.

"How's the arm? Wanna take a break?" Douglas said, even though he was the one with back pain.

"I'm all right. But sure, why not?"

They made the most of the pause to smoke a joint. While Douglas ground the weed, Washington studied his tattoo in the mirror. The first of many. He wanted a full sleeve with a ton of the city's landmarks: Carioca Aqueduct, Corcovado Mountain, Christ the Redeemer, Rocinha. Wesley walked out of the bathroom just as they were lighting up. He was looking a lot better.

"Y'all seriously gotta check out Praia do Meio. For real."

"The fuck is that?" The pain was making Washington more irritable.

"It's a beach, bro. A crazy, kickass beach. That's where I was, the beach. The place is insane. Way the fuck out there, too. You gotta go over this mountain, then hike a trail for like an hour plus, depending on how much gear you got. It's brutal, but once you're there, it's super chill. There's nothing around, feels like the city don't even exist. There's times you forget, like really forget, that the city's there at all." Wesley was rambling, and Washington wondered if it was his enthusiasm speaking or the cocaine. "There's these, like, locals, right? Dudes that've lived there for fucking ever and look after the place. Like, if you try and chop fresh wood for a fire or fuck with the drinking water, litter—those guys will crush you. I heard some crazy-ass stories about fights that went down there. But if you act right, respect the place and whatever, they leave you alone. Damn, you gotta see one of their houses, bro. It's made of wood, right smack in the middle of the forest, and cool as hell. Dude's real smart too. He's got a ton of books, surfboards, and stuff. So that's how he lives, right, just hanging on the beach, making his own schedule, reading books, catching waves, smoking weed. I mean, I couldn't stop wondering, why are we killing ourselves just to get by, bro? It's nothing but trouble, neguins living in shitty studios, no running water, power always cutting out, constant headaches . . ."

"Why didn't you say nothing, Wesley? You know how

bugged out Dona Marli's been these days . . . With the cops on the hill, she gets anxious as hell."

"It just happened, bro, I swear. I swung by my buddy's place in Dioneia. Him and his friends were about to leave—they had tents, food, the works. I didn't think twice, just followed. For real. I reckon that's what I needed, you know? Some peace and quiet. That's all. No motorbikes or cars, no neighbors or churches blasting music—nothing. Just the ocean and birdsong. And man were there a shit-ton of birds! Nights are crazy, too. The stars . . . I never seen so many stars in my life. It's like a whole other sky or something. The stars shine brighter. I mean it. We gotta go there together sometime."

Washington knew that working at the restaurant, with only Mondays and one Sunday off a month, meant he wasn't in any condition to be doing things like that, on a whim. Which made him even more pissed at Wesley; his brother didn't have a job anymore, didn't bring home any money, and he still got to have an awesome time while Washington busted ass around the clock just to be hard up again by the middle of the month.

After the joint, Douglas went back to the tattoo, wanting to give it one final push before calling it a day. They'd been at it for over four hours. Wesley watched for a while. Neither of them was up for talking, so he figured he should probably get a move on.

The short break had cooled Washington's blood. The pain was unbearable. He even suggested finishing up another day, but Douglas was dead set against it, as much as his back was killing him. The end was in sight. He wanted to take a photo of the finished piece. He could already picture the comments on Facebook, the likes, the DMs he'd get from people wanting to schedule a sesh.

They picked up the rhythm and only stopped now and then to smoke a cigarette. Washington would never forget the relief that washed over him when he heard Douglas turn off the machine. The only thing more memorable was the terror of it coming on again. He'd stopped checking out the design, couldn't for the life of him remember why he'd wanted it so bad, and even felt kind of pissed at Douglas for taking so long. But all of a sudden, as he screwed his eyes shut through the pain, the whirring of the machine stopped. He felt a paper towel clean off the blood on his shoulder and heard a satisfied chuckle.

"Check it out, my man!"

Washington opened his eyes and saw Pedra da Gávea. His shoulder was throbbing, but it was worth it.

He got up to shake Douglas's hand and thank him for his work, but Douglas went right in for a hug.

RIO—August 25, 2012

The second he got on that bus, Biel was sure shit would go south. He felt it in the pit of his stomach. That was his third time running contraband from Rocinha to its allies. He'd hauled that backpack to Vidigal, Chácara do Céu, and even farther afield, to Morro de São Carlos, in the city center. It was different this time, though. In his backpack were five kilos of coca base destined for Cruzada, the favela he'd grown up in.

After Biel had ditched his blacktop connects and quit selling on the beach, he'd made an honest effort to find employment. He never imagined it'd be so hard. His first foray into the labor market was as a builder's assistant on a construction site where Murilo worked. Things got off to a rough start: Biel wasn't built to carry heavy weight, didn't know how to mix mortar, and consistently got back late from lunch. The foreman fired him before the first week was up. Even with rent due and the fridge emptying out, Biel was relieved. As far as he was concerned, it made no sense to work all day long, come rain or come shine, just to take home a measly twenty-five reais.

The bus turned onto Avenida Niemeyer. Even though Biel had taken that road a million times, he was still awed by the beauty of the ocean, the color of the sky, the brilliance of the sun. The window was like a seascape. Maybe he was paying closer attention than usual because he knew that if he was busted with that backpack, he wouldn't get to see any views for a while. Just the thought made Biel shudder. As he tried to push that occupational hazard out of his mind, another, weirder notion began to occupy his thoughts. What if he was caught by the pigs and, instead of arresting him, they decided to lift the gear and sell it in another favela? Biel did the math. There were five kilos. Each kilo could be processed into another five, or a total of twenty-five keys of cocaine. Assuming each sold for eighty thousand, give or take, that meant he currently had 1.5 million reais just sitting in his backpack.

The bus approached VIPS motel, and Biel spotted the usual checkpoint. Two cops inspected a mototaxi while a third directed traffic. As much as Biel knew they never stopped buses around there, everything seemed so weird that he had something of a premonition. He saw the cops walk onto the bus and order the passengers to get out and line up next to the vehicle. Then he watched an officer open his backpack and flash that smile exclusive to pigs who knew they were about to fuck up someone's life. The premonition vanished, and he was back in his seat watching the cops pat down the mototaxi driver. The bus rolled through.

Once the checkpoint was behind them, Biel started asking himself where all the drug money ended up. One thing was for sure, the folks working the block saw almost none of it. The kids paid to keep their eyes peeled, risking prison time if they were caught, got max one hundred reais a week. A soldier with some standing in the narco-hierarchy—the kind on the front line of every shootout—who managed to get in with a heavy-weight gang made no more than five hundred a week. Dealers earned on commission, so depending on the boca, they could do all right for themselves, though not enough to justify getting charged with possession with intent. How much money went toward bribing cops? And what about the politicians, police officers, and military personnel who looked the other way when product was smuggled across international borders? Then there was the issue of having to pay the matuto, maintain the stash houses, and also figure out the logistics of keeping the shop open 24/7. All this made Biel feel insignificant in the grand scheme of things. They all were. Him, the soldiers, the pushers, the guys who weighed and wrapped the drugs, the ones who transported it in trucks, and all the people who pressed and mixed the substances on farms in Paraguay and Colombia.

Several passengers got on when the bus stopped at Vidigal. Biel could tell they were all residents, so he felt calm around them. Even though he hadn't spent a lot of time on that hill, he was drawn to the idea of living in Vidigal. Ever since they'd been forced to leave the place on Travessa Kátia, on account of their disagreement with Coroa, Biel had been trying to convince Douglas and Murilo to move there. The place had an awesome view, there were barely ever water shortages, and the cops were way less intense. The problem was that Vidigal was getting more expensive by the day. After the

UPP, hordes of gringos had descended upon the hill, leading to increases in rent and other amenities. In any event, with all three of them broke and struggling to make rent in Rocinha, a move to Vidigal was starting to feel like a distant dream.

The bus zipped past Leblon. Minutes later, Biel peeped Jardim de Alah, his destination. He stood up, then waited a bit longer before pulling the cord. If he got off at Posto 10, he could avoid the officers patrolling the canal.

He jumped off the bus and made his way toward Cruzada along Avenida Henrique Dumont. Ever since splitting with the playboy crowd, Biel had felt nervous near Ipanema. He was torn: at once anxious about being seen and recognized and scared of being totally ignored, of becoming a nobody again.

When he turned onto the street that crossed the canal, he saw his old middle school, Henrique Dodsworth. He thought back to the cigarettes he used to sneak during recess, playing soccer at Jardim de Alah, and his first time touching a girl's tits. He'd learned a lot at that school. It's where he realized that he could be different, a whole other person. The Leblon shopping mall had just opened behind Cruzada, and the gang used to go there all the time to ride up and down the escalators, drool over the sneakers they saw in shop windows and, obviously, get chased around by mall cops and glared at by customers and sales assistants. One day, for some reason he couldn't remember, Biel had gone to the mall on his own. It was a lot chiller. Even though he had on his school uniform, people let him wander around in peace. That was the day Biel understood that he was *special*.

Biel only had to walk into Cruzada to remember why he'd

left in the first place. The favela was exactly the same, except the buildings were older. Besides that, it was like the streets had been frozen in time: same rhythm, same smell, same vendors, and same trash bags sitting on the curb waiting for COMLURB to grace them with a collection. All that said, he had a sense of familiarity here that he'd never experienced anywhere else. It was so strong Biel got weirded out by the fact that no one said hello, even when he hadn't been there in months. The faces he recognized all turned the other way. The worst part was he couldn't tell if they'd forgotten him or if they were just ignoring him.

He walked into the building where the boca used to be. There was no one there, just two kids kicking a ball around. The backpack felt heavier and heavier, and Biel couldn't wait to deliver the package. He made up his mind right then and there: He was never taking on another job like that one for a measly two hundred reais. Not when the thing he was putting on the line was his own freedom.

"Yo, you lost or something?" one of the kids asked Biel. He'd never seen either of them.

"I think I'm in the wrong building. They all look the fucking same." Biel sweated all the way back to the entrance.

"What you're looking for isn't here anymore, menó. It's in building 6 now." The kids laughed, then went back to playing ball.

Biel had spent most of his life in building 6. It was where he took his first steps, spoke his first swear words. He could already see the cracks, the flaked paint, the stairwell, the walls covered in marker graffiti. Biel hadn't visited his mom in close to a year. Sometimes, he got up in his head about it;

at the end of the day, no one lives forever. But once his mom had found God and started living by the fire of Christ, things between them had gotten impossible. The tipping point was when she had a pastor and another dozen gospel workers pray for him early one Monday morning. As if that wasn't enough, she started getting on his case about going to AA. That's when Biel, who at the time only dabbled in weed, realized he'd be better off finding a place of his own.

He walked through the front gate and saw three guys sitting in school chairs. A customer had just bought something from one of them. All three were really young, and Biel had the feeling he remembered seeing them running around in the street as kids. The sound of people on the stairs got Biel worrying about what would happen if his mom walked past there as he was making his delivery. He went up to them, holding fast to the relief he knew he would feel when he handed over that backpack. But before he could reach the boca, he heard footsteps behind him. By the look of terror on the kids' faces, it could only be five-o.

One of the kids made a run for it and started scrambling over the wall to the other building.

"Stop, or I'll shoot!" a cop yelled. But the kid kept on climbing, shielded by the knowledge that, even though Cruzada was a favela, it was sandwiched between Leblon and Ipanema, and nobody wanted to scare the shoppers in the mall behind them with the sound of gunfire.

Biel heard the cops racing toward the kids and stood frozen in place. They caught two out of the three. Biel had the urge to run, but he couldn't seem to move.

"What the fuck you looking at? Beat it!" one of the cops
shouted at him while handcuffing the kids.

Dazed, Biel began walking away but then balked at the
sight of a cruiser and turned back toward the stairs. As he
took the steps one by one, never looking back, his backpack
felt heavy as lead. When he reached the seventh and final
floor, he prayed to God that his mom was home.

RIO—September 8, 2012

Wesley had been meaning to roll through the Rua 2 base for
a while. A buddy of his from school, a guy they called PhD,
was working as a soldier in the organization and kept writing him on Facebook, saying to come through, that it'd be lit.
But something always got in the way. The truth is, Wesley *did*
want to link up with his friend, but he also felt kind of lazy
about it. Plus, the thought of going there wigged him out.
These days, Rua 2 was another Gaza Strip, a place where bullets flew at all hours of the night and day.

Wesley had woken up with a raging hangover and no
money in his pocket to cop a joint. Time to take his friend
up on his invitation. It was around three in the afternoon
when he managed to coax himself out of bed. He walked
down Cachopa under the sun, still kind of treading water,
legs soft. The night before, they'd drunk vodka and done several rails each. Things were starting to come back to him—
with such vengeance that he even relived the dread he'd felt

when they realized they were out of blow. He'd actually considered searching his house for something to sell in Valão, the junkies' open market. The thought filled him with shame. It wasn't the first time Wesley was floored by the power that a small pile of dust, a scrap of nothing, could have over him. For a while now, he'd been telling himself he'd never fuck with that stuff again, only to go off the deep end the next chance he got.

Halfway there, Wesley began to regret leaving the house. He still had a long walk ahead of him, stairs to take up and down, and his head felt heavier by the minute. He should've just knocked on the neighbors' door, asked if they had any weed to spare, given that Washington was at work and hadn't left a shred of grass behind. The trouble with the neighbors was that their situation was so out of whack they probably would've gone with him to Rua 2 as well, looking to leech off the same joint.

Wesley stopped at a boteco for a baile cigarette. The way he saw it, the trick was to show up at the base with a smoke behind his ear, then light it the second somebody fired up a joint. If he passed around his cig, folks might be more inclined to share with him when they burned a fatty later. He asked for a glass of water and was relieved to see the vendor take a bottle out of the fridge instead of running the tap. Wesley took the glass from her and knocked the whole thing back in one go. The water was so cold, he felt this weird pressure on the left side of his brain. It was just what he needed.

"Another?" the woman asked, bottle still open.

Wesley nodded and once again downed the whole thing in one gulp.

"I'm sweating buckets in here. I can't even imagine what summer will be like."

"This heat's no joke. But the thing that's killing me today is this hangover. It's like I can't stay hydrated." Wesley handed back the glass, then tucked the cigarette behind his ear.

"Heavens! See, that's why I don't drink."

"And how do you manage with all the juicers who come by here every day?"

"Ay, kid. Since my husband died, I'm the one who looks after this place. The trick is to keep your ears open. That way shit comes in one ear and goes straight out the other. The only thing I have to stay on top of is the bills. Everything else is noise."

"Right on, tia . . ."

Wesley wondered how many times he'd been the drunk douchebag everybody crossed the street to avoid. He pictured junked-up guys, all twitchy and crazy-eyed, seeing shit that wasn't there.

"God be with you!" she called out before putting the water bottle back in the fridge.

The base wasn't too far now, and Wesley had finally started feeling like the walk was doing him some good, like he was sweating out the toxins. But he still couldn't shake the sadness. And he wouldn't, not for a while. After a night on the slopes, depression was practically a guarantee. Not that life needed any chemical assistance to bum a guy out. But the sadness of a comedown was different. Wesley felt it somewhere else, right in the pit of his stomach. Unlike life's other sorrows, this one was paralyzing; it made him want to stay in bed forever and took his mind to a bunch of weird places. That's why Wesley had pushed himself to go out that afternoon. Not only for the weed but so he could talk with other people, see things in a new light, hear stories from the other neck of the favela.

On the last stretch, Wesley peeped some duty boots pounding the steps. His first impulse was to do a one-eighty, avoid an encounter. The way things were on the hill those days, he knew it was best not to turn his back on police. He kept walking, head down, avoiding eye contact. In his mind, he was already running through the script of their interaction—it always went the same way.

"Stop right there."

Wesley stopped in front of the cops. There were five total: the three who'd approached him and two more who were hovering behind, all packing the same kind of heat.

"Where do you live?"

"Cachopa, officer."

"Then what the hell you doing down here?"

The cops always got riled up when they found Rocinha residents outside their own neighborhoods. Which is another thing that annoyed the hell out of Wesley. It made him want to ask those cops where *they* lived. He bet it was a lot farther than Cachopa.

"I'm gonna see my girl," was the most original excuse he could come up with.

"Does she live near here?"

"Around the corner," Wesley said, only to immediately regret it.

"All right, let's get going then." The cop pointed the way with his rifle.

Wesley started walking toward a house farther up. He didn't have a clue who lived there; he'd just have to knock on the door and hope for the best. He couldn't stall, either. If folks saw him spending too much time with a bunch of cops, they might peg him as a snitch. So he just matched the officers' stride and made for a house right in that alley.

"Hold up . . . Let the kid see his girl," said one of the cops farther back. By the way the man talked, Wesley figured he must be higher up in the chain of command.

"Got any drugs on you?"

"Nuh-uh, officer." Wesley was relieved to see their interaction go back to the usual script.

"And if I find something . . . ?"

"You won't, officer." After a year of being stopped all the time, Wesley had learned it was best to keep things short.

One of the cops frisked him. He pulled Wesley's ID out of his pocket and studied it for a while with glazed eyes. Before releasing him, the cop grabbed the cigarette tucked behind Wesley's ear.

"You shouldn't smoke this shit. It'll kill you," he said, then slid a lighter out of his pocket and lit the baile cigarette. The scent of cinnamon washed over the alley.

By the time Wesley reached the boca, his heart was going a mile a minute. He found his buddy PhD sitting in a chair, cradling his machine gun, not showing a care in the world.

"There's cops round the corner. I just got stopped," Wesley blurted out.

"Relax, menó. They're not gonna try nothing."

As PhD explained the agreement between the organization and the police, Wesley stared at him, trying to catch a glimpse of the boy he'd known in school. PhD used to be one of the quietest kids in class—sitting front row, always doing his homework, that kind of thing. Out of everyone Wesley had been to school with, PhD was the last person he'd thought would wind up in the trade.

"Anyway, it's been super chill these past three days. The pigs are on good behavior. Orders from up top," PhD said, rounding off his explanation. Then he introduced Wesley to the rest of the crew: four more soldiers, one dealer, and a half-dozen sympathizers. An old Ja Rule tune played on the speakers.

It wasn't long before somebody broke out a joint. The first smoke of the day is always special, particularly when you wake up on the wrong side of the bed. Wesley inhaled with relish. Even though the weed was nothing to write home about, his mind and body mellowed after a few drags. Right then, everything felt completely chill. Only after passing the joint did he start paying attention to the conversation around him.

"Nah, man, my other sister, Patrícia, the one that lives in bumfuck Padre Miguel, right by the OG favela, Vintém. The bike was hers. So, anyway, she let one of our uncles borrow it. My pops's whole family still lives round those parts. So my uncle borrows the bike, all good. Except one day he goes to the grocery store, locks it up outside, and when he gets back, wham, it's gone. The place is right near Vintém—folks should know better. But there's a ton of crackheads in the area, and it's hard to keep those guys in check. Anyway. So my uncle talks to a buddy of his. Dude's not in the trade or nothing, but he's from there, born and raised, an old head, friendly with a lot of the players. So this dude sends his guys after the bike. Like, everybody. He tells them: Bike's yellow, yada yada, go find it. The bike turns up not even three hours later. My uncle and his friend head over there to check it out. The thing's sitting in a junk shop in the favela. The owner says to them: Listen, a crackhead sold it to me, claimed it was his and the rest, I paid fifty for the thing. Turns out he wants his money back. The guys who'd gone there to track down the bike tell my uncle he should pay the owner half so he doesn't totally lose out, right? Also, that way the dude'll think twice before buying stolen shit without asking questions. Cool, so my uncle hands over the money, grabs the bike, and bounces. Except, as they're headed back, he turns to his buddy and says: Pô, I know this bike's yellow and all, it's practically the same as mine, but, if I'm honest, I don't think it belongs to me. Then his buddy says: C'mon, neguim, I've done my part. I'm not heading back there and telling the guys it's not your bike, after all the effort they went to. Just hold on to it. And my uncle doesn't know what to do, right? So his buddy says: Hold on to the bike but don't forget to throw on another coat of paint, cause if the real owner shows up and knocks you black and blue, you'll know why."

The kid finished his anecdote, and everybody stared at him like the story needed an ending.

"Shit, man, your uncle paid to fucking steal!" the dealer said, and everybody burst out laughing.

Things were like that, with everybody kicking back and taking it easy, when Wesley saw a kid dash inside and announce that the cops were coming their way. Everybody at the base looked at each other, unsure what to do.

"Let's head up. Orders are not to make trouble," one of the soldiers finally declared. The whole crew did as he said and made for the alley. Wesley hung back. The last thing he wanted was to bump into those cops again.

As they made their way up, people kept talking about how the cops were just messing with them, that nothing was going to happen. Wesley listened but couldn't help thinking that even though *they* could guarantee they wouldn't start anything, who was to say the cops would keep their cool? And there he was, right in the eye of the shitstorm, in the wrong place at the wrong time, all because he smoked weed.

It wasn't long before the crew came across other soldiers. They explained the situation, then continued uphill together. The news that the cops were still on their way reached them by phone and walkie-talkie. The crew plodded up the steps with their rifles, joking around, swapping stories from the last few days. As far as Wesley was concerned, all that laughter was just nerves, though they'd never own up to it. Suddenly, he had the sinking feeling something terrible was about to happen.

The stress brought back the hangover, the weed high, the exhaustion, all of it. As he walked, his vision seemed crystal-clear. He considered ditching the crew and dipping into another alleyway but worried the cops had called for backup. As terrified as he was of sticking around, he also, in a way, felt safer around those players. The farther up they got, the more people joined them, forming a longer and longer line in the alley. Every resident who passed them was startled by what they saw.

As much as he wanted to, Wesley didn't have the courage to bail. He wound up walking with them until Rua 1, where 157's crew was posted. Now that shit was no joke. There were like forty-plus armed men. Machine guns, pistols, grenades. Rifles everywhere you looked, some so new the sun bounced right off them. Counting the guys who'd come up from Rua 2, there were more than sixty players standing in the street. There were only three or four other civilians besides Wesley. Even around all those people, he couldn't not feel nervous. Wesley was dying to dip out, but first he had to see what the deal was with the cops.

The Rua 2 crew explained why they'd had to head up the hill and made a point of mentioning they were keeping their end of the bargain with the police. Wesley could already picture himself telling this story when he got home: how he'd watched the two gangs talking, seen Rogério 157 in the flesh, for the first time since his release from prison. And that he'd heard from 157's own mouth that they should sit tight. If the pigs came up, they'd show them.

After 157 gave that order, everybody stared down the hill. They didn't raise their weapons but also made no effort to hide them. Their eyes were all trained on the same alley, the one the cops were expected to come out of. Wesley felt time stop. His heart pounded in his chest. The crew stood like that for a few minutes, tense, but in the end the police didn't have the guts to show their faces.

RIO—September 24, 2012

Since leaving the military, Murilo had taken any job that came his way. No matter the headache, he welcomed it with open arms. Now and then he got a gig on a building site for a week or two, but most of the time he carried construction material, moved furniture, or unloaded crates of beer at botecos. His family was always on his case about him finding steady work; he couldn't go on like that forever, they said, without any security or paid leave. Plus, the manual labor could really mess up his back. He always agreed with them and pretended he had an interview lined up, then went back to his bullshit. The truth was that, barring the strain on his body, he enjoyed not having a fixed schedule or anyone to report to. Plus, he liked that some gigs came with unexpected surprises.

That day, Murilo had a job cleaning out a house filled wall to wall with junk. The owner, an old head who'd lived in there all his life, had a reputation as a hoarder. When Murilo walked through the front door and clocked all the stuff strewn on the floor, hanging on walls, and piled in corners, he saw for himself that the old man's reputation was well-deserved. Also, that he would need backup. So he went to find it at home.

"Are you outta your mind? On Ladeira da Cachopa, in this heat?! Fuck no." Biel was offended that Murilo had woken him up for something so stupid.

"Plus, it's right next to the cops. You ask too much, man." From Murilo's description, Douglas had worked out the house was right next to Mestre's old place, which had been turned into the UPP's headquarters in Rocinha. There were dozens of stories about people who'd been dragged there to get the living shit kicked out of them. Apparently, the story about the guy from Vila Verde who had a carrot shoved up his ass had taken place right there.

But Murilo was more annoyed than the two of them together. Who did they think they were, picking and choosing what kind of work they took on? He didn't hold back: he wasn't anybody's dad to be footing the rent and the bills, he said. They'd been having that argument a lot, ever since all three had quit their jobs. It was stressful being broke. Murilo often thought about jumping ship and finding a place of his own where he wouldn't have to worry about the challenges of cohabitation.

Douglas and Biel were a lot more committed to staying put. Biel, for one, didn't have the same work ethic as Murilo and knew he couldn't afford to live alone. Besides, he liked having roommates and hated the thought of an empty house. Douglas, on the other hand, did eventually want his own place, once he could afford it. But the time wasn't right, he knew that. First off, he didn't want another nine-to-five, not when he was so close to making a living from ink. The week before, he'd started tattooing at a new parlor in Valão. It was early days, so they didn't have a lot of business yet, and Douglas still hadn't gotten any commissions. But it was only a matter of time.

In the end, Douglas and Biel agreed to help. Besides getting an increasingly agitated Murilo to cool off, it was also a way for them to pocket some cash. The month was close to ending, and they needed to find a way to pay the rent. They walked down their street, then back up another hill.

It became clear when they got to the house that the situation was a lot worse than Murilo had let on. On top of the piles and piles of junk, the whole house stank of mildew, and every surface was covered in dust.

They gazed around at the furniture and objects, unsure where to begin. Douglas clocked several stacks of VHS tapes on a TV stand, so many he couldn't even make out the VCR. There were recordings of soccer matches, TV shows, random movies, Carnaval parades, all identifiable by handwritten labels.

"How'd the old man die, anyway?" Douglas asked, still sorting through the tapes.

"I bet the smell killed him," Biel said, lighting a cigarette. It was one of three loosies they'd bought on the walk up. They were meant to last them all day.

"All right, let's let grandpa rest in peace and get on with it. There's still a ton of shit to get through."

The house had two stories and a terrace that was also full

of junk. Murilo suggested they start there and work their way down to the first floor, but Biel countered that it made more sense to start at the bottom: that way, if they had to move something big downstairs, the path would be clear. Murilo and Douglas agreed with him. Thankfully, they had a hand truck to help with the heavier stuff, and several 15-gallon garbage bags.

"His daughter said it's all trash, that she came by earlier this week and took what she wanted."

They began filling garbage bags with the dead man's stuff but kept getting sidetracked. Biel couldn't tear himself away from a collection of branded yo-yos he'd found in the kitchen—Coca-Cola, Sprite, Fanta, all in perfect condition, as if no one had ever played with them.

"You know, we could make some money off these."

Murilo wore two hats that day: that of manual laborer and manager. Every new find seemed to slow his co-workers down, which meant having to stay on top of them. Douglas was intent on piecing together the man's life through the stuff he'd left behind: a collection of beer festival mugs, a stuffed piranha with bared teeth, a berimbau and other capoeira gear, a bag of old cameras.

It took them two hours just to finish the ground floor. First, they had to shove everything in bags. Then, they had to carry them downhill, only to hike back up again under the beating sun. Their only consolation was walking past the UPP headquarters and seeing the cops melting in their uniforms. Once they were done with the ground floor, they took a snack break: bread with mortadella and some sodas.

They went upstairs, digestif at the ready. While they rummaged through the dead man's junk, they blazed up. Murilo was really impressed by a huge trunk in the bedroom filled with Carnaval costumes.

"Dude must've been *wild*."

"I bet he sold some stuff at the flea market."

"The guy clearly couldn't move shit. The stock's overflowing!"

As they joked around, Murilo found a huge, heavy-duty contractor bag sitting on top of a wardrobe. He tried to grab it and nearly fell off the chair. It was a two-person job, so he called over Douglas.

"The fuck is that?" Biel asked when he saw them with the bag.

Inside were hundreds of photos—some big, some small, some 3x4 cm, some in viewfinders. They dove into the bag, hoping to track down a picture of the man of the house, to unearth a clue as to the life he'd left behind.

To their surprise, none of the photos were of his family or life. At first, there didn't seem to be a throughline. There were pictures of bailes and parties, of building sites, partially built houses, samba school rehearsals, the Day of Saint Cosmas and Damian. Douglas was the one who realized what all those photographs had in common: Rocinha.

This piqued their interest even more, to the point that Murilo didn't complain when they dumped the bag of photos on the floor. The pictures showed different stages of an ever-changing Rocinha. Biel noticed some had dates scribbled on the back, and they started hunting for those: 1987, 1994, 1965, 2002. The oldest ones dated to the 1950s and showed a handful of houses scattered across a huge, beautiful green hill.

"I guess now we know what killed the old man," Biel said. Murilo and Douglas didn't get it. "Disgust! Picture living your whole life here only to wind up with cops for neighbors."

"Say less, neguim. If he took these photos himself, then the man is OG Rocinha."

"The kind of dude that's always saying: When I moved here, there was nothing, just fields and trees." Biel loved it when old heads came out with that sort of thing.

"I wonder if he moved here before this place even had a name." Murilo had in mind a story he'd heard about the origin of the name Rocinha.

"What was it called before?" Biel asked, studying one of the oldest photos they'd found, a black-and-white print of a white chapel surrounded by vegetation.

"Fuck knows, man. But word is that, like, back in the day, all this was farmland. Tomato, corn, hell knows what else they grew up here. Anyway, apparently they sold their crops at a market in Gávea, and the stuff was out of this world, high fucking caliber. So, folks at the market would ask: Where'd all this awesome fruit and veg come from? Or whatever. And the guys would answer that it came from their farm, their *rocinha* up on the hill. And the name stuck. Rocinha."

"Pretty sure that shit you just said goes way the hell back, neguim." Douglas clearly remembered his history teacher telling them about the foundation and growth of Rocinha over the last century. "Like, that stuff about the market, about there being a farm up here, was early, early days, if I'm not wrong."

"You mean this favela used to be one big-ass farm?"

"Nah, I don't think so. There was more than one farm.

Vila Laboriaux was a farm too, though I don't know if it was around at the same time. All I know is that the dude who owned it was French, which is why it's called that. Same goes for Portão Vermelho. I bet there was a ton of farms up here." Douglas liked thinking about how different parts of Rocinha had gotten their names.

They could have spent all day poring over those photographs. But Murilo wanted to get paid ASAP so he could cop a pack of cigarettes, have a decent meal for dinner. He put his managerial hat back on and told the guys to get to work.

"What about the photos?" Douglas asked, gingerly placing the albums back in the bag.

"Fuck knows. Dump them or give them to his daughter . . . ?"

Judging by the state of the house, Douglas got the sense that giving those pictures to the family would be as good as throwing them in the trash. As he put the photographs away, he felt strongly that he couldn't let that happen.

"I'll keep them."

Murilo and Biel had also considered taking the photos. But the size of the bag and all the dust had dissuaded them. They figured that, at most, they could take some of the older pictures with them.

"These photos are Rocinha's *history*. We gotta do something with them. I don't know what. Something."

Now that the fate of the pictures had been decided, they went back to cleaning the house. The hours they'd spent among those objects had made the three feel close to the deceased. Maybe that's why they finished cleaning the room in silence. Out of respect for those stories.

By the time they made it to the terrace, it was past four in the afternoon. Not one of them was surprised by the piles of crates, the stacks of cardboard and Styrofoam boxes. Some were filled with records, others with books, but most held a random assortment of things. The biggest surprise of the day went to Murilo. There, in a corner of the terrace, between a beer cooler and a bicycle frame, he found a surfboard.

He walked up to the board, curious but not particularly hopeful. The three keels were perfectly aligned, and the only ding had been fixed with Silver Tape. It was a great size too, on the larger end, nearly a longboard, perfect for someone who hadn't gotten wet in years.

He thought back to his conversation with the dead man's daughter, to how she said everything, every last thing, could be thrown away. He decided to keep the surfboard. His heart raced. He pictured himself in the ocean, tasted the salt on his lips . . . Murilo tried his best to get back to work but couldn't.

"Y'all wanna finish up tomorrow?"

Douglas and Biel didn't understand. Tired as they were, they didn't want to stop. Murilo had been so adamant about getting it all done in one day that the two had become attached to the idea of being paid that evening. They wanted to get some cigarettes as well. And weed, which they were clean out of.

Murilo tried to come up with some excuse, like saying his back hurt. But if he wanted to do what he had in mind, he needed to be truthful. He told his friends that the reason he wanted to finish up tomorrow is that he had to get to the beach. Biel and Douglas thought he was kidding, but Murilo was dead serious. Ever since leaving the Army, he'd wanted to buy a surfboard, but money seemed to burn a hole in his pocket. Most of the time, he couldn't even afford the essentials.

For the first time ever, he told his friends why he'd resigned from the Army. They listened in shock, feeling both sorry for Murilo and suspicious of him. At the same time, they were confused. How exactly was that connected to the beach and the surfboard?

"I need to do my own thing again. I lost years of my life to that place. Time to go after what's mine."

In the end, they agreed to finish up the next day. The plan was to hit the beach, then swing by the woman's house and ask her to front them a portion of the payment. Murilo tucked the surfboard under his arm, and the three of them set off.

As they were heading down the main street, the weather began to turn. Heavy clouds rolled into the sky. Douglas wanted to go back home, but Murilo's determination to see things through kept him going. Besides, Biel and Douglas wanted to see if Murilo was any good, or if all that surf talk was just hot air.

By the time they reached São Conrado, there was no one left in the water. The few people still on the beach were getting ready to leave. They all turned to look at the trio when they walked onto the sand, wondering why they were there. The three friends remarked on the state of the ocean: the swell was weak.

"Safe to say you won't be needing a lifeguard!" Biel joked.

Murilo didn't stretch, his body warmed up from moving things around all day. He headed straight for the water. Douglas and Biel sat in a spot under the boardwalk, on the lookout for rain. Murilo stood at the water's edge. It was colder than he'd expected. Instead of taking it slow, he waded right in. Rain started falling. Big, fat drops warmer than the ocean.

He positioned the surfboard on the water. Only then did he realize he didn't have a strap or any paraffin. *What was he trying to prove, anyway?* he wondered. It didn't matter. He pushed his board through the water until it was waist-high, then mounted it. The waves seemed bigger from that angle. He started paddling. The first wave came, and he paddled over it. Then the second wave, and his only option was to nosedive. He did this without thinking, even though it'd been years. He sank the tip of the board into the water with his arms and knees, then dipped into the wave. His whole body was wet now. The rest of the set rolled in. Murilo nosedived into two more waves before finally breaking through the surf.

RIO—October 9, 2012

"What the hell is that shit on your nose?"

Wesley was startled awake by fingers touching his nostrils. He leaped off the sofa and recognized his mother, who was dressed for work. For some reason, he'd been sleeping in the living room. That much was clear, though he still couldn't process what was going on around him.

"What's up, Ma?"

Dona Marli walked up to her son and held his chin in her hand, lifting it so she could take a good, hard look inside his nose.

"Are you doing cocaine, Wesley?" she yelled. He didn't answer. "What I wanna know is where you're getting money for this crap when you're not contributing at home. Listen, son, I told you once, I told you a million times. If you got yourself mixed up in something, if you've started stealing or whatever to bank this stupid vice, then let me be clear: I swear to God, the day they call me from the police station, I am done. I'm not waiting in no line to visit you in prison. I'm not bringing you no cigarettes. I'm not doing anything, understand? If you get picked up, you're on your own."

Wesley was so out of it, he could barely react. He had no idea what to say to get his mother to calm down or to start a conversation. His throat was dry, his nose on the verge of leaking.

"C'mon, Ma, don't act crazy. I swear I'm not doing coke." Wesley lowered his head and tried to sniffle as discreetly as possible.

"Now I get why you don't chip in, why you never finished driver's ed . . . You're throwing it all away on this shit."

Wesley finally snapped out of it. He got the urge to tell his mom that the reason he was always broke was that he'd been born poor, was still poor, and would die poor. That most of the money he made gigging did make it back to the house. And that he could only afford to do coke when others contributed or somebody else spotted him. If he said that, though, he'd not only have to face the humiliation of hearing himself speak those words aloud, but he'd also be contradicting the lie he'd just told her.

"While your brother and me work our asses off . . . That's why people like us never win. There's always somebody dragging us down."

Washington walked into the living room. He looked like he'd just woken up, probably on account of the shouting. At the sound of his name, Wesley saw what seemed like a smug grin flit across Washington's face, and it made him angry as hell.

"You really wanna know, Ma? I *am* snorting coke. And I fucking love it. But before you start kissing Washington's feet, why don't you ask him who introduced me to this shit in the first place?"

Dona Marli turned to her eldest son, at a loss for words.

"The fuck you just say?!" Washington threw himself at Wesley with his fists, but before he could get a punch in, Wesley tackled him to the ground. The two started rolling around the floor, though without landing any blows.

"Stop! Both of you, stop it!" Dona Marli got between her two boys and broke up the fight.

The three sat in the living room in silence, the only sound their heavy breathing.

"I'm running late," Dona Marli said, fixing her hair as if she'd been the one rolling on the floor. "Make good choices, you two."

The brothers didn't move. Instead of staring at the floor as they had when their mother was home, they studied each other as if trying to determine whether or not they were still fighting. Washington saw his brother's face clearly then, and he looked terrible. Wesley moved his eyes back down to the floor, possibly cowed by his brother's gaze.

As Washington lay on the living room sofa, he could hear Wesley spitting up in the sink. No matter how angry he was at his brother for ratting him out, he needed to face the facts. When all was said and done, his brother hadn't lied. A few minutes later, Wesley walked out of the bathroom and toward his bedroom.

"Smoke?" Washington called out from the sofa.

He grabbed some weed from his bedroom, then joined

Wesley again in the living room. Rocinha grass was so dry those days he didn't even have to use the grinder, the stuff came apart in his hands. As Washington sprinkled the weed over the rolling papers, there was a sharp scent of ammonia.

"I'm dying for some good grass, this schwag is depressing as hell . . . But it's been rough not finding the time to go on a mission."

Washington was the only person who hadn't believed Wesley when he said the cops had busted him on his mission to Jacarezinho. He'd known from the jump that it was a lie but decided to keep quiet because it didn't feel right to bad-mouth his brother. Still, after that, he never gave Wesley money again, and Wesley stopped offering to run missions for them, even with all his spare time. Washington sealed the joint, then lit up.

"Tat's looking pretty dope," Wesley said.

"Douglas is a pro. He's killing it."

The two brothers seemed to have agreed not to mention their recent fight.

"I really like that you got Pedra da Gávea. I'm always thinking about how with, like, tattoos, you gotta really know for sure what you want. Cause that shit lasts forever." Wesley had been running through an apology in his head ever since they'd sat down to smoke. He felt bad about grassing on his brother.

"How are you, man?" Washington took a few more drags before passing the joint. "Been a while since we, like, really talked."

Wesley hadn't expected the conversation to take that turn. But on top of being surprised, he was also touched by the sincerity of Washington's question. He tried to put into words the chaos in his mind. The police occupation in Rocinha, all the times he'd been stopped and frisked, the cocaine, the way he'd left his job from one day to the next, the fact that he had no prospects, no money, no cigarettes. Busting ass every day just to stay afloat, and how the rationale behind this somehow made the future seem even smaller.

"You know I can help you, right, bro? But you gotta want it." Hearing those words made Wesley realize just how far apart they'd grown lately.

"Thing is, I do, menó. I know exactly what needs to be done. I just can't. Before I realize, I'm like right back in the hole again, with no idea how I got there. And my head, I can't explain it. It's like my head wants out. I keep seeing these weird things, images of stuff that already happened, that crop up again and again, out of nowhere, you know? I barely slept last night, bro. Got home early, you were already down for the count. I only came here and lay on the sofa cause, like, I guess I needed to be alone or something. Yesterday, some buddies and me carried a kilo of rock, and I made fucking pennies. Bro, I walked from here all the way to Chácara do Céu just to get hold of weed, cause folks were saying there were fat sacks of grass down there. I swear, menó, I didn't mean for any of it to happen. I just wanted some good weed. The stuff they're slinging up here is so shitty it pisses me off. You know how it is. But then, I bumped into No Arms. Bro, I see that dude every time I'm in Chácara. He's always kicking it with some neguim or other. Those two motherfuckers love doing lines, like you wouldn't believe. Then No Arms—and when I say *no arms*, I mean *zero arms*, no right arm, no left, nothing. Anyway, No Arms was alone yesterday. I walked past him on my way to the boca, no sign of the neguim that usually hangs with him. So, anyway, I had some weed in my pocket, and I was headed toward Vidigal—I'd even set aside two bucks for the van ride—when No Arms says to me: Hey, wanna do some rails? I brush him off and keep walking, but he comes after me and starts going on about how his social security's just come through, and he's got a nice chunk of change sitting in his account, except his buddy's at the hospital after getting into a motorcycle accident, and he can't access the money without his help, let alone cut lines, roll a straw. That dude was his literal right hand, and he was fucked cause it's not like he can trust any old fool with his debit card. So I tell him he doesn't know me either, that I *am* any old fool, but then he says the reason he trusts me is that he doesn't know me, that all the fiends who hang around the boca are favela fuckups. I don't know how he does it, but I go with him, menó. I go over to his house and grab his Caixa Econômica debit card from a drawer he showed me. Then we head toward Leblon looking to hit a 24Horas ATM. Bro, I only really clocked the name on the card when I slid it into the machine: Maria Aparecida something something. I started tripping but stayed quiet. There are three hundred reais in the account. He asks me to withdraw the whole amount, then we rush back to Chácara. On the way, I keep telling myself I can just dip out. It's not like No Arms could do anything about it anyway. Instead, I go with him to the boca, and we cop four eight-balls. The sacks are fat. I guess it must've been a new stash. We're feeling pumped, so we head down to the beach, where it's quieter at night. But it's windy as hell, right, so next thing we know we're hiking up the steps, back to where we'd started, then even farther up, to this spot in bumfuck Chácara that No Arms claims is really chill. By the time we get there, I'm beyond ready to leave. Instead, I start cutting lines. We're doing a ton of rails, one after the other, for real, it isn't long before the first eight-ball is gone. No Arms is geeked and running his mouth, even starts telling me the story of how he lost both his arms. Apparently, he'd been trying to untangle a kite from a power line and got electrocuted. Claims he's lucky he didn't die. He was still a kid back then, played a lot of ball. Apparently, he was on Fluminense's roster. That's what he said to me anyway, and I can't know if it's true or not cause there's loads of other stuff he's said that I know for a fact is bullshit. Dude's pathological. Anyway, I get in this really weird mood, and honest to God, while I'm cutting lines and holding the straw for No Arms, I can't get Maria Aparecida outta my head. Like, is she his mom, his sister? But listen, whatever this guy needs, somebody's gotta do it for him, right? Whether it's eating food, drinking water, wiping his goddamn ass. So this needy motherfucker goes and swipes a person's entire savings only to, what, snort the whole thing in a goddamn back alley? Shit, menó, I started getting so mad, just looking at him made me feel, like, disgusted, you know? I couldn't take it anymore, so I just fucking left. I was still wired but I needed to get outta there before I started throwing hands at him, cause I swear I was seconds from doing that, for real. Then he got all pissed off and started cussing me out, accusing me of stealing his drugs, so I dropped the capsules on the ground, and kept walking. But when I got home, I couldn't sleep, bro. I just couldn't get that shit outta my head."

Wesley relit the roach between his fingers and took another pull before passing it on. Washington could tell he was trying really hard not to cry and thought back to when his brother was a little kid and how he used to always pull the same face when he was choking back tears. That picture of his brother as a boy started mixing with the picture of Wesley snorting powder with some armless dude in a dark, dingy corner of Chácara do Céu.

"I'm so sorry, man. I never should've offered you this shit in the first place," Washington mumbled after a few minutes of silence.

"It's all right, menó."

Washington realized then that the best thing he could do for his brother was help take his mind off matters. So he broke out one joint and then another, and another, and even though the weed was of dubious quality, after a while, the two of them were stoned enough that they could finally relax and chop it up about anything. It wasn't long before they were laughing like they could only laugh with each other, about the stories they'd built together throughout the course of their lives.

Washington was about to roll another joint when he noticed the time and saw that he was late for work. He threw on some clothes, splashed water on his face, and brushed his teeth. Even running behind schedule, he made a point of giving Wesley a long hug, something they hadn't done in a while.

As he walked downhill, Washington tried to come up with some excuse for his tardiness. But he couldn't get his brother out of his head. He needed to do something to help

Wesley out of that downward spiral. He pictured him in cracôlandia and thought of how dangerous it was to be in the wrong place at the wrong time. How many people had gone down for some shit like that? No, Washington would do something. It was settled: as soon as a position opened up at the restaurant, he'd get his brother a job. He'd been there a year, his word meant something now. Wesley was a hard worker—things would pan out.

Washington was in the small alley that led to Casa da Paz, when some guy flew past him and almost knocked him over. He even turned around to cuss him out. But before he could say anything, his eyes took in the machine pistol in the man's left hand. Only when Washington stepped out of the alley did it occur to him he might be walking right into the police. He heard the gunfire, milliseconds before hitting the ground.

RIO—October 16, 2012

"On this day, as hope mixes with sorrow and we come together to honor those whom we have loved and lost, the resurrection of Jesus Christ is a beacon of light for our faith in eternal life."

The Our Lady of Good Voyage parish was packed for the seventh-day service. There were friends and family from Cachopa but also people who'd come from other areas of Rocinha after hearing about Washington's case on social media. Almost everyone from Cachopa was wearing a T-shirt with a photograph of Washington on Pedra da Gávea and the words "Rest in Power" printed below it. Some of the unfamiliar faces wore white T-shirts that said: ROCINHA WANTS PEACE.

"We are gathered here today to remember our brothers, sisters, and children, whom we hope and believe to be with God. In Our Lord Jesus Christ lies the assurance that, as we live and work to build His Kingdom on Earth, we shall also be granted the eternal inheritance."

Dona Marli settled into the front row of the church. As she stood beside her sister and other relatives, she thought about Wesley, who had left the house early that morning with no explanation. They began singing the first hymns. Even though most of the congregants stood throughout the songs, Dona Marli remained seated. Her body ached. All the crying had made her face, chest, and lower back sore.

"Job spoke and said: 'Oh, that my words were now written! Oh, that they were printed in a book, that they were graven with an iron pen and lead, in the rock for ever! For I know that my Redeemer liveth, and that He shall stand at the latter day upon the earth; and though after my skin, worms destroy this body, yet in my flesh shall I see God, whom I shall see for myself, and mine eyes shall behold, and not another, though my reins be consumed within me.'"

Dona Marli could not look at those walls and at those saints without remembering the day Washington was baptized in that very church. A beautiful celebration. She'd even made feijoada for everyone to enjoy after the ceremony. May 30, 1989. Twenty-five days after his birth on May 5. Only to return on another date: October 9, 2012. The distance between those two events was far too short. Twenty-three years. Dona Marli remembered the yellow onesie Washington wore the day of his baptism, his hands still small, his head bald, his cheeks round and plump. He weighed almost four kilos.

"Then, Jesus said to His disciples: 'Let not your heart be troubled. Ye believe in God; believe also in Me. In My Father's house are many mansions; if it were not so, I would have told you. I go to prepare a place for you. And if I go and prepare a place for you, I will come again and receive you unto Myself, that where I am, there ye may be also. And whither I go ye know, and the way ye know.' But Thomas said to Him, 'Lord, we know not whither Thou goest; and how can we know the way?' To which Jesus replied, 'I am the Way, the Truth, and the Life.'"

October 9, 2012. Dona Marli would never forget that phone call. She'd been vacuuming an enormous sofa at the house she cleaned, and the noise very nearly drowned out the ringtone. She turned off the vacuum, answered the phone, and heard the news. Her neighbor was calling from Wesley's cell because her son was too shocked to speak. Ten to four in the afternoon. Washington was usually at work at that time, they must have mistaken someone else for her boy. There was no way it could be him. But the neighbor was sure and told Dona Marli to fly home. And fly she did, leaving behind the sofa, the vacuum, everything.

The priest's sermon went in one ear and out the other. She couldn't concentrate on a word he said. At the same time, she never wanted that service to end. Because she didn't know what she would do with herself once it did. Planning the wake, the burial, scheduling the mass, sending out invitations—it all had a purpose, a precise number of steps to be completed. Steps that, in a way, had propped her up. Now, as the priest brought his sermon to a close, she felt suddenly afraid to go home. To face a life that had to go on even though a fundamental part of it was missing. Rent needed to be paid, the bills for the funeral service settled. And she needed to eat, shower, get dressed, day after day.

"Time and again, I have stood before this community and said that we will never understand God's divine plan. But I would be lying if I didn't express how deeply shaken I am by the death of Washington Pereira do Santos. As a member of the clergy and a follower of His teachings, I can guarantee that this boy's death was not a part of God's plan." The entire church sprang to attention. "What is happening today in Rocinha is a *political* plan. Those of us who live here are exposed to poor sanitation, blackouts, cramped living conditions. We have the highest concentration of tuberculosis cases in the entire state. Our school system is a disgrace. And what does the government do? It sends in hundreds of inexperienced police officers. Countless guns. But what of our sewage treatment? Where are the protective measures for at-risk areas? I've lived here for twenty years, yet this year, I've asked myself again and again: What has really changed for our community in the last twelve months?" The priest received a standing ovation. Dona Marli remained seated. He thanked the audience, collected himself, then continued: "To those families who mourn the loss of their loved ones, I say, Turn to God for the answer to this pain. Speak to Him. Open your heart. Though time cannot erase your pain or your longing, it can ease your suffering. When we are faced with death, our only recourse is to pray and put our faith in Jesus Christ. Meanwhile, to those of us who are still here, I say, We must fight for justice."

As the service ended, some congregants shouted, *Cops kill! Impeach Sérgio Cabral!*, while others went up to Dona Marli to share their condolences. She nodded and thanked them as her family ushered her out of the church.

Her relatives offered to walk her home, but when Gleyce,

Murilo, Biel, and Douglas went up to her, she sent them on their way. They all felt Wesley's absence, but no one had the courage to bring it up.

"Wesley left early this morning, without saying anything . . . He's not well, my son. He's not well," she explained while watching the goings-on outside the church. People gathered in small groups to discuss the situation on the hill and how they could get the media's attention.

"It's going to be hard. To be honest, I'm not sure what I can do for Wesley. I'm not even sure what to do with myself . . ." Dona Marli lowered her eyes and felt a strong desire to cry, a desire that had become all too familiar over the last week. "But I need you. I need your help, as his friends . . ."

"Don't worry, Dona Marli. We're here for both of you," Douglas said, speaking for everyone.

It dawned on Dona Marli just how downcast they all looked. So different from all the other times she'd seen them chatting and laughing. She studied their T-shirts. All identical, stamped with the same picture of Washington on the mountaintop. Identical to hers, too, and yet different at the same time, because they each represented the relationships her son had forged with every one of them. Her son, whom she'd taught to walk, talk, run. Her boy, who'd grown up and made friends of his own and been loved by those friends. Who'd won over girls and taken them to bed. Twenty-three years.

A police car slowly drove by the church, tailing the crowd outside. The residents cursed at them, banged their fists on the trunk of the car. The officers rolled up their windows and kept driving.

"You let us know if you need anything. You just gotta knock on our door if you need help with the groceries or anything in the house . . ." Biel said from the heart.

Everyone promised to do whatever they could. This gesture sent a twinge of happiness through Dona Marli. Their attention, their friendship—they were a kindness she'd inherited from her son. His legacy.

"The church was packed."

"For real."

"I enjoyed hearing the priest's perspective. Somebody had to say it."

They all chatted outside the church door, but it was a slightly odd conversation because every word was about Washington while, at the same time, they all went out of their way not to say his name. The sun started beating down, and they agreed it was time to get back to the house. The crew decided Dona Marli needed to eat something, so they all chipped in to get roast chicken. While Murilo, Biel, and Douglas ran to the grocery store, Gleyce walked up to Cachopa with Dona Marli so they could start making rice and the rest of lunch.

RIO—October 19, 2012

Even though his bus wasn't until two, Douglas got to the station around noon. All he had was a suitcase of clothes, a backpack full of tattoo equipment, and a folder with his favorite designs. Gleyce Kelly was the only person who came to see him off.

It was a Friday, so the bus station was busier and more chaotic than usual. People rushed around with their luggage, their children, their dogs. Some tearfully hugged their loved ones goodbye while others celebrated their return. Meanwhile, tickets were sold to nearly every city in Brazil. Douglas and Gleyce had to walk from one end of the station to the other before they could find the service counter for the Paraibuna bus company.

"One ticket to São João del Rei, Minas Gerais."

It was Douglas's second time leaving Rio de Janeiro. The first had also been to Minas, though he was a kid at the time, not even eight years old. All he remembered from that trip was playing soccer with his cousin and friends in a small, dirt field. Also, that people talked funny. He'd only seen that side of his family the handful of times they'd come to the city on vacation. He had no idea what the streets would be like in Minas, or the bars, or the police uniforms. The last point probably explained the relief he felt when he was handed his ticket.

Douglas and Gleyce wandered around looking for somewhere to eat. They were shocked at the prices. Douglas barely had any money left. The cash he'd gotten from selling his phone had mostly gone toward bus fare and a pack of cigarettes. He'd already made peace with the idea of not eating before he got to his aunt's. But Gleyce was concerned and decided to break out her credit card. They sat down at Bob's.

"You got any work lined up?"

Like everyone else, Gleyce had only been informed about the move at the last minute. Douglas had told no one what he planned to do in Minas, and he hadn't asked for any opinions. He'd just dropped the bomb two days before his scheduled departure. When he told Gleyce about it, he handed her the bag of photographs of Rocinha and asked her to do something with them.

"My cousin said he could hook me up with these guys that work with dengue prevention or something. That's what he does."

"Dengue prevention?" Gleyce was trying her best to hide her disappointment. Not that she didn't understand Douglas's decision. But of all the times to go, why then, when they all needed to be there for each other? It was difficult not to see what he was doing as selfish.

"You know, when guys show up at your house and check the backyard and terrace for standing water. There's a lot of houses over there. Like real houses, with backyards and shit. But, honest, I'd do whatever. I wanna try and throw some tattoos on my cousin and his friends. It's a small place so, who knows, might not be much of a scene there yet. Could be good for me." Douglas was staring down at the table, like he himself didn't entirely believe what he was saying.

"What about you?" Douglas got the sense they'd been talking about him a bit too much lately.

"I'm taking the ENEM early next month . . . Dunno, like, I worked really hard last year for this stupid test, but now nothing makes sense anymore, does it? I mean, I know it's important, that I need to get that spot at the university, but it's tough . . . When shit like this happens it's like this massive reality check. It's all just so intense, so heavy, that any goal, plan, or dream feels like a fucking joke. I mean, you tell me, what's the point in planning for tomorrow when you might not even be around to see it? I can't stop thinking about how my life and the lives of every resident in Rocinha are in the hands of a bunch of goddamn cops. And nobody's speaking up. Nobody's doing shit."

Gleyce's eyes were still bleary when they walked out of the station for a smoke. There were as many people hanging around the entrance as there were inside. The sun shone bright, and vendors hawked bottles of water, shouting at the tops of their lungs. Douglas clocked the scent of piss and the dozens of people sleeping under overpasses and canopies. Now that he was about to leave Rio, everything about that city seemed more intense and overwhelming than ever.

"Excuse me, sorry to bother you two, but . . ." Douglas was so distracted that he didn't even notice the old man walk up to them. ". . . I was passing by just now when I saw you, I swear to God I saw you and, suddenly, I don't know how to explain it, but I had this vision in my head of the two of you in your old age. And you were still together. Now, don't take this the wrong way or anything, I don't want to be sticking my nose in where it doesn't belong, but I work around the corner, and every day I see couples like you who are about to say goodbye, about to spend some time apart." The more the old man spoke, the more the smell of booze wafted off him. "But you two, I had to—no, I needed to . . . Maybe you won't believe me, but I saw this warmth between you, and I just wanted to tell you because, well, this isn't my first rodeo, I know how things are, and I just wanted to let you know not to worry. Things happen in their own time, the Lord's time. No goodbye is forever, I can tell you that much. Not even death is forever. You know, I've lost my mother, my son, and the thing that keeps me going day after day is knowing I'll see them again. Because we, all of us, we're made in God's image, and it's not me saying that, you know, it's the Bible. We're more than just flesh and bone."

The old man pulled a bottle of cachaça out of his backpack and took a swig. Gleyce and Douglas didn't know what to say, so they just thanked him for his advice and reassured him they were all right.

"If that's the case, son, then give us a smoke."

After the old man left with his cigarette, a string of other people started asking them for things. Money for diapers, powdered milk, cocaine. A woman of a certain age tried to sell them a RioCard for five reais, claiming it had twenty on it. Tired of turning people down, they went back inside.

They sat on a pair of metal seats, leaning against each other, and waited for the bus. Time slowed to a crawl. After hearing the old man's spiel, they began noticing just how many couples and families were saying tearful goodbyes at the departure area. At the same time, they also noticed the reunions, the hugs, the long, drawn-out kisses.

"Thanks for coming with me, really." The bus was leaving in fifteen minutes, and Douglas felt the need to say something. He turned to face Gleyce and started ordering his thoughts. "I realize we haven't been together a long time, but you know me, right? You know I wouldn't leave for no reason, just for the hell of it. This is my home, pô, my home." He stood up and gathered his things. They started walking to the departure area. "To be honest, I never thought I'd live anywhere else. I swear, I didn't. See, I know Rocinha. I know how things work there. The people. All of it. But now, after everything . . . Like, I kinda think that's why I have to leave. *Because* I know Rocinha inside out. And the hate I feel right now . . . it's too much. I swear, every time I see a police car, or even just some fucking cop standing around, strolling down an alley, I get the urge to kill everyone. Until nobody's left. I picture it. Right here. In my head. It's too much hate, Gleyce. And I guess I realized that unless I did something to get away from that hate, I was going to suffocate. Or else flip out and do something stupid . . . I can't, I just can't picture having to see those assholes every day and not doing something. All while knowing that if I'm not careful, I could go down anyway. I just can't . . ."

"Go on, your bus is leaving soon." Gleyce hugged him. "We'll be okay here, I promise. Not like we got a choice, anyway . . ." They headed toward the line of passengers at the departure area. They kissed one last time. A kiss void of passion and desire but filled with love and affection.

It didn't take Douglas long to find his bus. He put his suitcase in the luggage compartment and waited in line again a couple of minutes, then showed the driver his ticket and ID. He climbed on and was happy to realize he had a window seat. More passengers filed in and sat down. Their faces were completely unlike the ones he was used to seeing. Which made him feel like the life that awaited him would also be very, very different.

The bus pulled out and slowly started moving. Traffic was light, and it wasn't long before they were speeding down Avenida Brasil. As Douglas peered through the window, he saw not the cars or favelas or buildings that made up the cityscape, but a mental image of Rocinha aglow with the light of houses that drifted, little by little, into the distance.

RIO—October 20, 2012

Wesley sat on São Conrado beach, gazing out at the ocean. Weirdly, even though the sky was white and overcast, the water was bright blue. He watched the waves, their smooth faces and perfect tubes. There were no surfers or swimmers in the water, and the beach was deserted.

"Man, been forever since I spent any time down here!" It was Washington's voice.

Wesley turned around and saw his brother. All of him: feet, arms, hands, head. The person beside him, in a pair of red shorts and no shirt, really was Washington.

The brothers immediately started reminiscing about that beach. Sunny days when they'd cut class to bodysurf. Soccer matches and capoeira circles. Soon, they were also talking about the riptides, how hard it could be to get out of the water, the way Dona Marli never let them forget that the ocean was bigger and stronger than them.

"But it's calm today . . . No currents." Wesley still didn't know what this reunion meant, but there was one thing he was sure of: he never wanted it to end.

Washington lit a joint. The scent of fresh weed took hold of their corner of the beach. Wesley watched his brother smoke, relishing a smell he'd been missing a long time. When Washington handed him the joint, he pulled on it so hard he started coughing.

"Damn, son. Where'd you get this stuff?" he asked once he could finally talk again.

But Washington ignored his questions and started running back other memories of São Conrado. Lei's bodyboarding school, the Projeto Golfinho summer camp, their unconfessed love for some of the girls on the beach, the day there was a shark and everybody hightailed it out of the water. Wesley thought of the time they'd found a body floating near the rocks, informed the lifeguard, and watched the dead man being airlifted by helicopter. He decided not to bring it up.

"Wanna swim?" Washington asked out of the blue.

The two brothers ran toward the ocean and dove in, ignoring how cold the water was. With no riptides to struggle against, they were able to reach the waves in no time and start bodysurfing. Everything seemed hazy to Wesley. The past mixed with the present. He saw himself and his brother as little kids splashing around the whitewater, as teenagers taking a dip after a joint, and also there, in the bright blue ocean beneath the white sky. The weirdest thing was that, at the end of the day, they were all one and the same.

They headed back to the beach, happy and dripping wet. Wesley had forgotten how much fun it was to swim. Even though they hadn't left sarongs or anything on the sand to mark their spot, they went back to the same exact place. The beach was still deserted, which made it look even bigger.

All of a sudden, they were walking back home. Wesley wondered how Dona Marli would react when she saw Washington. It was tough leaving the beach and having to be around other people. Seeing his brother in a crowd made Wesley feel like it would all end, like he'd wake up any second. But Washington was unbothered. He just went on chatting about this and that as they made their way up the street lined with almond trees toward the foot of Rocinha.

Washington was talking about Flamengo, ticket prices, the weather. Meanwhile, Wesley did his best to tamp down an unavoidable question: Did Washington know he was dead? That the fact that he was there at all was no more than a dream?

They reached Via Ápia, where foot traffic was as intense as ever. The only difference was the total absence of police presence. There wasn't a single car, soldier, or armed officer at Rocinha's main point of entrance. The brothers crossed the street amid the hubbub of residents, the din of motorcycles, and the crying of children and street vendors. As much as Wesley couldn't get that thought out of his head, he also couldn't bring himself to ask his brother about it. He was scared that if he said those words aloud, they would become a truth as absolute as death.

They started making their way along Estrada da Gávea. Wesley didn't feel tired hiking uphill. He didn't even have to stop at Curva do S to catch his breath. Still, his heart beat faster and faster the closer they got to their house. Before reaching the 24Horas ATM, Wesley tried to hang a right on Vila Verde, which would take them to Cachopa through the side alleys. But Washington kept walking up the main street, and Wesley followed.

"You all right, bro?" Wesley had a hunch where Washington was going, and he wanted to steer clear of it at all costs.

As his brother crossed the street toward Casa da Paz, Wesley practically shouted that he couldn't go that way. Ever since what happened to Washington, he'd never walked on that street again. If he was coming up Via Ápia, he took Vila Verde. This meant going farther uphill, but he could just walk down the steps after. But never Casa da Paz. Still, Wesley didn't say anything, and he couldn't stop following his brother out of fear of never seeing him again.

Washington walked ahead, looking totally unconcerned, with the confidence of someone who'd been born and raised in that place. He had a slow but determined gait. The two finally passed the alley where Washington had been shot. As they walked through it, Wesley searched the walls for bullet holes and traces of blood. But it was the same alley as ever, the one he and Washington had run up and down countless times while playing tag.

On Cachopa, they bumped into several friends who all greeted Washington like there was nothing unusual about it. They stood in a circle, drinking beer, smoking weed, shooting the breeze. *Does no one but me realize Washington is dead?* Wesley kept thinking while also trying to distract himself and enjoy the moment.

Out of nowhere, the sky darkened. Washington wanted to get home; Dona Marli would be expecting them. The brothers said goodbye to the crew, then headed into the alley. Standing at their front door, Wesley watched his brother fish his keys out of his shorts pocket. For the first time, he thought that maybe, in some strange and mysterious way, it was all real, and that the nightmare of the past few days, the pain in his chest, the knot in his throat, were only that, a nightmare. Washington held the door open so his brother could walk in.

"You first."

———

Wesley opened his eyes. It took him a second to work out where he was. Lying on a thin rug, he scanned the room around him, trying to place the furniture and remember how he'd wound up there. Finally, he saw the host sleeping on a mattress near the wall, and everything came back to him. The place was in Valão, which is where he'd met the guy he was crashing with. They'd done a bunch of gigs together recently: carrying construction waste and beer crates, scavenging for copper wire to offload at the junk shop, stealing bottles of vodka from Extra to sell on the street. At the end of each day, they snorted every last cent they made.

The night before, besides blow, they'd also smoked a couple of rocks that one of the guy's buddies had copped for them in Cantagalo. But what really pushed them over the edge were the two bottles of Absolut they hadn't been able to resell. Just the thought of it made Wesley's throat close up, he was so parched. Staggering to his feet, he headed straight to the sink, praying for running water. There was a thin trickle, and Wesley collected it in his hands, drank it, then splashed it on his face. It was time to go home.

Wesley walked in without knocking. He found Dona

Marli sitting on the sofa in front of the muted TV. Hearing the door close, she turned around, then immediately jumped to her feet when she saw it was her son.

"God bless, Ma."

"God bless and keep you, son."

They hugged. Only then was Wesley able to let out all the tears he'd been choking back for the last few days. Dona Marli held him tight to her chest, as if wanting them to be one. But despite her best efforts, Wesley felt this emptiness, this hole between them. He tried to make up for it by hugging Dona Marli back as firmly as he could.

RIO—October 26, 2013

It took Douglas over a year to get back to Rocinha. He didn't plan it, either. One day, he just decided to go home and made it happen. Biel and Murilo weren't living together anymore, so he moved in with his mom. At least until he could find a place of his own to start over.

That night, Douglas was the first one to get to Via Ápia, where they were all meeting for a baile. Though the sound trucks and billboards on Estrada da Gávea hadn't announced it yet, word on the street was MC Marcinho was going to do a set. Or at least that's what Murilo had told him via text. Hopes were high. There hadn't been a legit baile at the foot of the hill since the UPP occupation.

It was eleven p.m., and people were still setting up their refreshment stalls. Onstage, a DJ did a sound test. Douglas went to the nearest vendor for a beer, then lit a cigarette. His head spun from the commotion: the racket of motorcycles and sound systems, of people honking and screaming. It was weird, a little jarring. Still, he couldn't deny it was good to be back.

"Yo, DG! I knew you'd get here early. Apparently, you can take the boy out of Minas, but you can't take Minas out of the boy," Murilo said. He'd come out of nowhere and hugged Douglas so hard he lifted him right off the ground.

"Back off, neguim. You know I'm Rocinha born and bred. No matter how long I'm gone, this place will always be home."

Douglas wanted to show Murilo how happy he was to see him, so he ran back to the vendor for another can of beer and a plastic cup. They toasted for the first time that evening, then sat on the steps of O China, facing Travessa Kátia. The stalls were nearly all set up, and the music was getting louder. Douglas tried to remember the last time he'd been to a baile on the hill. It was more than two years ago, a month before UPP's arrival, back when all of Rocinha was on pins and needles. He was so lost in thought that he didn't notice Murilo pull a joint out of his cigarette pack and spark up, right there in the street. Realizing the marola of weed was coming from his friend, he couldn't hide his surprise.

"It's cool, bro. Things are different now. You'll see," Murilo said.

Douglas nodded, and as he did he noticed the grass smelled fresh, sweet. After taking a hit, he asked Murilo if he'd gotten it there, on the hill.

"Nah, bro. A lot's changed, but our weed is still schwag. I copped this stuff from a guy I know at the beach. It's from Primavera. Dank bud. Everybody's been going there to buy it."

Murilo said he'd been manning this stall on Ipanema beach since last summer. The work wasn't easy. At peak season, he pulled twelve-, thirteen-hour days. But he made decent money, managed to stay afloat. Plus, he enjoyed working by the ocean.

"Been putting away a bit of cash to buy some paddle boards. The plan is to rent them out. The beach is crawling with tourists. Just pull a number out of your ass, and they pay it."

"You're gonna clean up." As Douglas slowly inhaled, two cops rolled by on a motorcycle. On reflex, he took the joint out of his mouth and stuck his hands behind his back. The pigs cruised past. Murilo cracked up.

"What was the quality of the grass like in Minas?"

"Real talk? Better than the stuff we used to get here but also worse than I'd imagined." Douglas had pulled into the bus station that morning and slept all afternoon. That was his first smoke of the day, and he could feel it. "Dunno, the city's, like, tiny, right? So I figured folks would be growing pot in their backyards and shit. But nah, it's brick weed, just like here. Nothing to write home about but smokable. What those dudes excel at is shrooms. Shrooms are the shit."

As Douglas talked, he was relieved to see he was getting back his accent, his vocabulary, his cadence. After a year around people who spoke mineirês, he'd naturally started slipping a couple of *trens* into his sentences for *cool*, calling his friends *véi* instead of *neguim*, and saying *nu!* when he used to say *puta que pariu*, or *the fuck!* After some time in São João del Rei, Douglas noticed the way he spoke beginning to change; he was cursing less and had a different lilt.

"Biel coming today?"

"You haven't talked? Biel left Rocinha, bro. He started seeing this chick, then, next thing you know, the two of them are shacking up over in Vidigal. Honest, the timing was perfect cause I was looking for someplace to live with my sister. So we parted ways. But we still talk every day and shit."

By the time they'd finished the joint, lights were flashing on the street, and folks were rocking up, dancing, looking fresh. They'd smoked the party's inaugural joint, Douglas proclaimed.

"I been following your work, DG. Your tattoos are awesome. You're killing it, man . . ."

"Thanks, neguim."

"When're you gonna do me?"

Douglas's phone started ringing. It was Gleyce. The second he picked up the call, he spotted her walking toward them. She spotted them too but stayed on the line until she was next to Douglas. They gave each other a long, confusing hug.

"Congrats," Douglas said once they were done with their hellos. "I knew you had it in you."

He'd already congratulated Gleyce on getting into journalism school back when she'd posted on Facebook. He'd texted her about it and called her up. But just then, he felt the need to tell her in person. Murilo congratulated her as well.

"Thanks, y'all," Gleyce said with a smile. "You know, PUC isn't as cool as everybody makes it out to be, especially if you're on a scholarship . . . Man, have I peeped some fucking dirt behind the scenes. I can't even get into it. Anyway, I'm not here to dwell on this shit—I'm here to tear up the floor!"

All three of them laughed in that full-bellied way of old friends reunited at long last. As Murilo lit another joint, Biel arrived with his girlfriend. He went straight up to Douglas, pulled him in for a hug, and kissed his cheek. Douglas remembered the day Biel had shown up at the house with the tattoo gun. After all that time, he finally understood what a huge gesture it was.

"This is my girl, Larissa. And these are the two fools I used to live with. You've met Murilo. This here is Gleyce. She didn't live with us, but she's good people."

They all said hello. As more and more folks arrived, the baile started coming together. The music got louder. A group of armed men rolled in and stood facing the street. Nobody looked bothered or worried about things getting ugly if the cops came through again.

"Damn! There's four speakers this time," Larissa exclaimed, pointing at the massive sound system sitting in the street. "You really think MC Marcinho is gonna play? Rocinha's a whole other world . . ." Even though they'd backed away from the stage, the thumping bass made it so they had to shout to be heard.

"This one thinks everything in Rocinha's the goat . . . I already told her she wouldn't last a week if we moved here."

Biel filled them in on their place in Vidigal. There was only one room and one bathroom, but it had a kickass terrace for churrascos, plus a sick view of the ocean. He also told them about his new hustle: selling imported clothes on the hill. A buddy of his brought the threads from the U.S., and Biel resold them around the neighborhood. They had everything you could imagine: Oakley, Nike, Aeropostale. Kicks, shirts, shorts. He invited Douglas over to check out his stock.

After all, what clients really want is to be tattooed by dudes who are styling.

"You and your side hustles, man. You're too much." It was slowly dawning on Douglas how much he'd missed the guy. "I'm gonna open a shop with Lari over in Vidigal. Become a legit fucking businessman!"

The joint had burned down to the roach by the time Wesley showed up looking like he'd just rolled out of bed. He greeted everyone in a daze and stared wide-eyed at the flashing lights, the shadows of people, like it'd been this huge effort to get there.

"Sorry, y'all. I was zonked. I got home from work, burned a fatty, started reading something, and next thing I know I'm dead to the world. Woke up like five minutes ago. Jumped outta bed, threw on some clothes, and grabbed a mototaxi down here."

Wesley worked as a custodian at Biblioteca Parque, a local library. He said that whenever work was slow, he read one of their books—they had a load of great stuff. Then he told them Dona Marli sent her love, that she'd woken up as he was getting dressed and was really happy to hear who he was meeting up with that night.

"Roll another J to wake this fool up." Douglas turned around and pulled Wesley in for another hug. The first one had been too short. "Let's toast, man. To the whole crew being together again." He instantly regretted those words. *Whole crew* implied nobody was missing. But everybody, probably even Larissa, knew that wasn't true. But Douglas went to the vendor anyway, bought some more beer and grabbed a half dozen plastic cups.

He started pouring beer for everyone, but when he got to Larissa's, she said no thanks, she was off the booze for a while.

"What's that about? Dry October or something?" Gleyce asked.

From the way Larissa and Biel looked at each other, there was no need for follow-up questions. Everyone knew exactly what was going on.

"Oh, snap! There's a mini Biel on the way!"

"Can you picture this dude as a *dad*?!"

"We just found out this week," Larissa said.

Everybody hugged, beers sloshing, thrilled to find out they were going to be aunts and uncles.

They toasted to the new kid, then decided to get closer to the stage, where everyone was dancing. The vibe was electric. The street smelled of sweat, weed, and Gudang Garam cigarettes, the famous baile smokes. They cracked open a few more beers, sparked up some more joints, started getting lit. Every now and then, one of them would stop dancing to talk.

"You know the library where Wesley works? You gotta go there," Gleyce yelled in Douglas's ear.

"Yeah, yeah, I'll hit it up soon."

"It's right near Rampa, you know, on Cachopa slope. You gotta go there. Remember the photos you gave me? The ones that belonged to that old head on Ladeira da Cachopa, right next to UPP's headquarters? They're at the library now." The music stopped for a second, and everyone turned to look at the DJ. "They've put them up on the walls. And there's also these texts about the history of Rocinha." The sound started blasting again. Gleyce couldn't tell if Douglas had heard the last part of her sentence.

"Is it open tomorrow? I can go there first thing."

The two of them danced again. A few songs later, Douglas started looking at Gleyce differently. As she moved her hips, he pictured her naked on his bed in his old apartment in Cachopa. He wondered if he still had a chance with her, if he still *wanted* a chance with her. The music got more and more intense. Douglas worried Gleyce would be able to tell he was turned on, so he went to get more beer.

"Yeah, it all happened after Amarildo disappeared. Nothing was ever the same again," Douglas heard Murilo shout to his friend. They were talking about how bailes like that one would've been a no-go just a few weeks back. How, after the UPP put a lid on street bailes, the best they could hope for were bailes at Clube Emoções.

"Real talk: that shit that happened with Amarildo needed to happen. Cause then the press finally started paying attention. Meaning cops had to be cool, take bribes again like they used to, keep a low profile." Gleyce downed the rest of her beer. The music didn't let up, making it harder and harder to talk.

Douglas remembered the piece about Amarildo that Gleyce had published in a local news outlet called Fala Roça. In it, she'd written that if people started organizing around murders in favelas like they had around bus fare hikes, the police would be forced to think twice before they shot someone.

"What's rough is all the people we had to lose before things started changing. And that none of us know how

much longer this situation will go on for," Biel shouted over
the funk. He sounded desperate. Everybody stopped talking
and started dancing again. Douglas topped up their plastic
cups with more beer. This time they toasted to Washington.

By the time Biel and Larissa were arguing in the middle
of the baile, everybody was buzzed. No one knew what the
fight was about, only that they'd started going toe-to-toe after
Biel came back from the bathroom. At first, everyone thought
they were just shouting over the noise, but their body language was charged. Then, all of a sudden, the two of them
left, without saying a proper goodbye.

"Biel was doing lines in the alley. I think that's what
kicked it off," Wesley explained. "He invited me, but I wanna
take it easy today. Be chill."

Murilo was next to leave. He was beat from working on
the beach all day. Besides, he had an early start tomorrow.
Nothing could change his mind, not even Douglas drunkenly
begging Murilo not to abandon him, saying he'd been gone a
whole year, that they had to stay up all night long, and YOLO,
just like they used to, the exact same way as they used to.
Murilo's mind was made up. He hugged everyone and left.

A few minutes later, the music came to an abrupt stop.
The only sound was of people talking over each other. Everyone was convinced the organizers had cut the music so they
could announce the next set. But nothing happened. Douglas
saw a man speaking to the DJ, up close. He couldn't tell if the
guy was armed or not, only that he was wearing gold chains,
which meant he was probably in the organization. For a second, Douglas wondered if he was a cop sent to shut down the
party, but he kept that thought to himself. Gleyce and Wesley

were also glancing around them, confused. Not exactly the warm welcome he'd been hoping for, he thought. But then the sound came back on, and the tension they'd felt in that silence became a distant memory.

By three in the morning, the baile was heaving. They couldn't have fit anyone else on Via Ápia if they'd wanted. Douglas peeped Gleyce and Wesley dancing—each in their own style, busting new moves—and started tripping about how deeply life could change in so little time, altering things that seemed unalterable. As he watched his friends, he remembered how abruptly Biel and Murilo had left the party. It struck him that they would never be as close as they had once been. At the same time, he felt certain that their bond was unbreakable. Everything they had lived through together had marked them. Like a tattoo. Every smile, every hurdle, every tragedy. Each and every one of them had been marked by the history of that hill, the history of that city.

MC Marcinho finally came onstage, and the crowd blew up. When he took the microphone and shouted, *Hello, Rocinha!* the speakers seemed even louder. He began singing acapella: *Nem melhor nem pior, apenas diferente.* Not better or worse, just different . . . Then the beat came on, and everyone got down. As the lights flashed at high speed, smoke from the fog machine mixed with smoke from the weed and cigarettes. And as the digital drums shot through those hundreds of bodies, it was life—always life, never death—that made the ground shake.